"Tired of the same old humdrum? Is one day just like the next and the one before it? Take a break and enjoy a relationship you will never forget. But be warned: Once you've decided, there's no turning back."

"Old-fashioned girl, intimidated by singles scene, new to city. Likes: Libraries, men who understand that intimacy and sex are not the same, long, aimless afternoons wandering through a sleeping city. If you need to ask for a picture, I don't need to meet you."

"I'M NOT LOOKING FOR PERFECTION. I'm looking for you! SWF, 25, slim, attractive. Are you ready to reach your full potential? If so, I'm waiting."

These are just a few of the ads you'll find placed and answered in this all-new collection of stories that range from the romantic to the magical, the humorous to the horrific. And in honor of the title, Tanya Huff has graced us with a brand new Henry Fitzroy story set after he and Vicki have gone their separate ways. These are the Personals the way you wish—or dread— they might be. But beware! That blind date you're meeting might be your true soul mate, or a night stalker with far too many centuries of experience!

SINGLE WHITE VAMPIRE SEEKS SAME

EDITED BY

Martin H. Greenberg
and Brittiany A. Koren

DAW BOOKS, INC.
DONALD A. WOLLHEIM, FOUNDER
375 Hudson Street, New York, NY 10014

ELIZABETH R. WOLLHEIM
SHEILA E. GILBERT
PUBLISHERS
www.dawbooks.com

First Printing, January 2001

1 2 3 4 5 6 7 8 9

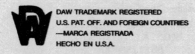

DAW TRADEMARK REGISTERED
U.S. PAT. OFF. AND FOREIGN COUNTRIES
—MARCA REGISTRADA
HECHO EN U.S.A.

PRINTED IN THE U.S.A.

CONTENTS

CONTENTS

INTRODUCTION

by Brittiany A. Koren

Are you bored with the current condition of your love life? How far would you go to find that perfect match? Would you be willing to answer a personal ad if you found someone who had written in black and white what you were looking for? Many people would say yes, and be willing to meet with a perfect stranger. After all, he or she might be "The One."

Most people think the personal ads are a last resort, used only because those who place them don't know where to look to find happiness, even though it may be closer than they think. They're tired of the usual meeting places and have run out of ideas on where to meet the love of their lives. Personal ads are an easy way to look for a match, and (hopefully) get the results you want in a timely fashion.

A quick e-mail or phone conversation takes care of setting up a blind date once the companion of your choice (or at least your choice of ads) has been determined. The actual date itself can be a frightening experience for some, or at least the minutes before that first meeting. Your hopes, fears, doubts, and worries all seem to become magnified while waiting for your chosen person. *Will they like me? Does my breath*

smell all right? I hope I don't make a fool of myself.
Then the other person arrives, and, for better or
worse, your blind date begins.

Of course, there have been those dates that don't
quite start out right, but still end up happily. My own
first date with my husband started over spilled soup
in the doorway of a restaurant. But we're still together,
and have survived many embarrassing moments since.
You just have to have the courage to go on that first
date and take a chance on someone you've never met.

Most think it is only the desperate who place a personal ad, but what if there were those out there who
were so desperate that the personal ads were their
only hope of finding someone, anyone? With that in
mind, we asked some of the best fantasy authors writing today to give us their own unique spins on personal ads. The results were as varied as the ads
themselves often are. Brad Sinor tells of a man willing
to defy his rather unusual family to be with the woman
of his choice, if only for a little while. In Nina Kiriki
Hoffman's story, three teenagers answer what appears
to be the perfect personal ad, only to find a seductive
older man who puts their very friendship at risk. And
in Kristine Kathryn Rusch's story, a woman finds the
companion she was looking for right under her nose.

In the end, whether it's a one-night stand or for
eternity, these stories are an adventure for the people
who meet up with their blind dates. And take a chance
on what it will bring them—eternal happiness or a
broken heart.

PERSONALS WISHES

by Mickey Zucker Reichert

Mickey Zucker Reichert is a pediatrician whose fantasy and science fiction novels include *The Legend of Nightfall*, *The Unknown Soldier*, and two trilogies about the Renshai. Her most recent releases from DAW Books are *Spirit Fox*, with Jennifer Wingert, and her own *Flightless Falcon*. Her short fiction has appeared in numerous anthologies, including *Battle Magic*, *Zodiac Fantastic*, and *Wizard Fantastic*. Her claims to fame: she *has* performed brain surgery, and her parents *really are* rocket scientists.

SWF, Italian, early 50s, nice, nonsmoker, good cook seeks stable, kind, fifty-something man. Looks don't matter.

The subway lurched, flinging a wave of humanity into a backward lean, then righting it a moment later. Clemente Romando tightened his grip on the pole momentarily, regarding the small stranger who studied him with brows inching upward. A mop of black hair haloed childlike features: large brown eyes, an upturned nose, and heart-shaped lips. Like Romando, he carried about twenty extra pounds, but the smaller man's limbs appeared disproportionately thin. He had given his name as Keller, though Romando did not know if that was his first or his last.

"That's it?" Keller said incredulously, in a voice too deep to match his features.

Romando shrugged as the subway rattled and puffed down the track. He hitched his newspaper further under his armpit, and, beneath his heavy coat, straightened a suit rumpled by a full day of work. Usually, he liked to relax on the way home, quietly ignoring the other riders with the same uncomfortable purpose as on an elevator. "That's it," he confirmed. "My ideal woman's personals ad."

Keller shook his head, fine hair flying. "No supermodel? No five foot eleven? No size 2? No early 20s?"

Romando ran a hand through his graying hair and across the smooth skin of his ever-spreading bald spot. He thought of his hawk-nosed features, his common light brown eyes behind their glasses, his freckled, undimpled cheeks becoming jowly with age. "I have no romantic notions that a woman who looked like that would want a man like me."

Keller wiped his palms on his jeans, then returned one hand to the pole. He scanned the crowd.

As Keller turned his head, Romando once again tried to guess the smaller man's age. Now that he no longer weathered the direct attention of those depthless dark eyes, Romando found his companion's appearance much younger. He split the difference. *Thirties, maybe?*

Keller's gaze returned to Romando. "But this is supposed to be your fantasy woman's ad. Remember?"

Romando forced himself not to. His ex-wife still haunted the far corners of his mind long after alimony had ended and she had married her second, third, and fourth husbands. "I tried the looks thing once. Didn't like it." Against his will, he pictured Grace's supple curves, her well-shaped breasts, her long dark hair. She had been beautiful, yet his current thoughts of her made those same attractive features seem the very description of ugly. Not content with half, she had robbed their bank account, run up their credit cards, and stolen his paychecks from the mail. A bat of her blue eyes at the judge, a low-cut bodice and a high-cut hem for the police; she had gotten away with all of it. He had even had to pay her lawyer's fees and court costs. "This time—" He flushed. "If there is to be a this time, I want a woman whose self-respect comes from something stronger than a pretty face. A skill, perhaps. Wit. Personality. A woman who can see beyond looks, beyond money, and love me for . . . me." He laughed. "Cliché, huh?"

"Actually . . ." Keller smiled. "Less cliché than the skinny twenty-something supermodel. Most guys fantasize about having a woman who doesn't care how he looks but cares ever so much about how *she* looks."

Romando rolled his eyes. "Most men are . . ." Noticing others watching their conversation, he softened the word. ". . . inexperienced." His gaze fell on a slender, young man with piercing green eyes and neat, name-brand clothing peeking through the open zipper of his leather winter coat. "Inexperienced," he repeated. "Not necessarily sexually, but with love. With real relationships." Long-forgotten, a scene from his youth filled his mind. He and some male coworkers lunched in a mall food court, rating the passing women. He still remembered Wade calling one of the women a "cow" despite his own beer gut and tree-trunk legs. None of the others seemed to notice the irony.

Incomprehensible muffled noise blathered from the speakers. The subway jerked to a stop, the passengers falling into their accustomed sway. The doors hissed open.

Keller grunted. "A sensitive guy like you should have a date for Valentine's Day."

The holiday was still a week away. "How do you know I don't?"

"Do you?"

Romando lowered his head, watching strangers funnel through the opening, down the steps to the frigid, concrete platform below. He planned to do the same thing he had done on Valentine's Day for the last ten years: watch rented comedies over a TV dinner and play with his cat until he became too tired to remember the date. "No."

"Well, maybe a personals ad isn't such a bad thing."

Romando grunted. He glanced back toward his companion, only to find the space beside him empty. He jerked his attention around the car as the doors clapped closed and the train spluttered from the station. He saw no sign of the odd little man who had occupied his attention for the last ten stations. *Must have slipped out.* Romando shrugged, found a recently vacated seat, still warm from its occupant, and commenced the familiar routine of ignoring his fellow passengers.

The doorbell chimed. Elena Piazano put aside her broom, turned off a syndicated sitcom, and tucked stray wisps of mouse-brown hair beneath her kerchief. She walked from the kitchen through a living room filled with tidy bookshelves containing a pleasant array of books and knickknacks and opened the door. A small male stranger stood on the stoop, a clipboard on his coat sleeve and a pen tucked behind one ear. With a mittened hand, he held out her newspaper, still in its plastic wrapper. His breath steamed in the cold air.

"Oh." Anticipating a sales pitch, Piazano attempted to head it off. "I can save you some time. I don't buy anything door-to-door. And I'm happy with my religion."

The man loosed a pleasant, silvery laugh. Black hair rimed with frost lay tousled as a boy's, but his dark eyes held age and wisdom. His cheeks had grown pink as a cherub's. "I'm not selling anything. I'm just doing a survey. Completely free. Do you have a few moments you could spare?" His expression turned pleading.

Piazano studied the little man. She deemed herself a competent judge of character, and he appeared safe and friendly. She guessed many people had chased him away, too busy or suspicious to spare even a minute. Likely, he had to survey a certain number of people to finish for the day, and the February chill had to have become uncomfortable. She certainly had the time; and, she would actually enjoy the company. "Come on in. I was just about to have tea and fresh banana bread. Would you like some?" She stepped aside.

The small man's features seemed at once grateful and relieved. "Thank you." Carefully, he wiped his feet on the mat, though nothing came off of his shoes. He closed the door, handing Piazano the newspaper.

Piazano accepted the offering, gesturing him through the living room, down the hallway, to the kitchen. She dropped the paper on the tabletop. "Let me take your coat. My name is Elena."

"Thank you, Elena." The little man pulled off his mittens, placing one in each pocket. He eased off his coat, arranging it over the back of a kitchen chair rather than handing it to Piazano. "I'm Keller." He sat, laying the clipboard in front of him.

Glad she had nearly finished cleaning the kitchen, Piazano looked around the familiar furnishings. One door led to the living room, the other, closed, led into a laundry room. Gauzy curtains of blue and white shielded a large window overlooking the eighth of an acre lawn where her vegetable and flower beds grew in the summer. The teapot sat on the left front burner, shadowing the flickering blue fire of the gas. Between the stove and the sink, a white marble countertop with gold flecks held the cooling banana bread on a rack. The refrigerator hummed near the living room door.

By the time Piazano cut and buttered two large pieces of banana bread, the teapot whistled. She poured two mugs of hot water, dropped a tea bag into each, and set one in front of Keller. "Would you like sugar or lemon?"

"No, thank you." Keller smiled at Piazano. "It's fine like this. And the banana bread smells delicious."

"I made it from scratch." Piazano enjoyed the compliment and the conversation, though superficial. She placed the larger piece of banana bread in front of him. Returning to the counter, she put a teaspoonful of sugar into her own tea, removed the tea bag, and stirred. "Now, what's this survey about?"

"Love," Keller said, completely unselfconsciously.

Piazano blinked. "What?"

"Love," Keller repeated, looking at Piazano. "Is that okay?"

"I—I guess so." Piazano carried her bread and tea to the place across from Keller. She eased her plump body into the chair. Nervously, she laughed. "Though I think you're asking the wrong person."

Keller's deep voice reassured. "If we only asked people who gave the answers we wanted, it wouldn't be a very useful survey."

"No," Piazano agreed. She blew on her tea and stirred it again, then tapped the spoon on the edge and laid it beside the mug. "So, what do you want to know?"

"Let's start with your age."

"Fifty-two."

Keller wrote diligently, then looked up. "Are you married?"

"No."

Keller made a check mark. "Would you like to be?"

The question roused a desire long squelched. At forty, the media claimed she had a better chance of being struck by lightning. By fifty, the odds had only worsened. "It seems silly to yearn for something I can't have."

Keller studied Piazano, his dark eyes sweeping from the kerchiefed hair, past the generous nose and lips, to her stocky frame. Finally, he met her hazel eyes. "Are you ill?"

Piazano stared back. "Is that one of the survey questions?"

Keller laughed, that same pretty sound. "No. I just wondered why you couldn't get married."

Piazano flushed, unlocking her gaze from his. "It's not a matter of 'can't.' It's a matter of . . . of . . . age. Appearance. Needing a–a . . . man . . . first."

Keller made a thoughtful noise, tapping his pen on the clipboard. "That leads me to my next question." He cleared his throat. "If you were constructing the personals ad of your fantasy man, what would it say?"

"Personals ad?" The question caught Piazano off guard. "Oh, I'd like him to be a well-tempered man. A—"

Keller cut Piazano off with a wave. "In the form of a personals ad, please."

Piazano narrowed her eyes. "But I've never—" What she had been about to say was not wholly true. She had glanced at them once or twice but never considered answering one. She had not paid much attention to their construction. "All right." Awkwardly, she tried to string together an ad. "Uh, fiftyish male . . . uh . . . Italian descent . . . sweet, funny . . ." She remembered her previous words, ". . . well-tempered." She looked directly at Keller again. "And he can't be married to someone else."

Keller's forehead crinkled. "You mean single?"

"Yeah, single." Piazano considered. "Or widowed.

Or even divorced, I guess. Everyone's entitled to one mistake, right?"

Keller diligently wrote it down. "Which would you prefer?"

Piazano considered for the first time and found the answer different than she would have expected. "Well, I'd rather he wasn't always single, I guess. There's a reason a man makes it to his fifties without marrying, and it's usually because he's immature or unlikable or inflexible or some such. I'm not sure I want to compete with the ghost of a past wonderful woman, so maybe divorced."

"Go on," Keller said.

Piazano pursed her lips, then declared helplessly, "I forgot where I was."

Keller obliged: "Divorced male, 50s, Italian descent, sweet, funny, and well-tempered . . ." He inclined his head toward Piazano.

"Well," she started, worried to sound greedy. Savings from her years of substitute teaching and a modest inheritance kept her in groceries and clothing. She owned the house, the mortgage paid off by her late parents. "I'd like it if he could support us."

Keller tapped his pen against the clipboard. "Rich?"

Piazano felt her cheeks grow hot. "Who wouldn't want that? But I'd settle for a decent poor man who brings food to the table." She choked out a nervous laugh. "Sometimes, I think I'd settle for any man at all."

Keller crossed out and wrote. "Does this sound right now: 'sweet, funny, well-tempered, and financially secure'?"

It sounded like another way of saying rich. "How about financially . . ." Piazano considered. "Comfortable" and "well off" sounded even more euphemistic. "Okay?" A better word occurred to her, "Or stable?"

"Financially stable," Keller corrected, then looked at Piazano with brows raised.

Realizing Keller wanted more, Piazano smoothed her dress. 'What usually comes next?"

". . . seeks. Then a description of what he's looking for."

Piazano nodded.

"Unless you want to get more specific. Maybe something about looks? Habits? Children?"

The last word startled Piazano. "Goodness. It's a bit too late for children."

Keller smiled, with his eyes as well as his mouth. "I meant from the previous marriage."

Piazano's cheeks reddened again. "Oh. Well. No." She considered his previous suggestions. "I really have no right to specify appearances." She folded her hands sheepishly over her rounded belly. "How about 'seeks nice fiftyish woman'?"

Keller complied, pen scrabbling over the paper. He stuffed the last of his banana bread into his mouth, chewed, and swallowed. Clipping the pen securely to the board, he started to rise.

"Oh," Piazano said, disappointed. "Are we finished?"

"That's all my questions. Was there something more you wanted to add?"

"No." Piazano answered honestly, though she wanted him to stay. Visitors came so rarely, and she had enjoyed entertaining. *I really am lonely to consider lying to keep the company of a stranger.* "Thank you."

Keller finished rising and tossed on his coat. "And thank you, Elena." He held out a stubby hand.

Piazano shook his proffered hand, then escorted him to the door and out into the frigid day. She watched him go, his step bouncy and the faint sounds of tuneless whistling accompanying him into the distance.

Shivering, Piazano shut the door. For several moments she stood in icy silence, a sadness she had not contemplated in months washing over her. The emptiness of the house seemed echoing, her loneliness an unbearable burden. Unable to muster the energy to work, she returned to the kitchen and her tea. The mugs still sat on the table, Keller's plate empty and hers with a partially eaten slice of banana bread. She sat in her place, leaving his dishes on the table, finding solace in their presence. She scooted the newspaper to her, caught up in the suggestion left in the wake of Keller's questions. For the first time in her life, she deliberately sought out the personals.

Amid three columns of women hunting wealthy, unburdened men and men pleading for slender, younger women one ad captured her attention:

Divorced male, 50s, Italian descent, sweet, funny, well-tempered, and financially stable seeks nice, fiftyish woman. Respond P.O. Box 14058

Clemente Romando returned to an apartment that suddenly felt more like a prison, surprised to discover that he missed the scant company Keller had provided. He already spent far too much time alone. *A Valen-*

tine's Day blind date? The thought seemed madness, beyond contemplation. *Maybe, just maybe, he's right.*

Too tired to rummage through the refrigerator for leftover pizza and flat ginger ale, Romando flopped down on the couch and stretched his legs across the coffee table. It was a position of power and freedom he had assumed in the years since his divorce; Grace had never let him put his feet on the furniture. Feeling like a fool, he opened the newspaper to the classifieds. He turned past the cars, the real estate, the pets to the singles ads. His cheeks felt hot. Despite the quiet sanctity of home, he found himself peering around the pages to make certain no one watched him, his paranoia stemming from an ingrained dislike for the personals. They seemed dirty and desperate, for the young and adventuresome. Just reading them made him feel like a voyeur.

Romando's eyes went immediately to an ad in the upper middle column:

SWF, Italian, early 50s, nice, nonsmoker, good cook seeks stable, kind fifty-something man. Looks don't matter. Respond P.O. Box 20330 . . .

Shocked, Romando blinked rapidly several times, then looked at the ad again. It remained, its words a perfect duplicate of his own. "How?" He stared until the page blurred into black-and-white obscurity, closed his eyes tightly, reopened them to clear vision, then read the same ad again. He mouthed it aloud, uncertain whether to feel thrilled or disturbed. Finally overcome by a sensation of creepy terror, he folded the paper, tossed it to the table, and headed for a dinner of cold pizza and soda.

Candlelight flickered across the gold-and-scarlet-patterned wallpaper of Columbo's, and tuxedoed waiters passed like wraiths between the tables. Love songs crooned over the speakers, from Sinatra to muzak renditions of top 40 rock bands. Nearly every round table held a couple, but Clemente Romando had eyes only for Elena Piazano. Dressed in a modest, pale purple dress well-cut for her generous curves, she seemed self-assured and secure. Frequent touches to her kerchief revealed the anxiety she otherwise elegantly hid. Beneath it, Romando caught a glimpse of silky black hair, worn longer than most women of her age, barely touched by gray. Her dark eyes held an exotic touch of green. Her nose revealed her Italian heritage, as did his own. Her lips were full, glistening with a deep rose lipstick that made them seem exquisitely inviting. He suddenly felt very glad he had answered her ad, at the same time worried that the sight of him would send her scurrying for excuses to leave.

Piazano looked at her hands, ringless and slightly wrinkled. "I don't usually so much as open the personal—"

"Me either," Romando added as swiftly as possible. "But this time—"

"Yes, this time . . ."

They both laughed. It seemed almost magical how swiftly things had come together. Piazano's letter to him had come only two days after he had answered her ad. She had enclosed her telephone number, and he had called it to arrange a Valentine's Day date. It

23

seemed as mysterious as Keller, as if the post office, perhaps the universe itself, wished to hasten the process and bring them together for the holiday.

Romando caught Piazano's hand and held it.. He lost himself in the depths of her eyes, reading a possible future there. Neither noticed the waiter who bustled to their table to take their order, waited politely several moments, then quietly glided to the next customers.

They talked about childhood, the oddities and comforts of growing up in a traditionally Italian home, the irritation of companions assuming a family connection to the Mafia. She laughed genuinely at the antics of his mother, finding an easy comparison in her own home life. Her laughter sounded like music to him, and he sought it with a quiet joy. Her nervousness vanished, and she leaned across the table, truly and deeply interested in his stories, in him. The candlelight sparked red-and-blue highlights in the hair that escaped Piazano's kerchief, and Romando found his attention riveted to its beauty. And, inextricably, to Elena Piazano.

One year later, darkness settled across the heavens overlooking Clemente and Elena Romando's tidy cottage. The lovers sat in one another's arms long after the vivid wash of the sunset disappeared behind the distant mountains. Their breath left clouds in the frigid air, but they seemed not to notice the cold. They stared upward, each clearly believing the other had written the ad that had brought them together. Forever.

A touch startled Cupid from his reverie. He sidled

with a shocked squeak, plummeting from his cloud. Air slammed his face, whistling past his ears for a moment before he realized his danger. Quickly unfurling his wings, he soared back to his perch. There, Apollo crouched, howling with laughter, his face brilliant in the moonlight.

"Very funny," Cupid groused, though even the fall could not wholly banish the grin from his face.

"I thought you heard me," Apollo finally managed around his laughter. "Sorry, little buddy."

"Oh, very sincere." Cupid dropped to his haunches beside the god, still studying the couple. "I'm touched."

Apollo followed Cupid's gaze. "Your doing?"

Cupid rolled his eyes. "You know it is."

Apollo grunted and settled to a more comfortable position. "What happened to the bow-and-arrow thing?"

Cupid's wee shoulders rose and fell. "With the divorce rate what it is, sudden intense love just wasn't working anymore." Suddenly feeling the heavy scrutiny of his companion, Cupid turned his attention to Apollo.

The sun god shook dark hair from his shoulders, his golden tan and perfect musculature a glaring contrast to the pudgy couple below. "This wouldn't have anything to do with Jove's new quotas?"

Cupid shrugged. "Maybe." In truth, only partially. Over the centuries, he had suffered a decline in his own sense of self-worth as lovers parted when the initial rush of his potioned arrows waned. "It seemed time to join the twentieth century."

"Just in time for the twenty-first."

Cupid smiled. "Just in time for the twenty-first," he agreed. "Next year, I tackle the Internet."

"The Internet." Apollo grunted. "Good luck." He strode toward the horizon, where his 2000 Ford F250 waited to—once again—haul the sun across the sky.

FOLK LURE

by Kristine Kathryn Rusch

In 1999, Kristine Kathryn Rusch won three Reader's Choice Awards for three different stories in three different magazines in two different genres: mystery and science fiction. That same year, her short fiction was nominated for the Hugo, Nebula, and Locus Awards. Since she had just returned to writing short fiction after quitting her short fiction editing job at *The Magazine of Fantasy and Science Fiction*, she was quite encouraged by this welcome back to writing. She never quit writing novels, and has sold more than forty-five of them, some under pseudonyms, in mystery, science fiction, fantasy, horror, and romance. Her most recent mystery novel is *Hitler's Angel*. Her most recent fantasy novel is *The Black King*.

M folklorist seeks F vocalist with large repertoire and great knowledge of history/culture. Send demo tape and photograph to #4778.

"I don't know," I said. "Doesn't sound like an audition to me."

"Sometimes they list auditions in the personals," Karen said. "You have to know how to read the ads."

We were sitting on my sofa, newspapers spread between us. My computer hummed on the desk pushed up against the couch. The front door was open, revealing the concrete walkway that led to the other apartments, but the windows were closed. Sunlight was trying to sneak in, but I wouldn't let it.

"I know how to read the ads," I said gently. No sense trying to tell her that I often read them for my job. Did *DWM, 37, Professional, financially secure, spontaneous* really mean what it said or was it a cover for one of my clients' husbands? Was *Seeking Punk-Girl Type for athletic independent GWF* confirmation that another client's wife was getting some female companionship on the side?

The personals were a giant boon to my business. I scanned them every week and used them for more cases than I liked to think about. In fact, the *Eager, willing & able SGWM* ad, the one that sought *active willing partners* and claimed to be *ultra discreet, Bi & Married welcome* was mine. Not that I was Single—I was Divorced; not that I was Gay—I wasn't; and not that I was White—I only looked that way. My heritage was Creole, Comanche, Black, and German. For some strange reason, my skin showed only the German. That ad was a fishing expedition and with it, I caught more philandering husbands than I did with my zoom lens.

"See?" Karen said, pointing at another ad beneath the *Common Interests* category. "This one says, 'Seeking Female Vocalist for postrock group. Inf. incl. Pale Saints, My Bloody Valentine—' "

"I get the picture," I said. 'Why don't they advertise in the regular classifieds?"

"Because they're just starting out and can't pay."

"There is a Volunteers Wanted section."

She shrugged. "Not the same. Bands want personal relationships with each other."

"And folklorists?" I asked. "Is that what they want, too?"

"Come on, Drew. You're being too harsh."

I studied the ad again. "It's one of those cute ads, like *'Gilligan seeks life raft. Divorced white male 41 feels alone on island. All rescue attempts have failed . . .'*"

"I read that one," she said. "It's stupid. He's trying to win the Personal Ad of the Week, not get a date."

"And the folklorist isn't?"

"It's not a funny ad."

"True." I folded the newspaper and set it on top of the pile. Karen was my next door neighbor. We met on the concrete walkway one afternoon when she dropped two grocery bags of food and I caught one. We both dove after the navel oranges trying to escape beneath the blue iron railing, and missed. We lay on our bellies and winced at the oranges rained—and exploded—on the cars parked two stories below. We had laughed, cleaned up the evidence, and decided the crime wasn't worth confessing to; most of the cars were so rusted and damaged anyway that one more dent wouldn't make much difference.

We'd been friends ever since. Karen was one of the first people who, when she learned that I was a private detective, didn't go all starry eyed on me. She rarely asked me about my work, and she hadn't imposed until now.

"I don't like it," I said. "He wants to audition a date. He's trying to snare you through your dreams, Karen. Not a good thing."

She brought a leg to her chest, and grabbed her ankle, resting her chin on her knee. It was her favorite reflective pose, and one that made me realize that she was very young, too thin, and much too sad.

"I wouldn't mind seeing a man who shares my interests," she said. "And I have no illusions. He obviously works at the university, and he clearly is doing some sort of study on folk songs. So he meets women along the way? What can it hurt?"

I hated those words. Whenever I heard them, I knew something would happen that I would later regret.

"I'm not companion enough for you?" I asked.

She laughed and kissed my ear. "You're a great friend, Drew. But you don't know Bach from Bachman Turner Overdrive."

I did, but I didn't say anything. I remembered when BTO was topping the charts. She'd only heard them as a nostalgia group. No wonder she linked them with Bach. They were Not Modern in her mind.

"At least, let me tail you on the first meeting," I said.

"If there is a first meeting." She tucked a strand of her beautiful auburn hair behind an ear. "He might listen to the demo and decide I'm not worth the time."

Right. Her voice was husky and warm. When she sang, she sounded like a cross between Ella Fitzgerald and Aretha Franklin, with some of Billie Holiday's sadness thrown in for good measure. No music aficionado would pass up Karen's demo tape. And when he saw the photo—those dark eyes whose color mysteriously matched the hair, the pure pale skin—no freckles for this redhead—cheekbones so high that her cheeks were always in shadow—he'd be calling her so fast the phone lines would burn.

"Promise you'll let me," I said.

Her smile faded. "You know I will."

Three kinds of people lived in our apartment complex: folks on the way up like Karen; folks on the way down like most of the residents; and folks who got stranded in this 1940s former motel purgatory like me. Most of the time, I didn't socialize with my neighbors, but Karen was close, we'd shared a laugh, and it was clear that she needed someone to watch out for her.

She had just come out of one of those relationships that wasn't significantly bad, but wasn't good either. It had eaten her self-esteem—although I doubted if she'd had much in the first place—and it had reduced her to a kind of genteel poverty. Her clothes were upscale department store, but she used sheet-covered boxes as end tables. She worked as a waitress while she saved money for school, and this year, she started at the university as a sophomore. She was going to be a music major, even though she didn't know it yet. She'd aced last semester's music theory course, and she made it through a grueling audition to get into the U's chorus.

I'd held her hand the night before the audition, preventing her from talking too much, taking up smoking all over again, and practicing until she went hoarse.

She'd come back so jumped up, I'd thought she was high on something. I'd never seen her happy before.

Which was why this whole personals ad thing worried me. If this guy cheated her in any way, used in her any way, I was afraid the damage to her self-esteem would be lethal.

She let me listen to the demo tape, and I made a few suggestions I now regret. I had her drop "Me and Bobby McGee" because it sounded too much like Joplin and not enough like Karen. I had her add Cole Porter's "Miss Otis Regrets" because Karen sang it with a nasty sweetness, and I questioned her use of Sheryl Crowe's "All I Wanna Do (Is Have Some Fun)" not because she sang it badly but because I was afraid the guy would get the wrong message.

Karen took all of my suggestions and then some. The new improved demo was such a knockout that I wanted her to send to a local studio. Instead she sent it to M Folklorist along with a photograph she'd paid too much for at a professional's shop in the mall.

Of course he called. What red-blooded American male wouldn't? He had, she said, a Barry White sort of voice, deep and throbbing and sexy.

More trouble, I thought.

He wanted to meet her at the new Starbucks on the north end of campus at four in the afternoon. She would be able to recognize him by the Celtic knot he wore in his hair.

Stranger and stranger, I thought.

By now, she couldn't have shaken me off this first date if she had tried. A Barry White voice, hair long enough for jewelry, that strange note—all sent out warning signs for me.

Karen said I had spent too much time looking at the seedy side of humanity, and maybe I had. Divorce cases showed the worst sides of people, and those were most of the cases I had. Occasionally I'd get insurance fraud or the rare security double check, but mostly, I watched people cheat on their spouses, rob their own bank accounts, and sabotage their life partner's jobs so that they'd win custody of children who had become more of a prize than objects of affection.

What I didn't tell Karen, couldn't tell Karen, was that I had come to appreciate her throaty voice running scales on the other side of my apartment's paperthin walls. That I now preferred her rendition of "Makin' Whoopee" to virtually anyone else's. Sometimes I lay on my couch with the lights off, listening to Karen rehearse as if I were listening to a brandnew prize CD.

When she made it that next step up the ladder—and I had no doubt she would—when she would be singing in the bars instead of waiting tables, when she got heard by her first scout—I would cheer her like I had cheered no one else from our little dump on the wrong side of the tracks.

And I would miss her like no one else either.

I stationed myself at Starbucks at three-thirty. I wore a pager in case M Folklorist decided to change the date's venue. I brought along *Civilization and Its Discontents*, a thin paperback of Freud's masterpiece whose very cover looked dry. People wouldn't think twice if they saw me scanning a room, not with that book in my hands. I sat at a wobbly table near the muted blue back wall, and ordered a thin double tall that I nursed for the next half hour and an oversized shortbread cookie that didn't last five minutes.

M Folklorist arrived before Karen and staked out a table in the middle. He faced the door and watched it as if he were meeting a long-lost lover. I got a good view of his profile, and I was close enough to hear his fingers drumming on the table.

He was, as I expected, every hopeful man's nightmare. Tall, broad-shouldered, muscular in an athletic sort of way. His wavy black hair trailed to his shoulders, and he tamed it with the aforementioned Celtic knot. A woman would call what he wore a barrette, but it looked too masculine for that. It was an aggressive piece of jewelry, one that defied challenge and made other men, men less comfortable with their sense of self, wonder if they should wear such a piece. He had a diamond in his left ear—I couldn't see if he had one in his right—and he wore an open weave cotton shirt that looked as if he'd stolen it off the cover of a romance novel.

His jeans were one size too tight—I was praying for them to split as he sat down—and he wore boots with enough heel to make him look exotic rather than an inch or two too short.

I had no idea why this man needed a personals ad. Every woman in the place was staring at him, and a few were actively drooling. The men were looking at him, too, either with reluctant and angry envy, like I was, or with sheer unadulterated lust. I hoped he was dumber than a salmon in mating season; I didn't think it was fair for a man to be blessed with good looks, athleticism, and brains.

Karen arrived promptly at four. She stopped in the doorway for a half second. She had worn a dress, a cream number with trim that matched her auburn hair, and a side cut that revealed a length of thigh. For a moment she looked at M Folklorist as if she couldn't believe he was the one with the Celtic knot. Then he stood, nearly knocking over the table, and said in a voice more Barry White than Barry White's, "Karen?"

The women in the shop gave her the evil eye, the men nodded as if they understood how this couple came to be, and I felt my shoulder slump. I'd hoped I was wrong, that this was not the guy. I'd hoped that he'd stand her up in favor of a soprano with Beverly Sills' vibrato and Whitney Houston's talent for over-singing.

Karen was standing beside the table, hands clutching her schoolbooks to her chest. "You're Tom?"

Tom? She hadn't told me his name. Of course, I hadn't asked either. Hard to believe a studly guy like this was named something as mundane as Tom.

She studiously avoided looking at me. I took a long sip of my double tall and realized how much I hated cold coffee.

"I was afraid you weren't going to come," he said.

She shrugged.

He extended a hand to the chair opposite him. "Please, sit. I'll get you something to drink."

"Tea," she said in typical Karen fashion. She was an original. Starbucks specialized in coffee, but she wasn't the type who got sucked into a trend.

He did not seem amused by her little peculiarity, at least, not like I was. "Tea it is."

He went to the line, and it suddenly lost its form as the women who were in it turned to look at him. He had to be giving off pheromones like a mating experiment. I leaned back in my chair and crossed my arms, Freud overturned on the table.

Karen set her books on the far side of the round table, and ran fingers over the pages of the top one— *A Dictionary of Musical Terms*. She was watching Tom the Folklorist as if she wanted to peel off those tight jeans right then and there. I felt an irrational urge to get in line, wait until he'd been served the steaming coffee and the boiling water, and then bump him so hard that the liquid would scald him, sending him to the hospital and ending the date forever.

But if I did that, Karen would send me packing, and she'd be alone with the male cover model/ potential serial killer, and I'd never forgive myself.

I decided to bide my time, hoping that his flaws— whatever they were—would reveal themselves in conversation.

He handed her the tea and a red rose that seemed to come out of nowhere. Then he went back to the counter and retrieved his cappuccino. He stole three rock candy swizzle sticks off the counter and put one in his mouth like he ate raw sugar all the time.

If he did, that svelte male physique took more work than I had initially imagined.

Then he sat down. Karen was hiding her face in the rose. Its bloom made her hair look pale.

"So," he said, "you're a music student."

"I haven't declared my major yet." Her voice was soft. "Do you teach here?"

The first swizzle stick was clean. He picked up the second and twirled it in those long fingers. He ignored his cappuccino, didn't even suck on the foam like most New Age coffee drinkers.

"I'm on sabbatical," he said. "I'm doing a special study. Traditional songs of vanishing cultures."

Karen laughed—nervously, I thought. "Well, this culture isn't vanishing."

"Parts of it are." His deep rich voice warmed even more. I had never heard a speaking voice with so many tonal qualities. Back in my musical days, days I had never told Karen about, I had learned quite a bit about vocal color and brightness, about subtlety and shadings, all as they related to song. I'd never heard the same technique used in speaking.

"Yeah, right," Karen said.

He leaned forward. Clearly this was a subject he loved. "Once upon a time," he said as if he were telling a story he had no part of, "the Earth had thousands of cultures. Even within a dominant culture, like the British Empire, individual nations existed, their cultures surviving the ravishment of war and indoctrination."

I raised an eyebrow. This guy, for all his great speaking tones, would be a deadly dull lecturer. I couldn't believe Karen was looking at him so raptly. If I had tried something like this on a first date, the girl across from me would dump the hot tea on my head, grab a swizzle stick for herself, and leave.

"We still have a lot of cultures," Karen said. "And the British Empire is gone."

"Let us take the United States," he said. "Since you have learned how to mass produce culture, through radio and television, smaller enclaves have watched their traditions merge into the mainstream. The native cultures, for instance, now . . ."

His voice became background noise for me. Like Muzak, only smoother, more relaxing. I looked around the room. The women were still watching him. The twenty-something behind the counter, her hair in spikes, the dog collar around her neck filthy, the jewelry pierced into her eyebrows colored black, was staring at him as she ran the espresso machine. The middle-aged hippie who clearly managed the place was running her tie-die scarf back and forth through her hands as she listened to his every word.

". . . and in Appalachia," he said. "Soon these traditions will be all gone."

"I don't understand how I fit in," Karen said.

"I'm studying music," he said. "Recording and preserving songs that are mostly forgotten."

"I don't know any songs like that." Karen was still clutching her music dictionary. So she wasn't entirely at ease with Tom the Folklorist. That pleased me a bit too much.

"I'm sure you do," he said. "The songs you sang as a child. The songs your mother sang to you before you went to sleep. The music you heard in religious services or over a campfire. Those are the songs I'm interested in."

"You've probably heard them already," Karen said. "I grew up in a pretty whitebread community."

I hadn't, but I doubted Tom wanted to hear from

me. A couple of the women had moved closer, as if they knew some songs they wanted to share with him.

"You'd be surprised at what you know," he said. "Why don't you sing something for me?"

"Here?" Karen blushed a deep red. "I can't sing here."

"I thought you were a performer."

He'd caught her. I wondered how she would talk her way out of this one.

"People don't sing in Starbucks," she said.

"Then let's go to the Music Hall," he said. "I'm sure there's a practice room open."

Karen sipped her tea as if she hadn't heard him. "Um, I'm a little confused," she said. "A friend of mine said—" and she managed to say that without looking at me or inclining her head in my direction, "—that this is just a unique way of hitting on me. I mean, that was a personals ad."

He smiled. Half the room backed up with the power of that smile. The other half moved toward him as if he were the sun and they needed warmth.

Karen, bless her, didn't move at all.

"I go to communities," he said. "I interview elderly women and little old men. I talk to tribal leaders and I listen closely to the voices of children at play. I can get my material without putting an ad in the paper."

Now I was leaning forward. I hadn't expected him to take this tack.

"But," he said. "I have not met any women who share my interests. I adore music and beautiful voices. I love old songs and new ones as well. I like the emotion of a well balanced voice. It is, to me, more sexy than a well proportioned face."

A well proportioned face? Well, the guy wasn't going to pass any charm tests.

"So I took out a personals ad and hoped I would meet a woman who shared my interests." He lowered his voice to a whisper—or, more accurately, a rumble that could be heard in all corners of the coffee shop. "I hope that woman will be you."

Karen's blush deepened. Her eyes sparkled and this time, her glance darted to me. I rolled my eyes, but by the time they were in their proper place in their sockets, she was looking back at Tom the Folklorist.

With a look of complete infatuation.

I suppressed a sigh. I never pegged Karen for someone who would fall for a deep voice, a red rose, and a practiced (not very good) speech.

"So," he said. "Would you like to go to the Music Hall?"

Karen smiled at him. A soft sexy smile I had never seen before. My fingers clenched around the Freud.

"All right," she said.

The Carrington Carruthers Music Hall was an old stone building with the best acoustics for twenty miles. It had been part of the U's original campus way back when and had always been used for music.

The practice rooms were in the basement and in the '70s, they had been modernized. They had been soundproofed so the student playing Bartok in Room A wouldn't be distracted by the student playing Scott Joplin in Room B. Part of the soundproofing had been the addition of thick wooden doors with a small window made of triple paned glass, so that the people inside would be visible with a little work. It was designed so that the practice rooms didn't give complete privacy—seems in the '60s, they'd often been used for nefarious purposes, from dope dealing to sex parties.

But that little window didn't solve my problem. I wouldn't be able to see or her what was happening in Karen's room—not without seeming like a voyeur. If she got in trouble with good old Tom, it would happen in the practice room, and there wasn't a lot I could do about it.

At first I thought I would have to walk back and forth in front of the room like a lost student waiting for the practice room. Then I realized that the room they took was across from the vending machines. I got my binoculars and my kit from the car, sat at a sticky plastic table, and watched.

Tom sat on the metal folding chair while Karen sat at the piano. She would hit a note, and then she'd sing. I couldn't hear that sultry voice, but I could imagine it—its depth, power, and range filling the small space, echoing off the stone walls. Tom looked rapt, his cheeks flushed, his mouth open, his eyes slightly glazed. I had the horrible disconcerting feeling that this was how he looked when he had an orgasm, and I wondered if Karen noticed that too.

She didn't seem to. She laughed between songs, flirted a bit, and then came out of the room. Tom remained inside. Her hair was curled, the edges damp with sweat as if she had been working out. Her eyes were too bright, and her smile was a private one.

She started when she saw me. "I thought you'd gone home," she whispered.

"And leave you with pretty boy? Not a chance."

"Well, he's safe enough," she said.

I crossed my arms and leaned back in the chair. "And you base that on what?"

She shrugged. "He just seems nice."

"So did Ted Bundy."

She went to the soda machine, put in a dollar, and a can rumbled out. "You worry too much, Drew," she said. "It's okay. Go home now."

"I made you a promise," I said. "I'm staying until the bitter end."

"It might end privately," she said.

"I thought you didn't do that on the first date."

Her dark eyes met mine. "I haven't had a first date since I was sixteen. Maybe I've changed."

"I hope you haven't."

Her lips thinned. "Sometimes you really are an old fuddy." Then she turned her back on me and headed to the practice room without waiting for my response.

An old fuddy. Not a lean, muscular poster boy with a penchant for songs no one cared about. An old fuddy. I guess I was. But I still planned to stay in my chair. I didn't trust Mr. GQ Folklorist, and I wasn't sure why.

They stayed in that room until eight o'clock. Tom listened to her sing with rapt attention. I had to continue drinking Diet Cokes to keep from falling asleep. Watching someone sing wasn't the same as listening.

Nothing betrayed him. He barely moved. Once or twice he shifted in his seat. Halfway through his private concert, he fiddled with his diamond earring, and once he checked his Celtic knot. But other than that, he gave Karen his full attention.

That was probably the best thing he could do to appeal to a lonely woman like that.

When they left the practice room, he had his hand on her arm. She leaned into him as if she'd had too many drinks. Still, she found the chance to glance at me and shake her head. He didn't even seem to notice.

He was talking, and as they passed, I caught part of it: ". . . scientific basis that song came before speech. Not worded song, but organized sound, emotions put to music. Singing is one of the most primitive and primal urges. If you think about it, survival can be tied up in musical notes. A man can sing longer than he can shout, and a trained man . . ."

Well, a trained man should have put a gun to that guy's head years ago for being criminally pedantic. But Karen seemed to be appreciating it.

I didn't know what I'd do if she decided that the folklorist was the man of her dreams. Blind dates weren't supposed to work that way. In a rational world, a blind date would show the datee that she was better off with the people—well, the person—right next door.

As they left the building, Karen's hand slid around Tom's back. He stiffened visibly and she looked at him, surprised. I was a bit surprised too. The man had seemed enraptured with her. He disentangled himself from her arm, then slid his hand along her skin until he held hers captive. It probably felt romantic, but from the back—which was where I got my view—it looked manipulative.

And even more suspicious.

He walked her to her car—a five-year-old paid-off

Taurus that was one of the few things she'd salvaged from her marriage, and kissed her hand. She leaned into him eyes closed, but he was the one who stepped back.

I caught only a bit of what he said. That low rumble, which carried so well in Starbucks, dissipated like the wind outside. The words I heard were "old-fashioned," "first date," and "a bit of mystery."

He was more than a bit of mystery to me. I didn't know any man who would turn down a woman like Karen. Any heterosexual man, that is.

They spoke for a moment longer, and then he handed her a card which had, I assumed, his phone number on it. She smiled at him, got into the car, and drove off, her right hand raised in a small wave.

I didn't know if the wave was for him or for me.

It didn't matter. This guy was strange enough, and Karen was hooked enough, that I wanted answers. He stood in the parking lot for a few moments, staring after her. When her red taillights disappeared into the darkness, he reached up to his ear and removed his earring. Then he rubbed the earlobe as if he had been in pain the entire time.

If I had been a betting man, I'd have wagered that the Celtic knot was coming off second and then the belt on the pants would be undone so Tom could take a deep breath. But none of that happened. Instead he caught and held that earring as if it were a precious treasure, and walked across the parking lot to the foot-path that went around the lake.

I followed him.

The trail was dimly lit. A handful of yellow street-lights, fashioned to look like gaslights, illuminated small patches of the path. That was better than it had been when I was in school. In those distant days, there wasn't any light at all, and the female students had protested, saying that it was dangerous after dark. I thought it was more dangerous now, with the patches of light and shadow. It gave the illusion of safety whereas before the path proclaimed walker beware.

He walked with a loping, almost unnatural gait. I kept a discreet distance behind him. The lake was calm, the lights reflecting across its waters. This close, it smelled faintly of dead fish.

We were the only two people on the path. I worried that he would turn around and notice me, but he seemed preoccupied. He walked faster and faster, then stopped suddenly beside the Kissing Tree.

The Kissing Tree was an ancient oak that had been split by lightning, then had grown around the wound. The split formed a perfect love seat, and more than one couple had been found entwined in its branches.

Tom climbed onto the split and I eased into the shadows. Here was where it would get interesting. Here I would learn what he really wanted with Karen.

While he waited, he pried a piece of wood off one of the forking branches. He held the wood in his left hand and covered the hole he had made with his right. Then he replaced the wood, slid off the tree and headed back toward campus.

I moved deeper into the shadows. He was humming as he passed me. I didn't recognize the tune, but his rumbling hum was both engaging and uplifting. I found myself wanting to hum along.

Then I realized what I was doing. I would have revealed myself if I had made a sound. He continued down the path, and I hesitated. If I followed him, I might make it to my car in time to trace him all the way home. There I could see if he were married or single, straight or gay.

But somehow I didn't think those questions were as relevant as the one behind me. What had he done to the Kissing Tree? And why? He'd been in such a hurry to reach it. Had he put his earring inside it? Was that some sort of signal? Or was he returning a gift?

I waited until I couldn't see him any more, then I went to the tree. I had to hoist myself onto the split.

The wood was flat and rubbed smooth from the years of use. I ran my hands along the area Tom had touched. At first I felt nothing, and then I noticed it. A deep indentation along the side of one of the branches. I dug my finger inside, and pulled out a perfectly carved lid made of wood. There was a hole underneath and inside it felt shallow and empty.

I pulled out my flashlight, and turned it on, aiming the beam at the hole. There was nothing there. And then I noticed an even smaller hole in the center. I shone the light at that, and it seemed to reflect the light back. I took out one of my lock picks and poked at the hole with it.

The hole swallowed the edge of the pick and almost tugged it out of my hand. I pulled back, and the tip of the pick had been broken off.

I cursed softly—I didn't have the budget to constantly replace my tools—and then I dug the pick in harder, poking at the edges of the hole until I made the hole wider. Then I pulled out the pick and shone the light inside.

Again, it reflected back at me. Then the mouth of the hole closed up, like the mouth of a fish. And try as I might, I couldn't find that opening again.

I was being strange. The man had come out here because the tree was some kind of message center for him. He'd opened the hole to see if someone had left a note, and when no one had, he walked away. For all I knew, this had nothing to do with Karen, nothing to do with me. I was being thorough when I didn't need to be. Maybe when I got home, Karen would come over to my apartment and tell me that the date had been a bust. Maybe she would come over and ask me why good men were so hard to meet.

Maybe she would forget all about the gorgeous folklorist.

But somehow, I didn't think that was likely.

The next morning, I woke up to the sound of singing. Karen was in her shower and over the squeal of pipes, I heard "Me and Bobby McGee" at full Joplin. I frowned and rolled over. Karen had long since moved away from her imitation phase. Even though she felt that "Bobby McGee" was one of her best covers, she rarely sang it anymore. She only wanted to include it in her demo to show her range.

What about her date with Folklorist Tom had driven her to sing such a sad song? After a date, you'd think Karen wouldn't be singing the blues—any kind of blues.

I waited until the shower shut off and the singing stopped before getting into my own shower. Sometimes, if I lay in bed when Karen was singing, my eyes closed, warm covers around me, it almost seemed as if we shared the same place, as if we belonged together.

Almost.

Maybe I should have been the one singing the blues.

I was making toast when there was tentative knock on my door.

"It's open, Karen," I said.

She came in. I offered her some sourdough with peanut butter, but she declined.

"I wanted to thank you for coming along last night," she said.

"My pleasure," I said, even though it wasn't.

"What did you think of him?"

I suppressed a sigh. I had been up half the night trying to figure out how to answer that question. If I went too far, she'd know I was jealous, and if I didn't go far enough, she'd see him again.

"What did you think of him?" I asked.

"Come on, Drew, no games."

"Not a game," I said. "It's just safer if you go first."

She giggled and put in a piece of toast for herself. Then she helped herself to some of my coffee. She banged through the cupboards, found some ancient honey, and put it on the table.

"I think he's sweet and old-fashioned and incredibly gorgeous and a little too obsessed with his work and just about perfect, and that really scares me."

"Being obsessed about his work?"

"No," she said. "The fact that he looks like my dream date. God, I sound like something from the *Patty Duke Show!* My dream date."

She was too young to remember the *Patty Duke*

Show, too. Thank the cultural reference gods for *Nick at Nite*.

It took me a moment to get past her gushing to what she was actually saying. "Your dream date?"

"Yeah. If I had to describe a man that I wanted to date, physical attributes and all, I'd describe him."

"Down to his job?"

"No." She laughed. The toast popped up and she grabbed it out of the toaster with her fingernails. Then she put it on one of my chipped plastic plates, grabbed a knife, and took them to the table. "Just the way he looks. And his voice. Oof. All he'd have to do is shut out the lights and talk to me and I'd be jelly for the next two days."

"You and half the women in the world."

She looked at me, honey-covered knife clenched in her right fist. "What do you mean?"

"Didn't you see the reaction at Starbucks? I swear every woman in the place was infatuated with your folklorist."

"You make that sound suspicious."

I nodded. My toast had gotten cold. "Why would a guy like that go to the personals?"

"He's not searching for a face," she said. "He's searching for a voice. He says that voices are the essence of a person's being, and that he is searching for the most suitable voice."

Stranger and stranger. "Suitable for what?"

"For him."

"So," I said slowly, "you could weigh six thousand pounds, have acne so bad that no one could see your skin, and not bathe for a year, but if you had the right voice, this guy would want to spend his life with you?"

She smiled. "That's right."

"I don't believe it," I said.

"Why not?" she asked, her smile gone.

"There's got to be a catch. Men don't work that way."

Her eyes grew cold. I had insulted her. Karen was not the kind of woman who whined. She would never have said something like *You don't believe he could be interested in me!* But she thought it. She clearly thought it.

"Maybe he does." But she didn't sound confident any longer.

"Maybe," I said.

"I'm going to see him again." She spoke almost defiantly.

"I knew that last night."

"I don't want you following us."

"I knew that last night as well."

"What do I owe you?"

This time it was my turn to bristle. "I did it as a favor."

"All right," she said. "But now the favor's over and done."

I nodded. She was right. Now the favor was over and done. Now I worked for me.

I refrained from following them on that second date. And the third, and the fourth. But I did use my trusty computer to dig up information on old Tom the Folklorist. I didn't have a lot to go on. With some reluctance, Karen gave me his last name and his phone number, but only because I told her that I needed a way to track her when she was away.

She never asked why. I hadn't ever called her at work or in any sort of need before.

Tom didn't work at the U like I thought he did, nor did he seem to work anywhere. He didn't have an easily available home address or a home phone—the number Karen was using was a cell phone that he seemed to carry all the time—and, even more upsetting, he didn't seem to have a social security number.

For all intents and purposes, Tom the Folklorist didn't exist.

I wanted to tell Karen that, but I wasn't sure how to do it, not after I had promised I would leave her alone. Besides, she seemed happy. She smiled more than she ever had, and she sang a lot too, although her taste in music seemed to have changed. Instead of singing ballads and blues rifts and popular songs from the '30s and '40s, she started singing golden oldies, songs I'd always hated. One morning she went through an entire set of teen death songs from "Teen Angel" to "One Last Kiss" and I thought I would scream. The next day, she did teen angst songs, including five different versions of "It's My Party (and I'll Cry if I Want To)."

Finally, I saw her on the concrete walkway, and I asked her point-blank why she had switched material.

She blinked at me uncomprehendingly. "I hadn't realized I had."

"Karen," I said, "there're only so many renditions of 'Teen Angel' a man can take."

She flushed lightly, but didn't apologize.

"What about 'Miss Otis Regrets'? Or even 'Me and Bobby McGee'? I don't care how Joplin you sound."

"I sound like Joplin?" she asked, frowning.

Then I frowned. Had she forgotten? We had talked about it for an entire evening.

"Or 'Shenandoah,' 'The Red River Valley,' 'The Streets of Laredo.' Anything instead of those teen angst songs."

She put a hand on my arm. "Teach them to me sometime," she said, "and I'll sing them for you."

Then she walked away from me down the stairs.

I watched her get into her car, feeling chilled. Teach them to her? She knew them all. But she had watched me blankly, and there had been no recognition in her face when I mentioned the song titles.

It was as if she had never heard of them before.

A few days later, I saw her in the parking lot in front of the building. She hadn't come by my apartment much since she'd started seeing Tom, and I missed her.

I told her that, and she shrugged.

"I've been busy," she said.

"Classes?" I asked, not wanting to mention Tom.

She nodded, but looked distracted. "I'm spending too much time in the practice rooms."

"With Tom?"

She nodded again and set her books on the roof of her car. "I've been thinking. I don't enjoy the singing as much anymore. I guess I wasn't meant to do it for hours on end. Do you think I should change my major to English?"

She hadn't been singing in the mornings at all, not since we last spoke. And she looked wan.

"Has Tom been criticizing you?" I asked, knowing I was on dangerous ground.

She blinked at me, as if she couldn't believe I had asked the question. "No, of course not. He loves to hear me sing. We go almost every night."

"Those have been your dates?" I blurted.

"Sometimes we have dinner."

"And that doesn't seem odd to you?"

Her eyes narrowed, then she grabbed her books. "He likes voices. My voice."

I stared at her. "Karen," I repeated softly. "That doesn't seem odd to you?"

She puled open the car door, then leaned on it. "I always thought I'd want a man who moved slow."

"But?"

She set the books inside and put her hand on the wheel as if she wanted the conversation over. "I'm beginning to think all he wants to do is hear me sing."

"He hasn't touched you?"

"No."

"Kissed you?"

"No."

"Held you?"

"No."

"Then he's a fool," I said, a bit more strongly than I should have.

She smiled. It softened her face. "You're sweet, Drew."

Sweet. That was enough to cool any man's ardor. Sweet, indeed. "All he's been doing is listening?" I asked, trying to take the attention off me.

"Yes," she said. "New songs every night. I didn't realize I knew so many. And now I'm getting so tired I can hardly remember what I've done. I'm afraid I'll repeat myself."

"Sing him the teen angst songs," I said. "Those'll cure his desire for new music."

"Teen angst songs?"

" 'Teen Angel' or 'One Last Kiss.' The ones I complained about two days ago? The ones that stopped you from singing in the morning?"

She blinked at me, her eyes blank. "Sometimes," she said, "I wonder where you get these ideas. Teen angst songs. I don't suppose you want to teach them to me."

My breath caught in my throat. "No," I said. "I don't."

How do you find a man with no permanent address? If I had nifty equipment, I could triangulate his cell phone, but I wasn't that high tech. Instead, I checked the very place that I had first seen him, the place he met Karen.

Starbucks.

"Oh, the gorgeous guy?" asked the twenty-something behind the counter. Her spiked hair was green and curly today. "The one with the sweet tooth?"

I nodded.

She ran a hand possessively over the rock candy. "He comes in every morning at ten, every afternoon at one, and every evening at five. You just missed him."

"That often?" I asked. "Does he work nearby?"

She shrugged. Her dog collar was moved up and down with her shoulder blades. "I have no idea where he works. I'm not that interested. He's a user, you know. Pretty and knows it."

I didn't like the way my fists had automatically clenched. "A user?"

"He meets a woman at each time slot—a different woman, and they seem to last with him about a month. They're all goo-goo-eyed, I mean, who wouldn't be? But he isn't. He wants something from them, and if it's sex, he's good."

"He's good?" I asked.

"He never looks tired or trippy, you know. Always energetic and put together. You'd think a guy who gets it regular three times a day would be mussed at least once in a while."

You'd think.

"Do they stay here?"

She shook her head. "Why do you want to know?"

"Because," I said. 'I think he's just used the wrong girl."

So that day I had lunch at Starbucks—a cold sandwich, an almond biscotti, and a double tall. My camouflage book this time was Proust's *Remembrance of Things Past* which I had discovered, coffee-stained and torn, in the shop's lost and found.

Just before one, Tom came in and exactly at one, a fresh-faced young thing who made Karen look old, scampered to the chair beside him. She looked smitten and he watched her with the same guarded warmth he'd used with Karen.

Then he got up and left. I followed as he took her to the practice rooms in the Music Hall. Someone needed to charge this guy rent.

Sure enough, she sang to him. They stayed for three hours, then he walked her to her car. She tried to kiss him and he deftly maneuvered his way out of it. He sent her on her way, then hurried down the lake path to the Kissing Tree.

This time, I didn't wait until he was out of sight. I opened that wooden storage space immediately, in time to see his diamond earring circling the interior like a marble about to go down a drain.

I caught the earring. It looked like any old earring except that the crystal inside the gold prongs wasn't a diamond. It looked like some kind of chip.

I clutched the diamond in my hand and hurried after Tom. I only had a half-hour or so before he met Karen.

He was sauntering past the lake, like a man with no concerns in the world. I came up beside him and matched his step. He gave me a startled look and then walked faster.

I kept up and then opened my hand. "You mind telling me what this is?"

His face went pale, then it turned gray, and then an odd shade of green. "Where did you get that?"

"From the tree. You mind telling me what's so important about it?"

He had another in his ear. I remembered watching him fidget with it as he listened to Karen.

I put out a hand and stopped him. "Okay, here's the deal. I'm a friend of Karen's, and I don't like what's going on. So you tell me what you need her for and I'll give you back your toy."

"Karen?" he said.

"Don't play dumb with me, pretty boy," I said. "I tailed you on the first date."

"You're some kind of stalker?"

"I'm some kind of private detective. Now tell me what you want with Karen."

His lips thinned. They were almost purplish. He wasn't as handsome when he got riled. "I only want her to sing to me."

"Yeah, and every time she sings for you, she forgets the song."

His eyes widened so far that they seemed round. "Forgets?"

I nodded. "And now she tells me she doesn't enjoy singing anymore. What the hell are you doing to her?"

"I am," he said, reaching for the chip, "recording her."

I closed my fist over the earring and moved it away. "For what?"

"I am a folklorist."

"Yeah? And I'm Sam Spade. Should we try again?"

"I am not lying to you," he said. His Barry White voice now had a bit of a reedy, whiny quality to it. It suddenly didn't sound human. "I am taking the songs from this culture back to my own."

"Your own? And what would that be?"

He reached for the earring again. I moved my hand out of his reach. I felt like I was in kindergarten and we were playing a game of keep-away.

"I suppose you've been taping the other women, too," I said.

"Recording," he said.

"Let me take you around the corner. There's a CD shop there. You'll be able to buy any song you want at that place and then some. You don't need to lure pretty women into practice rooms."

He let his hand fall to his side. "I have heard your recordings. They are flat and lifeless, without spontaneity or warmth. They do not have emotion. Only rehearsed and spliced sound. That is not song. That is something else."

"And on this little device, I'd find song?"

"If you knew how to play it back."

In spite of myself, I was intrigued. "I thought song was just a musical composition for the human voice."

"It is emotion," he said. "The first and most primal source of communication among most sentient races."

"Sentient races?"

He looked away from me. His skin changed from greenish to grayish to greenish again. "Tell me again what is happening?"

"She's losing her music. Every line of it. She doesn't even sing to herself anymore."

"And you know this because you are her lover?"

I didn't answer that. If he could pick and choose which questions he wanted to respond to, so could I.

"It has never done that before," he said more to himself than to me. "That alters what I have been doing."

"What were you doing?" I asked.

"Recording love songs." He let out a watery little sigh. His hair fell limply around his face. "I cannot give them back. Oh, this is terrible. I must cease until we find equipment compatible with your physiology."

Compatible with our physiology? "What kind of game is this?"

"Not one that I should be participating in. I shall remove myself quickly, and inform my companions. We are not ready to continue this work." He took my hand and pumped it like we were old friends. His skin was scaly and vaguely gooey. I pulled away.

"I must thank you for informing me," he said. "You will give her my regrets, no? And Lisha and Anne. I meet them during the day. You will tell them as well?"

"I—"

He had taken the earring from me. He studied it for a moment, and then he put it in his pocket.

"One should never interact with a culture one does not entirely understand. I am so, so sorry." He bowed to me, his hair thinning on top, revealing skin mottled and brown. Then he stood, ran a hand over himself, and shrank to nothing.

I looked down. There wasn't even a brown spot on the pavement.

The Celtic knot clattered against the asphalt. It looked old and dented and somewhat sad. I left it there, a marker to something I didn't entirely understand.

By the time I reached the Music Hall, I had convinced myself that I had imagined his disappearance. Almost. My nerves still jangled from the clatter of the barrette, and my skin crawled from his gooey touch.

I went back to Starbucks and saw Karen, sitting alone at the table, looking both hopeful and relieved at the same time.

I didn't go in.

I went home instead and put on some Billie Holiday, the good old bluesy stuff about lost loves and horrible men and ruined affairs.

Hours later, Karen came to my door. This was the Karen I had met, the one whose self-esteem had been whittled away by a husband who hadn't loved her, the one who'd barely survived that messy divorce. Sometimes, it seemed, a person could steal bits of another person and not even realize he was doing it. Not even realize that what he took might never come back.

I put my arms around her and we sat on the couch. She curled against me like a child. Billie Holiday was singing "I'll Never Be the Same," her voice old beyond her years.

"Have I heard this song before?" Karen asked.

I didn't tell her that I first heard it when she sang it to me. I didn't tell her that it had been one of her favorites. Instead, I stroked her hair and held her close, feeling how frail and fragile she was.

But her bones were solid, and her heart beat against mine. He had taken her repertoire, not her self. And she could regain a repertoire with time and practice, and desire.

The CD ended. She stirred against me.

"I have more," I said. "You want to hear it?"

She sat up, rubbed her face with her fist, and gave me a sad, sleepy grin. "I think I *need* to hear it. Isn't that strange?"

"It's not strange at all," I said. It was the first thing in weeks that made sense to me.

A KISS AT MIDNIGHT

by R. Davis

R. Davis lives in Maine with his wife Monica
and their two children, Morgan and Mason. He
writes both poetry and fiction in a variety of
styles and genres. His work can be viewed in
numerous anthologies including *Black Cats and
Broken Mirrors*, *Merlin*, and *Catfantastic V*. Current projects include more work than he can
keep track of, and trying to keep up with his
extremely energetic children.

"On Sunday mornings I remember the first girl
I loved, red hair so dark it looked like a
bonfire."
　　　　　　　　　　—from *Waltzing With the Dead*

*Very attractive, SWF in search of passionate SWM
for one-night stand. Must understand the hungers
of the flesh. Guaranteed unforgettable evening.
Discretion a must. Send picture and bio to Box
8267-473.*

I imagine her this way:
　　She wakes to red velvet and lace. Though there is

not the tiniest sliver of light in the darkness, her green eyes can make out the tiny swirls in the fabric of the cloth canopy above her with ease. She licks her dry red lips, and her delicate, pale hands move over the white silk sheets of her bed. She rises, her long red hair a pillow-cloud around her shoulders, and she greets the night once again—a beautiful angel of love and lust and death. She wakes in this manner every night, as she has every night before. . . .

I fell in love with her in a single night. I answered her ad, expecting nothing more than an evening of enjoyable, commitment-free sex. I didn't get what I expected—nor, I suppose, did she. For long months, I have been thinking only of her. Trying to find her once again so I can tell her now I understand that true love does not care about the murky boundary waters between life and death, good and evil, or right and wrong. Love is the desire to consume oneself in the flames of another person—the flesh, minds, and souls combine and grow into a fire that burns with starlike heat at its most passionate, or burns out into the cold oblivion of darkness when it fails. . . .

I started browsing the personals a year after my wife, Anaka, was killed in a car accident. At first, I found them grimly amusing—the desperate acts of people who were unwilling or unable to meet others in the real world. I didn't realize then how desperate I myself would become; when the long days at work would become longer nights at home, sitting in a silence that no music or television program could breach. I became a recluse of sorts. I didn't go out, didn't meet people, and didn't start my life over as I'd planned when the shock and grief of losing my wife had passed. I was alone, and reading the personals—at first a joke to me—became a quest to connect somehow with someone else, to live again.

I was scared of course. Who wouldn't be in this age of unreason? I read the ads in the paper, over and over, searching for the ones that would interest me enough to answer. I had a process of reading them in no time at all—ignore every ad that involved men, couples, or home videos, and read every ad that involved a single female. It shortened the list considerably.

Occasionally, I would find the courage to respond to an ad, only to find that the people who placed the ad had misrepresented themselves. The women would—in actuality—be men, or unattractive to me, or simply undesirable in some other fashion. I went on several unsuccessful first dates before I decided to approach it from the other direction.

The day finally came when I placed my own ad, to generally poor results. Usually it read something like:

> *SWM, 30-something, not hard on the eyes, seeking SWF for relationship, possible long-term commitment. He is secure, honest, and intelligent. She must demonstrate similar qualities. Reply to Box 9673-626.*

More often than not, a brief phone conversation ended any hope of meeting in person—the results from this direction were the same as they were from the other one. It didn't seem to matter whether I was the advertiser or the respondent, everyone seemed to be something other than what they said they were. After one such phone call, I realized that I was being too particular. I also realized that I didn't really care. I was looking for someone who could replace my wife, my soul mate—and that didn't seem possible anymore. How do you go about replacing someone who is irreplaceable? I didn't want to risk love anymore, or face the pain of losing a loved one.

At night, I would lie awake and remember Anaka in vivid detail. The way her dark hair curled when it was wet, the color of her eyes in candlelight, the sound of her voice, husky and low, after we'd made love. I didn't believe that anyone could measure up to her. The very idea of love began to seem a little sad to me, like finding out that your religion is based on a falsehood.

Yet there was no doubt in my mind that I still longed for the touch of a woman. I became more and more lonely, and as the days and nights passed, I found that almost more than anything else, I missed physical intimacy. I would walk along the pier, fascinated by the way a woman's hips looked inside her jeans, or the press of her breasts against the fabric of her shirt. The scent of women's perfume mixing with the smell of the ocean in an intoxicating blend, the fading light of the day turning faces and forms into silhouettes that could—in my mind's eye—be a replacement for my lost Anaka.

Finally, I decided to ignore my continuing quest for true love, and find a way to appease my physical desires. Perhaps by extinguishing my lust I could find a path back to a place where love was possible again. I felt my desires were perfectly normal, and at the very least I would be on the same page as the other lost souls who were investing their time in the personals. My temporary hold on finding true love again would, if nothing else, save me from continued disappointments.

And then I saw her ad for the first time:

Very attractive, SWF in search of passionate SWM for one-night stand. Must understand the hungers of the flesh. Guaranteed unforgettable evening. Discretion a must. Send picture and bio to Box 8267-473.

The hungers of the flesh. I liked the sound of that a great deal. That is what I was suffering from . . . a hunger for the touch of flesh. How I lusted for the sweet scent of a woman's skin, the taste of her lips on mine. I sent her my picture, and a one-page description of myself and my life—such as it was. And I waited, in a strange state of trepidation and excitement, hoping for the phone to ring.

The call came an hour after sundown.

"Hello?" I asked.

"Good evening," the low-voiced, female caller said, "Is this Jameson Servais?"

My heart pounded. Was it her? Telemarketers never pronounce my name correctly, and I had mentioned the correct pronunciation in my letter to her. I swallowed hard, and my tongue clicked once, dryly.

"Hello?" she said. "Are you there?"

"Yes," I managed to croak. "This is Jameson."

"Hello," she said. "You answered my ad."

"I guess I did," I said, feeling nervous.

"I'm glad," she said. "I was impressed."

"Well, uh, then I guess I'm glad I answered," I said, then added when I caught up with myself long enough to remember my manners, "What's your name?"

"Alexa," she said. "Alexa McKnight."

"It's nice to meet you." I was beginning to feel embarrassed. Plagued by an out of control libido, perhaps I had gone too far.

"Would you like to meet sometime, Jameson?"

"You mean like at a hotel or something?" I asked, floundering.

She laughed. It was a warm, throaty sound that sent a tingle up my spine. "Actually, I thought dinner might be nice. We can proceed to other things if— and when—it suits us." Her voice was a low tenor, and brought to mind hundreds of movie maidens who speak in just the same way before succumbing to the charms of the hero. I didn't feel like a hero, but like a teenager, fumbling with my words and my proverbial zipper at the same time.

"Dinner would be great," I said. "When and where?"

"You pick," she said. "I like to get to know a man before inviting him for . . . other pleasures."

I hesitated, then, in a rush, "How about tomorrow," I asked, "Around seven?"

"That would be fine," she said. "Where?"

"There's a Greek café on the corner of Ninth and

Mitchell. They've got good food, and even better atmosphere. Do you like Greek?" I asked.

"Very much," she said. "Who doesn't like a good bite of Greek now and then?"

"It's called 'Sybil's Rock.' Do you know it?"

"I've never been there, but I'll find my way. I'm relatively new in town, but I'm starting to know my way around."

"That's great," I said, thinking that I was sounding more and more like a teenage boy whose dream date had just said yes to the prom *and* a midnight roll around in the back seat of his parents' car. "So I'll see you around seven?"

"Absolutely," she said.

"Good," I said. "I'm looking forward to it."

"So am I," she said.

"Wait!" I said, thinking she was about to hang up. "How will I know you? I don't have your picture."

"I have yours," she said. "And besides, I think you'll know me."

"Oh," I said. "Then I guess I'll see you then." Somehow, I could imagine her smiling, thinking I was a fool. "Good night, Alexa."

"Good night to you, Jameson."

As you might guess, I slept very little that night. I thought of Alexa, and the things we might do to—and for—one another the next evening. The short conversation replayed itself like a scratched record in my mind. I thought of Anaka—I had not physically been with anyone since her death—and I thought of betrayal. Would she approve of this strange, dark liaison? I didn't think so, and my separate thoughts of two women—one whom I loved, and the other I didn't know—stayed with me even in my dreams.

The café was dimly lit and pleasant, though it was busy. I had arrived a full half hour early to assure that we would have a good table. I sat in the semidarkness watching other couples talk and sip shots of Ouzo. When she walked in, I realized she had been right. I knew her in an instant.

Her feet were clad in black leather ankle boots, and she wore black denim jeans that hugged her slender waistline. Her shirt was crème-colored raw silk, open at the neck, and underneath, between the swell of her breasts, I could make out the faint lines of a dark purple, or perhaps red, lace brassiere. An embroidered black vest accented the outfit, and she carried a small, black purse in her left hand. I noticed her long nails, perfectly kept, and how flawless her hands seemed. Her neck was encircled with a slender gold chain and a locket. Her face was pale, and unblemished except for a small, circular birthmark just above her right eye. Her eyes were green—not the green of a forest glen, or a meadow in springtime, but the green of kelp washing onto the beach. And her hair . . . it was a dark, luxurious mane of red. It was a cigarette ember in the dark of night. It curled softly about her shoulders, a bonfire.

Her eyes met mine for the briefest instant, and she smiled. She was not what I had imagined on the phone, or while tossing and turning during the night . . . she was much more. As she made her way through the crowd, her eyes never left mine, and I did my best to appear composed. She walked effortlessly, somewhere (or so it appeared to my admiring gaze) between a glide and actual flight. The crowd seemed to melt away for her, clearing a path.

When she reached the table, I rose, and held out my hand. "You must be Alexa," I said.

She nodded, and set down her purse. "And you are Jameson," she said, taking my proffered hand lightly in hers, and clasping it gently.

"I am, and I'm pleased to meet you," I said, feeling a wild urge to kiss her hand.

"And I am pleased to meet you," she said. Her voice still carried that warm quality I had noticed on the phone.

I suppressed my gallant urges, and as we were seated, I gestured vaguely around the restaurant. "Will this be okay?"

"Oh, yes," she said. "Perfectly fine." She glanced around the room. "You were right about the atmosphere."

"I'm glad you like it," I said. "My wife and I came here often."

"You mentioned in your letter that your wife passed away a few years ago."

"Yes," I said, still feeling the guilt and grief from my thoughts of the night before. Seeing Alexa, those feelings were more distant, but there nonetheless.

"I don't wish to cause you pain, but may I ask . . ." she trailed off.

"Car accident," I replied. "'Drunk driver. His third offense, if you can believe it."

"I believe it," she said. "I'm sorry for your loss. How long have you been alone?"

"A little over three years," I said.

Just then the waiter arrived, rattled off the evening's specials, and took our drink order. I chose a bottle of Red Zinfandel, and we waited in agreeable silence until he came back with it, and took our dinner order. Both of us selected the feature—a cucumber salad, lamb chops, and pasta, with new potatoes. After he left, we continued our conversation.

"Has it been difficult for you?" she asked. "Being alone all this time?"

Fidgeting a little at the scrutiny, I said, "At first, I thought I would start over. Find love again, make the lifelong commitment, but I've found that facing that prospect is asking too much of myself. It's been more difficult than I thought it would be."

"I find that hard to believe," she said. "You're the first person I've ever met through the personals who was honest about themselves and actually matched their picture. In the photo, you have dark brown hair, streaked with white, and lo and behold—in person you're the same. I suspected you were too good to be true."

I laughed. "So, you've had the experience of meeting people through the personals who didn't quite match up to their descriptions of themselves?"

"Oh, yes," she said. "Quite a few times. I decided that it was pointless fooling around with the whole quest for true love thing. I hadn't really been getting anywhere."

"That sounds familiar," I said.

She smiled. "I understood how you felt when I was reading about you. I've been alone for a long time, too," she said, "but isn't it interesting how our feelings

70

about love or lust can change rapidly from one moment to the next?"

"Yes, it is," I said. "You have me at a disadvantage, you know," I added. "You've read all about me, and I know next to nothing about you."

She laughed, lightly. "Just the way I like it," she said, grinning. "It's good to have mystery in a relationship of any kind, don't you think?"

I nodded. "Mystery is fine," I said. "But that doesn't mean complete unfamiliarity. Tell me about yourself."

So she did. She said she had been born in London, but had moved to the United States with her parents when she was less than a year old. Her mother stayed at home, and her father was a professor of cultural anthropology at the University of Nebraska. There were no other children. She had grown up in a fairly normal environment, finished her Ph.D. in human biology, and then moved out to California for her work as a researcher.

While she talked, I watched her in growing fascination. Her voice, her gestures—they seemed uniquely understated, as though she were holding back a growing level of internal excitement. I couldn't seem to take my eyes off her hair, and I found myself wanting to reach out and touch it, to bury my face in its fiery softness and smell her perfume. When she finally wound down with her brief history, I felt disappointed as I enjoyed listening to her melodic voice.

"So," she concluded, "I guess that's enough about me for a while. I haven't told anyone that much about myself in a long time." She shrugged. "Tell me something more about you. What do you do for a living?"

"Crosswords," I said, still distracted by the play of light in her hair.

"I beg your pardon?" she asked. "Did you say crosswords?"

"Oh, yes," I said, then, seeing her confusion, I added, "I write crossword puzzles."

"I see," she said. "That's refreshing."

"How so?"

"Well, you just don't meet someone every day who does that for a living. Write crosswords, I mean. Do you like it?"

"I suppose I do," I said. "I enjoy the challenge of constructing clues, and I've always liked word games."

When our dinner arrived, we paused our conversation long enough to get a good way into our lamb chops. Finally, she said, "So you enjoy word games? You must be well read, then."

"Yes," I said, "Mostly personal ads."

And we laughed again. The rich warm sound of her voice cascaded around me, and I literally felt myself grow warm as I watched her. "You have a fine sense of humor," she said.

"Thank you," I said. "But in all seriousness, yes. I do read quite a lot."

This set off an entirely new discussion of different books and their merits. We ate, and talked, drinking the wine, and drinking in each other. By the time our coffee arrived, I somehow knew that I loved her. The poets speak of this phenomenon, but for me it was as real as any love I'd ever known. And though it seemed foolish, I found I was comfortable being a fool. It was senseless and fast, but she was, in every sense, a lady of intense qualities. It was also then that I realized I couldn't tell her my feelings. She actually deserved better than a one-night stand, and I suddenly knew that for all my recent cynicism about love and relationships, I had to respect her wishes about a relationship. She had been up front about what she wanted, and it wasn't my place to try and make her change her mind. I felt a little like a child. I was a weak man who had fallen to his knees at the first sight of her qualities.

When dessert was over, the conversation slowed, and then stopped. I watched her, trapped between my desires for her physically, and the bitter knowledge that what I now knew I really wanted, I couldn't have. "Well," I said. "That was a fine meal, but your company was better."

"Thank you," she said. "You mentioned the excellent atmosphere, but I had no idea it would be this good," she added.

I smiled. "What happens now?" I asked.

"Now?" she said. "Would you like to take a lady for a walk along the pier?"

I nodded. "It would be a pleasure," I said, and I meant it. "Besides, I need to work off this baklava." I couldn't tell her no, and I knew I couldn't say yes to the implicit want in her eyes.

I paid our check, and we left. As we stepped out into the darkness, I took the liberty of taking her hand in mine, and in companionable silence, we made our way to the stone pier that borders the ocean.

* * *

For a long time, nothing was said. We listened to the water lapping onto the shore, and the snap as it rolled over jetties of rock where people who couldn't afford real docks tied up their small boats. Occasionally, we would pass another couple walking along and enjoying the night. Orange-colored arc sodium lamps provided the occasional island of light, but mostly there was darkness, and boat lights distant on the water that looked like stars. It was the most comfortable I'd been in years. Even though it was dishonest to continue on, I didn't want it to end.

Still, I was the first to break the silence. "Alexa, I've enjoyed tonight," I said. "Very much."

"As have I," she said. "More than I expected."

"Yes," I said, "Even more than expected. But . . ." I trailed off, looking for words.

"But?" she said.

"Well, I guess I've misjudged myself."

"How do you mean?" she asked.

"I thought I wanted a one-night stand. Something purely physical and by extension, something simple. But being with you tonight reminded me of all the reasons I loved Anaka, and I realized that I still want love, even more than I do sex."

She nodded, "I understand."

I was startled. "How so?"

She shrugged. "I find that I'm in the same boat. You see, I, too, lost my soul mate, and even though he isn't dead, I can no longer be with him. Being with you reminded me of him, much as you being with me reminded you of your late wife. I was wrong about what I wanted, and the only thing I can say is how happy I am that we're both in agreement of a sort."

I laughed, and she turned on me, a little hurt and angry. "This is funny to you?"

"No, no," I said. "Not at all. It's just that here we are, two adults dancing around the idea of sex, and both of us are thinking about love, and lost loves."

She smiled then. "You're right. There is something strangely funny about that."

"Look," I said, "I like you, Alexa. A lot. But I can't sleep with you because you deserve better than a one nighter with no commitments. I thought I was ready for something like that, but I guess I'm not, at least not with you. Maybe I'm not as cynical about love as I thought."

She softened visibly. "That's really quite sweet, Jameson. And spending time with you has helped me change my mind, too. Love exists, even for someone like you," she said. "Or me."

"Don't get me wrong, though," I added. "Alexa, I was watching you tonight, how the light played in your hair, the little gestures you make while you speak, and I hungered for the touch of a woman—but I want something more. Something permanent like I had before. I want to wake up every morning knowing that you're—excuse me—that someone's there."

"Someone?" she asked.

We were standing in a pool of that orange lamplight, and she turned toward me, her eyes upturned. "I want . . . well, that is, I think that . . ."

"Oh, shut up," she said. Then, with unexpected strength, she pulled my face down to hers, and kissed me. In the distance, the waves continued their rhythmic pounding of the shoreline, and somewhere in the city, church bells tolled the midnight hour.

* * *

Was it the bells sounding the midnight hour? Was it the passion of the moment, the way we seemed to join together in that instant? I still do not know. As our kiss deepened, the bells tolled, and I felt her lips tracing a small crescent along the line of my jaw and down to my neck. Then, a sudden pain as her entire body tightened—every muscle locked rigid, and she clasped me so strongly I thought my ribs would shatter. She held me this way for a few moments, and I could sense her struggling with something. Her lips moved against my neck, as though she were praying or nuzzling me. Finally, as though she could stand no more, she pushed me away.

"I can't," she said, so quietly that it was hard to hear her.

"I don't get it," I said. "You can't what?"

"I can't be with you," she whispered. She was turned away from me, staring out into the dark ocean, her body visibly trembling.

"I don't understand, Alexa. It's obvious you want to be with me."

She shrugged. "You don't have to understand. Just accept it. I can't be with you."

"Be fair, damn it! I want to be with you—you at least owe me an explanation!"

"I can't give you that either. I'm sorry, Jameson." The bells had faded to silence, and over the waves, the city sounds resumed. "I've got to go," she said.

"Wait a minute," I said, grasping her shoulder and turned her around.

"No, Jameson!" she cried, but it was too late. I had seen her face.

Her eyes were now the color of blood; even in the orange light I could see they were red. Her skin looked vaguely feverish, and pale, though she had appeared healthy enough earlier. But the worst was her teeth. They had grown! They were so long and pointed that her canines jutted down past her bottom lip.

"What the . . ." I said, before she quickly turned away.

"So," she said. "Now you know."

I was dazed. "What do I know?" I asked. "That you aren't who you appear to be?"

She laughed, and now it was a grim sound, full of old disappointments. "You like word games, Jameson. You've seen me, you saw my ad. What am I?"

Still reeling, I tried to piece it together. Her ad said she wanted a one-night stand. What was so significant about that? And then it hit me—all at once, and I was stunned I hadn't seen it before. Her box number . . . when you signed up for the personals service, you selected your own box number. Mine, 9673-626 spelled out "word-man" on any standard phone pad. Hers, 8267-473, spelled vampire! Her ad had said that the respondent must "understand the hungers of the flesh." I put a hand to my head, which was suddenly aching.

"You're a vampire?" I asked. "A vampire?"

"You really are good at word games, Jameson," she said. Then, "Yes, I am a vampire. And now you know why I can't be with you." She was still turned away.

"A vampire?" I asked again, still floundering.

"Yes!" she half-screamed. "A vampire! You know, a bloodsucker. Creature of the night. The whole thing."

Feeling like my head was buried in cotton, I tried again. "Why are you dating?" I asked.

She spun around, and I took a not-so-involuntary step backward. "Do you think that being a vampire is proof against loneliness?" she hissed. "Do you have any idea how long forever is?"

Taken aback, I gestured vaguely around. "I . . . I guess not. How the hell would I know, anyway?" I asked, annoyed. "I'm standing here having a conversation with a vampire. Either that or I'm cracking up. It's not like you take a vampire to dinner every . . ." I trailed off as a thought struck me. Vampires don't eat dinner. "Wait a minute," I said. "Vampires don't eat, right? What'd you do with your food?"

"Simple illusion," she said. "One of the few benefits of being what I am."

"How did you . . . oh, never mind," I said. Then another thought struck me. "You weren't looking for a date, were you?"

She turned away again, but I could see her response. "No," she mumbled. "Not really."

"You were going to *feed* on me, weren't you?" I asked, nearly shouting myself. "Jesus Christ! Do you do this often? Let guys take you out to dinner and then drink their blood!"

She didn't answer, and that was answer enough.

"So this wasn't a date, wasn't even cheap sex. It was how a vampire hunts in the modern age, right? Everything you told me was bullshit."

"It's not like that," she whispered. "Not really."

"Then what's it like," I snapped. *"Really."*

"It's a little more death every day," she said softly. "Always aching to be alive again, to feel something besides the hunger—and always being denied. It's too late to lie to you, and I don't really want to anyway." She turned back to me, and for a moment, I saw *her* again. Not the monster within her, but the real woman trying to escape. "You're right, of course," she said. "Everything I told you before about me, who I am, was a lie. A necessary lie, but a lie nonetheless. And, usually, this is how I feed. I hate it, but that's a hunger that cannot be denied. Some desperate soul responds to an ad that appears to be for sex, he takes me out, and then I feed on him. It's not pretty, but it gets the job done."

"Then why didn't you feed on me?" I asked. "I'm pretty desperate. In fact, you might say that death would be a blessing."

She nodded in understanding. "For many of them, it is. But for you . . . I couldn't do it. That's just it. When I read your letter, and then I met you in person, I thought that . . . well, I thought that you might be the one. And when we kissed, I knew for sure, and that's why I pushed you away—before it went too far."

"Before what went too far?" I asked.

She pointed at my neck. "Touch yourself," she said. "There on your neck where I kissed you."

I did, felt the small wound, and pulling my hand away, I saw blood. "You were sucking my blood?"

She nodded glumly. "Yes," she said. "But I stopped in time. You may feel a little weak for a short time, but that is all. I stopped because when I tasted you, the essence of you, I knew you were the one."

"The one what?" I asked.

"Even vampires can love," she said. "Isn't there a

saying that there's someone for everyone? Well, it's essentially true, but in the case of a vampire it's more than basic. It's part of the deal."

"What do you mean?"

"I mean that all vampires have soul mates. We don't run around making other vampires. We only make other vampires out of our true soul mates—sometimes a good friend, more often, a lover. Some vampires find theirs right away, while others search for years before finding the right person."

"So your lost love is a vampire, too?"

"Oh, yes," she said, bitterly. "And that's why I have to go now. He's coming here, this night, and I can sense him drawing closer to me."

"But why would you leave?" I asked. "If he's your soul mate, why can't you be with him? I would give anything—anything at all—to have my Anaka back."

"Because he's not who he was then. He's become a true monster, feeding on those he chooses without regard. Two hundred years ago, he was nearly killed by a mob of peasants, would-be vampire killers, outside of London. He was horribly scarred, physically and emotionally by the ordeal. He lost his love of the world, and those in it, and slowly, I lost my love for him."

Thinking on this, I felt a little bad for her. 'What about you, Alexa? How long have you been alone, looking for another soul mate?"

"Most of the last two hundred years," she said. "But who's counting?"

"Will I become a vampire now?" I asked, a little frightened.

"No," she said. "It didn't go nearly far enough. I stopped in plenty of time."

"I'm flattered, I guess," I said. "It's not every day that one meets a vampire who thinks you might be their soul mate." I paused, thinking, and added, "That is that what you meant when you said you thought I was the one, isn't it? That I am your soul mate?"

"I haven't changed my mind, Jameson," she said. "You *are* my soul mate."

"But I can't be a vampire!" I said.

"Not yet," she said.

"Not yet?" I echoed.

"I can tell you're not ready yet. Not ready to make a true commitment. This is a true commitment, Jameson. There's no turning back, no divorce. It's forever and ever, amen." Then she added, "I don't mean us per se, because even soul mates can lose their way in the darkness. Love can fade and people can change. I mean becoming a vampire. There's no turning back into a human."

"I think you're wrong, Alexa. I'm ready for a commitment, but not this fast and not this sudden. And I don't think I'll ever be ready to be a vampire."

"You will one day," she said. "I can see it when I look at you. I can taste it." She turned, scanning the pier with her eyes. "He's coming closer, now. You must go."

"I think you're wrong about me, Alexa. If you think I'm destined to be your soul mate—to be a vampire for God's sake—then fine. But I'm glad you didn't turn me into a vampire or kill me. This is just way too much, Alexa, and way too weird. Thanks for an interesting night." I turned, and began walking down the pier. For some distance, I was alone with my morbid thoughts.

"Jameson, wait!" she cried, running toward me.

I turned. "What is it?"

"It wasn't my choice, you know," she said. "To be a vampire."

"I didn't assume so," I said. "Who would choose that?"

"You'd be surprised," she said. "But the point is that the vampire who made me didn't ask, or give me a choice. He simply said, 'You are one of us' and made me what I am. He was a good person, but he had no sense of timing and certainly no subtlety. I'm giving you the choice I didn't have."

Looking at her then, with the city and ocean sounds surrounding us, I almost said yes. Part of me wanted to scream yes with all my strength. But I couldn't then, and I could sense her fear, too. Whatever her maker had become, it scared her. And if it scared a vampire, it must be quite horrible. Her observation of me had been correct. I wasn't ready for an eternal commitment, not really. And I certainly wasn't ready to face a scorned lover from her past, who happened to be an angry vampire. "I'm sorry, Alexa, or whatever your real name is. I can't. Not now, and probably not ever."

"I understand," she said. "But, one day, you'll change your mind."

"Maybe," I said.

"Love is funny that way," she said. "Once you feel it for somebody, once the fire has begun to burn, there's no turning back, only turning away. Sooner or later, your heart leads you to find that person again, and to warm yourself next to whatever flame they will offer."

"Maybe," I repeated.

She tensed slightly, and I could see her fangs once more. "I have to go now," she said. "The hunger grows. It's long past time for my dinner. I will lead him away from here, and you. I can sense your fear." She began walking away, then she stopped and looked back at me. "We are connected now, Jameson. When you are ready, I will know it, and we will meet again."

And with that, she walked away. Her long red hair flashing like fire in the lights along the pier. I watched her until I couldn't see her anymore, thinking about what she'd said. Thinking how cold it was at home with no one there and nothing to comfort me but old memories of a wife three years in her grave. Thinking that she was probably right—sooner or later, I'd want to be warm again.

I returned home, alone, and wondering.

Two weeks later I saw him for the first time. I was coming home from a late night walk to the corner store for ice cream, and I saw a man who had once been quite attractive, but now bore the scars of someone who had been in a horrible fire. He walked behind me for some distance, and I waited, trying to control my urge to run, certain that at any moment he would pounce on me, perhaps drain my body of blood and leave me lifeless on the pavement, a bizarre headline for the following day's newspaper. Finally, with my heart racing, I couldn't stand it any longer, and I turned to face him, only to find myself alone on the sidewalk. With my breath rasping in my throat, I made my way home.

That night, I wondered how long it would be before we actually met. His intention, no doubt, was to confront me, perhaps kill me, so that I could no longer be of interest to Alexa. Had he found her that night, I wondered? I didn't know for sure. I had long since realized that Alexa was right about one thing. I thought about her constantly, and was soon searching for her along the pier, and once, I accosted a red-haired woman who was perfectly human—and quite startled by the madman grabbing her and calling her Alexa.

Sometimes, during quiet moments alone, it seemed as though we were connected, that I could feel her inside of me. I wondered where she was, if she was safe from the machinations of the monster that now stalked me. I wanted to talk to her again. To watch the light play in her hair like little children made of fire. How had he found me? Was he watching us that night from some great distance? Could he feel her, as I seemed to?

For another month, I watched for him. Sometimes, I caught the merest glimpse of his shadowed form in the distance. Once, I thought I saw him staring through my window, but when I looked closer, I saw only my reflection. Seven weeks after Alexa had gone, her lost soul mate and I met, though not in the way I had expected.

Shortly after sundown, the doorbell rang. When I answered it, he was there. The scarred face I had seen earlier stared in at me, and I jumped backward, holding up my hands to ward him off.

"Stop," he said. "If I meant to harm you, no force in the world could stop me." His voice carried a vague accent, and was quite deep.

My pulse was racing. "What do you want from me?" I asked.

"Nothing you will not freely give," he said. "You have already—in a sense—done what I desire. I merely wish confirmation."

"Why have you been following me?"

"To see what kind of man you were," he said, and then gestured into the house. "May I come in?" he asked, "So that we may speak as civilized beings?"

"I've done my homework, vampire," I said. "You cannot enter here unless you are invited."

He smiled and stepped into the entryway. "Not everything you read is accurate, fool. A writer, even one such as yourself, should know that. I was being polite."

I nodded. "Okay," I said. "Come on in, as it seems I cannot stop you."

He stepped the rest of the way into the house, his long stride carrying him past me and into the living room. He was quite tall, and moved with easy grace. His hair was long and black, and tied into a ponytail with a length of dark silk. Turning back to me, I saw that his eyes were dark blue. "Why don't you sit down," he said, "and we can talk."

I sat in the wingback chair I preferred and gestured him into the other. "All right, talk," I said.

"You are a direct man," he said. "That's good. I find it refreshing."

"I think we can dispense with the compliments and polite necessities for the most part," I said. "What do you want?"

"Your word," he said. "Your word that you will not pursue Alexa. She is mine, for now and eternity."

"I think you're mistaken," I said. "She is her own. You can't own somebody like that. Love doesn't work that way."

"I think your opinion of such matters is of little value. I made Alexa, when your long-dead ancestors were still trying to fight off the natives of this land. I have loved her from the first, and she has loved me. She cannot deny that. She mustn't."

"For someone as old as you apparently are, you haven't garnered a lot of wisdom in those years. Love is something that cannot be permanent by its very nature—it takes work and sacrifice, it is built on those foundations, not on a flimsy base of want or desire. Like any fire, if you leave it untended long enough, it will go out."

"So you're wise enough to instruct me in the ways of love between immortals? Bah! Alexa doesn't understand me. That is all. She thinks I am some sort of monster, when all I am is a realist. Humans despise and fear us. Caring about them will only get us hurt or killed, because sooner or later, humans—who are no more than animals that walk upright—will strike out at that which they despise and fear."

I was frightened of him, then. Truly scared. Not because he could kill me, though that was scary enough in its own right, but because he saw us as animals. And when you see something as an animal, it usually has less value in your eyes than others of your own kind. I thought of Alexa, and I knew why she had left this . . . thing disguised as a man. "What is your name?" I asked.

"My name?" he said. "What does it matter? Give me your word, and I will leave you in peace. You will not see me—or her—ever again."

"Your name, please?" I said again. I was still thinking of Alexa, and then I could feel her. Somehow, I could feel her as though she were in my arms, and I felt safe.

"Don't be foolish, human," he said. "I do not like games."

"This is no game," I said. "Your name—what is it?"

"Very well," he said. "My name is Demetri Vasile."

"Okay, then, Demetri Vasile. I'm Jameson Servais, and I cannot give you my word."

He looked at me then, and I watched in that slow moment as his eyes turned from their dark blue color to the icy blue of arctic frost. He hissed. "Do you wish to die, fool?" he asked.

"No," I said. "I don't. But I'm not a liar, and I won't append my name to a lie. I love her, which is more than you can truly say, having kept her away from everything she's wanted for two hundred years. She was right. You are a monster."

He leaped to his feet then, and I was certain that he would reach out and kill me with one blow. His fangs were bared, and I found that his eyes, which had changed again to become the color of blood, impaled me. "Then you've made your choice," he snarled, reaching toward me.

When Alexa spoke from the doorway, he froze in amazement. "Demetri! Stop!"

He turned to her. "Alexa!"

And then it happened, so fast that I barely saw it. Her arm whipped forward, and a long wooden spike flew across the room and buried itself in Demetri's chest. He howled, an animal sound of rage, and pain, and love finally broken and betrayed. I stood, stunned, as she crossed to his writhing form on the floor. He tried to pull the stake out, and couldn't seem to find the strength.

"I'm sorry, Demetri. You don't know how sorry. But now it's truly over, as it should have been years ago. The stake is barbed, and you cannot remove it. In a few more moments, all the years you have cheated death as a vampire will return for you, and you will be nothing but a withered husk that will blow away in the night wind."

He looked up at her then, and I could suddenly see the man he'd once been. "Alexa," he said. "Why?"

"Because you are no longer my soul mate," she said. "The bond is broken." I felt a strange internal snap, and the connection I felt with her grew even stronger.

"You cannot!" he said. "To be soul mates is to be together forever."

"You are not who you were," she said. "I'm sorry."

His struggles slowed, and age lines began to appear on his face, wrapping around the scars from that long ago bonfire. "I love you, Alexa," he whispered.

She shook her head. "No, Demetri, you don't. Or it never would have ended this way."

Suddenly, his whole form stiffened, and he howled in anguish one last time. Alexa and I stood silent, while the returning years took their terrible toll. Finally, he fell still, and his clothing collapsed in on itself. Nothing remained but the cloth, the stake, and a few pieces of bone.

She turned to me, then, tears the color of blood tracing paths down her face making a bizarre complement to her hair. I wrapped her in my arms and held her, very glad to be alive and with her once again. "I loved him once," she said. "Long ago."

"I know," I said.

For nearly half an hour we stood just like that. Our arms around each other, knowing that the storm was over, and wondering how we'd managed to survive. Then she gently pushed me away. "I have to go," she said.

"Why?" I asked. "I want you to stay. I was wrong before. I am ready."

She smiled at me. "No, Jameson. You weren't wrong before. You're not ready for this yet. I didn't destroy Demetri for you, or even for us. I did it for me, and even for him."

"I love you, Alexa, but I guess you know that."

"I do, Jameson. And I love you, too. But you need more time to truly accept what becoming a vampire means. I'm giving you the time."

I didn't say anything, realizing she was right. For the first time since Anaka had died, I was truly glad to be alive. I nodded in acceptance, and said, "You won't forget about us, will you?"

"No," she said, softly. "I will be waiting for you, and when the time is right, I will come and we will be together." She reached down and gathered up what was left of Demetri. "I have to go now. It's getting late."

I nodded again. "When will I see you again?"

"When it's time, Jameson. When you are ready."

I kissed her then, once, softly, and I could see that this was not easy for her either. "You're right," I said, wanting to make it easier for her, maybe even easier for me. "I'm not ready yet. But I will be one day, and on that day, I want you to come for me. We can be warmth for each other."

"You are already my fire," she said. Then, quietly, she left.

And when I knew for certain she was gone, I sat down in the wingback chair, put my head in my shaking hands, and cried.

Many long months have passed since that night. And I think I'm almost ready now to face what being a vampire really means. Sometimes, I can feel Alexa nearby, so I know she is watching over me. Does she keep me safe from whatever other creatures hunt the night? I do not know.

Of course, I don't read the personals anymore—there is no real need, even for the grim amusement I might feel once again, now that I have found love. At night, I lie in my cold bed and wonder if this will be the night she comes. I wonder if she is not also waiting to be ready herself, if the wounds she must have felt when she destroyed her lost soul mate Demetri have begun to heal? Those wounds will heal, in time.

And we have a long time. I can wait for her, though I am impatient to hold her, wrap her long hair in my hands, and taste her lips. When we are both ready, she will know it. She will come to me in my darkened bedroom, my angel of death, and love, and lust. When that night comes, whatever warmth she brings, I will welcome her. I will bear my throat to her gentle fangs. And we will consummate our relationship with a kiss at midnight, in blood the color of roses, the color of her hair, the color of fire.

For Misti

STARLESS AND
BIBLE BLACK

by Gary A. Braunbeck

Gary A. Braunbeck is the acclaimed author of the collection *Things Left Behind*, released last year to unanimously excellent reviews and nominated for both the Bram Stoker Award and the International Horror Guild Award for Best Collection. He has written in the fields of horror, science fiction, mystery, suspense, fantasy, and western fiction, with over 120 sales to his credit. His work has most recently appeared in *Legends: Tales from the Eternal Archives*, *The Best of Cemetery Dance*, *The Year's Best Fantasy and Horror*, and *Dark Whispers*. He is the coauthor (along with Steve Perry) of *Time Was: Isaac Asimov's I-Bots*, a science fiction adventure novel being praised for its depth of characterization. His fiction, to quote *Publishers Weekly*, ". . . stirs the mind as it chills the marrow."

"I long to talk with some old lover's ghost
Who died before the god of Love was born."
                    —John Donne, "Love's Deitie"

SWM, 36, steady employment, owns own home, seeks SF for companionship and possible romance. Appearance not at all important. "Who, being loved, is poor?" Do you know who said that? If so, we might be right for each other. Respond to P.O. Box 18012, Cedar Hill, Ohio, 43055.

Come, and I will teach you the disillusionment of the body as it perishes in the rain of grief, the death in fading roses never sent to one you admire from afar, the emptiness of lonely orgasms in night-flooded, loveless rooms.

How many starless and Bible black nights had those words come to him while he was asleep and just about to hold his dream lover in his arms? How many mornings had begun with the bitter taste of *alone* in his mouth?

Too many; far, far too many.

And so he came to find himself writing, then rewriting the ad. Short but not too short, and there must be no hint in the words of the desperation in his heart.

Come, and I will teach you the disillusionment of the body as it perishes in the rain of grief . . .

No more, he thought as he stood before the post office box, the key in his trembling hand. No more.

He inserted the key and turned the lock.

Inside was only one envelope. He knew that he should be happy that at least *someone* had responded, but he'd hoped for more than—

—no. He would not do this. Someone out there cared enough to reply.

He removed the envelope and opened it. Inside was a single sheet of stationery.

The script was delicate and exquisitely feminine, the spaces between each word painstakingly exact, the angle of her slant almost Elizabethan in its fluid grace, each letter a blossom, each word a bouquet, the sentence itself a breathtaking garland: *Oscar Wilde*, read the first two words. *One of his plays, I believe.*

No more the death of fading roses, he prayed.

No more.

The morning had been filled with frantic activity around the office, and Wayne's thoughts of his impending blind date retreated to the back of his mind where they curled up in a corner, covered themselves against the cold and snapped off the light.

When lunchtime arrived, he pulled his paper bag from lower desk drawer, took the elevator to the lobby, and went outside to his usual bench.

Someone was sitting there.

No one all that special, really, just the most beautiful woman he'd ever seen.

Shaking and perspiring, Wayne picked up the pace of his steps and crossed to the bench. He stood in front of her for a moment, noting that she was alone, wore no rings, and didn't seem to be waiting for anyone.

She looked up. "Hi."

Wayne gave her a smile. "Hello. Do you mind if I sit down? I always like to eat my lunch here and this is . . . well, you're the first person I've ever seen sitting here."

"Please, join me."

He sat down—not too close—and opened his lunch: a tuna sandwich, a bag of potato chips, an apple, and an eight ounce bottle of cranberry juice. Boring.

He glanced at the divine woman next to him. She probably knew well the taste of caviar, rack of lamb, things exquisite. Chicken of the Sea from a tin can never came near those lips, nosiree. Nothing common for this beauty, and beauty always has her way.

She looked at him. Her eyes were a deep, soft green.

He felt his grip tighten on the sandwich.

"Are you all right?" she asked.

"Uh . . . yes, fine, thank you. I didn't mean to stare, I'm very sorry, please excuse me."

"That's all right, I'm used to it." She said this with a laugh, but her lips never formed a smile.

I'll bet you are, thought Wayne. Her statement lacked the edge of arrogance he usually associated with women this stunning; it was almost self-deprecating. He found that refreshing.

"Are you sure you're all right?" She seemed genuinely concerned, and Wayne wondered why until he looked down and saw that he'd completely crushed his sandwich. He shrugged, embarrassed, and began rummaging through his bag for a napkin.

He wished she'd smile at him, just a little something to let him know that she didn't mind his being clumsy.

She turned away. Wayne cursed himself.

He began eating what was left of his lunch, chewing slowly hoping she wouldn't leave, feeling the food land in his stomach with all the tenderness of a baseball bat shattering a kneecap. Maybe it wasn't too late to salvage this; he could strike up a conversation, get her to talking, show her that he wasn't a total loss. It would be nice to know her name, where she worked, if she was seeing anyone seriously or if there might be a chance—

—don't send out the wedding invitations just yet, Don Juan.

He gave her a quick glance. She was staring at something.

"Zombies," she said.

"I beg your pardon?"

She pointed to a group of well-dressed business people who were rushing past, briefcases or files in one hand, some kind of sandwich in the other, trying to balance everything with all the dexterity of a circus performer as they raced their way up the ol' corporate ladder. Wayne always got a kick out of watching groups like this, wishing that just once they'd get so caught up in their wheeling and dealing they'd lose track of what was in which hand and take a bite out of a briefcase. It's the little hopes that keep you going.

"Sad," she whispered.

"What makes you say that?"

She looked at him, expressionless, and shrugged. "I just can't imagine anyone functioning in that type of environment for long without shredding their individuality, their specialness, if you know what I mean."

"But it's possible not to sacrifice that . . . if you're careful and have your priorities in place." He heard himself and almost gagged; why did everything he said sound as if he wrote it down ahead of time and memorized it? He was trying to think of a way to sound spontaneous when she said:

"And what are your priorities, Wayne?"

He started. "How did you know my name?"

A light in her eyes. *"A Woman of No Importance,"* she said.

"Pardon me?"

"The Wilde line. I knew it from one of his plays, I just couldn't recall which one. It was *A Woman of No Importance.*"

Wayne felt his stomach turn to marble. "Y–you're—?"

"I know that our 'official' date wasn't supposed to be until tomorrow night, but I couldn't wait. I hope you don't mind."

"I, uh . . . no, no, of course not," replied Wayne. But inside he was screaming *Oh, shit, shit, shit, Shit, SHIT!*

"Besides," she continued, "you always hated the formality of 'official' first dates—let alone the pressure of a *blind* first date, so I thought we could have our lunch together out here and consider *this* our first date. Is that okay with you?"

Something occurred to him. "How did you know where to find me? I never told you."

"You always eat your lunch out here, weather permitting."

"Yes, but . . . I never told you that. How did you know?"

"I know a lot about you, Wayne Bricker. I know that you've worked as an accountant with Burton, Kroeger, and Denver for the last eight years; I know that you live alone and have never been married—or had a steady girlfriend, for that matter; I know that you spend your weekends reading and going to the movies or renting a video if there's nothing playing that you want to see; and I know that you go to the nursing home three times a month to visit your mother, sometimes even take her out to dinner if she's having a good week and remembers who you are. Of course, if she is in good shape, she usually chews you out for spending all your time with your nose in some kind of book."

The food had set his stomach on fire. He swallowed hard as a cramp passed. *"Who are you?"*

"And if none *of* those activities appeal to you, you just ask for one or two weeks of the thirteen months of vacation time you've piled up over the years, hop in your car, and drive somewhere. You never tell anyone where you went or what you did because you think they aren't really interested." She moved closer to him. The warmth of her minty breath tickled his chin. They were so close it probably looked as if they were two young lovers about to kiss.

"You know me,' she said. "It'll take you a second, but you'll remember."

Definite panic now. "I'm sorry, but we've never met." He looked around, half-expecting to see some of the office staff hiding behind a bush somewhere, laughing at their little, well-staged joke.

"Yes, we have," she said, her voice low, sultry; the sexiest he'd ever heard. "You've made love to me thousands of times. Sometimes my hair is a different color, and the last time we were together you gave me green eyes." She moved her face even closer. "How do you like them?"

Wayne couldn't speak. This was outrageous, even cruel. He'd done nothing to deserve this kind of treatment. Maybe he wasn't the most debonair of men, but he prided himself on being courteous, so why—

—and then, in the back of his mind, something threw back its covers, rose up, wiped the sleep from its eyes, and turned on a light.

Come, and I will teach you the disillusionment of the body . . .

"Remember me now?"

". . . oh god . . ."

"While I was waiting out here, I got to thinking about our first night together. Remember that? Your father had gotten drunk and slammed his car into a parked semi. Your mother zoned out when the police told her about his death, so her sister came over and took her to the hospital, leaving you alone. You were thirteen years old. You were so sweet. Didn't have any close friends—"

"Still don't," he said.

"I know." She took his hand in hers. "You rummaged around in your father's room until you came across his cache of girlie magazines, took them into your bedroom, and cried while you looked at the pictures and tried to . . ."

. . . the emptiness of lonely orgasms in night-flooded, loveless rooms . . .

"You did this," she went on, "because you didn't really love your father, though you wanted to. He was just a very cautious man, but that caution came across as coldness. You couldn't find any women in the magazines who did it for you, so you threw them aside, put a Monkees album on, closed your eyes, and when you heard 'Daydream Believer,' there I was."

". . . yes . . ." he whispered, closing his eyes, bringing back the memory of that night.

"I'm glad you remember," she said, brushing his cheek with her lips.

"I . . . I took the record off and you asked me to sing to you while you taught me how to dance."

"You wanted to learn so you could ask Michelle Gibney to the spring dance."

"I never did, you know? Ask her."

"You wouldn't have liked it. You would have felt awkward and foolish."

"What did I sing to you that night?"

" 'There Will Never Be Another You,' the Nat King Cole song."

"That's right! I was pretty bad."

"But your heart was in the right place."

He opened his eyes and looked at her. Her eyes were warm and sparkling, but her face was a stone mask.

And her eyes were now blue—

—and her cheekbones were higher—

—and her nose was smaller—

—and—

"Want me, Wayne. Want me now. Think of me the way I was in your dream last night."

He pulled her close, kissing her, a deep wet kiss, full of awkward but honest passion, his mind folding in on itself, turning drawers upside down, shaking out all the excesses and trivialities of the day until he found himself gliding backward in time to the moment last night when she'd come to him, her body ripe and sweaty, her desire strong, her breath coming in bursts as she held him and moved with him, gasping and crying out, loving him as no other could, then lying in his arms afterward, looking up, her face sheened in sweat that reflected like diamond dust in the candle's light, and he saw her face clearly.

He pulled back now and opened his eyes.

She was as she should be.

"I need your help."

Images from an average life swirled around him, reminding him that he had never had a grand moment and never expected one and now here it was; signed, sealed, delivered.

"Anything," he said.

She wrapped her arms around him, hands caressing the back of his neck. "Make me yours, all yours."

"But you are," he whispered. "You always have been."

She shook her head. "No, Wayne. You're not the only person who's ever been lonely, who's scrambled to the back of his mind to build a lover and soul mate. Do you remember that old saying about monkeys and typewriters?"

"Yeah," he cupped her face in his hands, reveling in the glory of her eyes. "If you put enough monkeys in a room with enough typewriters, eventually they'll write Shakespeare."

"Yes . . . and if you have enough lonely people who search their minds for a mate, eventually some of them will invent the same one. Oh, maybe this lover, this soul mate, will differ slightly from person to person: one might give her blue eyes, while another dreams her with green; someone may make her cheekbones higher and her nose smaller, but the thing is, she's never so different that she can't be recognized. Do you understand what I'm saying?"

"How many others are there?"

"Seven, eight, I'm not certain."

"And out of all of them, you . . . chose me?"

She brought her hands around, touched his face, pulled him close and kissed him. "*Of course* I chose you. You were the one who first gave me life. You made me real. The others, they only added to me. But none are as sweet and kind and loving and gentle and decent as you." A tear crept to the corner of her eye, glistened in the afternoon sun, and dropped onto her wrist.

"I can't stand it anymore, Wayne. I have nothing of myself to hold on to, only what they give me. But you'll give me a real life, a fuller life, you'll let me become something *I* want to be and not just what you dream me."

"Of course, you know that."

"Take me home. I need to be with you now."

They rose, arm in arm, and walked quickly to the parking garage, found Wayne's car, and left. Wayne Bricker didn't care about his job at this point; he didn't care about anything except being with the woman next to him, the woman who was as real as he, who was flesh of his flesh, blood of his blood, desire of his desire.

In the sweet darkness, they made love for hours. Her body held discoveries for Wayne, her touch answers, her sounds the power of clarity and destination. Wayne moved with a grace of which he'd always thought himself incapable, never fumbling or making foolish mistakes he associated with being an average, unimaginative thirty-six-year-old man.

When, at last, they finished, when there was no strength left in their limbs for anything other than holding on to one another, when their achings had been soothed and solitude had fled forever with its head hung in shame, only then did she ask him.

"Give me a name."

"Esmeralda," he said. "My Esmeralda."

"Such an elegant, exquisite name."

"No other would suffice." He wished she would smile.

She traced over his lips with her finger. "But why do you always imagine yourself to be so . . . ugly?"

"I don't know. I've just never felt much like I'm the type women give second glances to."

"That's your father's caution coming through."

"I know." He lifted her head and kissed her. Her lips were different, not as full. And her hair was shorter—

—and her hands thinner—

—and—

"It's time," she said.

He tried to put her back to the way she was but hadn't the strength.

"Don't waste your time," she said, her voice tight with panic. "You don't have it in you to pull me back every time this happens."

"Then tell me what to do."

She held both his hands tightly. Her eyes filled with pleading. "Do you love me?"

"Yes."

"And I love you."

His soul, until that moment trapped in a rain of his own making, was lifted from a cold damp place with those words.

"Then there's nothing I can't do," he said.

"God, I hope."

His name was Dan Rosen. He wore thick glasses and had a club foot. He was a short order cook at a truck stop in Baltimore. When Wayne first walked in and took a seat at the counter, Dan looked across at him.

In a way, they recognized each other.

Wayne wasn't sure he could go through with this, but then remembered Esmeralda's words—"I love you"—and realized that he would, indeed, spend the rest of his life lonely and miserable and a little bit dead, filled with average and unimaginative activities that would help him pass the time until people would smile at him and his failures and whisper to themselves that, well, he was Old, and you know How They Can Be.

He ordered a hamburger and fries, ate them slowly, checking the clock. Dan's shift ended at three AM. Then he'd go home to his dim and dirty studio apartment over the Wagon Wheel Bar and Grill where he filled his evenings with model ship-building and dreams of Esmeralda—called Lori by him, the name of the girl who'd broken up with him in public one night, saying she had no desire to spend the rest of her life tied to a nearsighted, going-nowhere cripple. He'd cried, Dan had, more out of humiliation than a broken heart, because Lori had just left him standing there as she ran to a car driven by Dan's ex-best friend, calling, "Why don't you run after me?" He'd gone home that night to a house where his drunken, widowed mother was snoring in front of the television, locked the door to his room, laid on his bed, and tried to guess whether or not the ceiling beams would take his weight. As he lay there cursing himself and his affliction, he imagined Lori apologizing to him, declaring her love. But then he decided to change her just a little bit, the hair at first, then the eyes, then lips and cheeks and body, running through hundreds of combinations until, at last—

—Wayne shook his head. He hadn't really wanted to know all that, but Esmeralda had said it was important he understand. The lonely road toward True Love was littered with casualties.

"I've never cared about the physical," she said. "Danny's very nice, if a bit on the self-pitying side."

"What am I supposed to do once he leaves?"

"You'll know when the time comes."

And that time, Wayne noted with sleepy eyes, was just five minutes away. He pulled out his wallet and took out a five and two ones to cover the bill and a tip, thankful that he'd been so frugal over the years about dipping into his savings; he had more than enough to last him for a while and he'd been building up a lot of vacation time at work, anyway. Following his sudden disappearance after lunch the other day, Wayne's department supervisor had called to see if he was all right. In eight years, Wayne had not had a sick day. A quick lie about problems with his mother cleared that up and enabled him to take three weeks' vacation—

—he stopped his tired musing as Dan walked by

him and out the door. Wayne followed him from the truck stop to his apartment, waiting until Dan was out of the car and on his way up the stairs.

Wayne walked up behind him and said, "Dan?"

He turned, startled, eyes wide. "What the fuck do you want?"

"I need to talk to you."

Dan reached into his back pocket and pulled out a switchblade, which he quickly and expertly flipped open. "I got nothing to say to anyone at three-thirty in the morning, pal, so get away from me."

A figure appeared on the landing behind him and said, "Danny?"

Both men looked up. It was Esmeralda, *Wayne's* Esmeralda.

"What happened to your hair?" asked Dan with deep sadness. He lowered the hand that held the knife.

Wayne wasted no time. Throwing one arm around Dan's neck, he used his free hand to wrench the knife from Dan's grip and then hit him hard in the center of his face. Dan stumbled backward, tried to regain his balance, but his damned foot got in the way again, and he fell to the ground.

"Jesus, Lori," cried Dan, in more than one kind of pain. "Who is this guy?"

She started down the stairs, her eyes clear and glistening. 'You can't have me anymore, Danny. I'm sorry."

"I don't . . . how can you . . . what's with . . . I—"

Her eyes met Wayne's.

You said you loved me.

He froze for a moment. This Dan wasn't a bad guy,

his sad little fantasies were almost all he had, and Wayne felt his heart fill with pity for the man who now lay there shaking with a knife pressed against his jugular. He thought of loneliness in all its forms of expression: of snipers in towers whose pleas for attention and acceptance were carried on tips of bullets, of plain teenage girls pouring their souls onto paper in the form of poetry that would embarrass them someday, of shabby men wandering into clean, well-lighted places, buying coffee they didn't like, listening to music that was too loud, watching younger men who were too stupid and shallow, all for the sake of not spending another second alone.

Wayne pulled Dan to his feet, whirled him around, and stared deep into his eyes.

"Don't take her away . . . please?" pleaded Dan.

Wayne looked at Esmeralda, who handed him Dan's knife, which she had changed; it was now a dagger of crystal and jade.

"I love only you," she said.

Wayne looked at Dan's foot. And knew.

"I'll take it away," he said. "I'll take it all away."

And Wayne set about his task.

"It's odd," said Wayne to Esmeralda as they drove back to his home.

"What is?"

He pointed outside. It was raining. A blinking traffic light scattered rubies across the windshield. "I always used to find the rain so sad. I don't anymore."

"Rain's very pretty," she said.

Wayne looked at her. "I used to imagine that, when

I was finally in love, I'd be able to run between the drops and never get wet."

She almost smiled at that, but only almost.

The task became easier with each successive person.

The next was a harelipped woman of sixty in Gettysburg who spent her days doing volunteer work for the county childrens agency. Having never married because of her sexual preference, she had no grandchildren. Wayne caught her one afternoon as she was making a run to McDonald's for the once-a-week hamburgers she brought to the children. She'd gone to the ladies' room and found Esmeralda on the other side, backed away in fright, and turned to find Wayne pushing her back in. He'd felt a little funny about her; she reminded him of his mother.

Then came Joe in Brownsville, Texas, a gas station attendant who'd lost one of his testicles to a landmine in Vietnam; next was Jerry, a library bookmobile driver in Binghamton, New York, who was lucky to have the job because of having only one good eye, the other having been burned partially closed in a furnace explosion a few years before; after that came Cindy with the facial cleft and Alan in Topeka who was a midget and then that guy in Los Angeles with the shriveled arm that looked more like the flipper on a fish, all of them so full of pain and regret and pleadings, all of them so happy to finally see Esmeralda in the flesh, all of them so easy—

—well, maybe not "easy," but when Wayne looked into the eyes of his true love, he knew there was no hardship he could not overcome.

Still, he wondered why she would not smile for him.

But that was soon forgotten, at least for a while.

Wayne had begun to taste Purpose. Yes, it was terrible that he had to take her away from all of them—there was always that moment where they would plead with him—but Esmeralda had chosen him, the only woman ever in his life to choose him, and so he never hesitated to use her magic dagger.

He was taking away their suffering.

He was destroying their pain.

He was making Things Better.

And there were moments when it didn't really matter that she wouldn't smile for him, because Wayne felt a sense of power that he'd never known before.

To take away pain and suffering, to destroy loneliness.

God must feel a little like this.

They traveled many · places on the lonely road toward True Love, saw many sights, made love as often as possible, whispering of their plans.

All things considered, it was as close to heaven as Wayne had ever come.

Or as close as it had come to him.

Now his heaven was on Earth, and he was its ruler, the Remover of Pain, the Destroyer of Loneliness, the Taker-Away of Affliction.

This holy knowledge made the physical aspect of what was happening to him easier to accept.

Her love grew more intense with every minute of every day. She had no regrets, she said. It really didn't matter what Wayne looked like.

It didn't matter.

Appearances weren't important.

The physical was illusion.

Come, and I will you teach you the disillusionment of the body . . .

Then came the day, finally, that the last of them was found. Wayne claimed what was rightfully his. At that moment, his true love seemed to shimmer, whole and clean and alive, no longer the particles of a diamond but the jewel itself, one that Wayne felt himself melt into until they were one.

Peace. Clarity. Fulfillment.

Everything had been worth it. He was no longer average, no longer a man who'd been denied his golden moment, his grand accomplishment.

Hand in hand, in the rain, they went home. Their home.

Between the drops, all the way.

He awoke in the middle of the night and found her gone. He sat up and saw her silhouette by the window.

He reached over to turn on the light.

"Don't," she said.

"What's the matter?"

"Please come to me."

He rose to go to her and felt his center of balance shift drastically, throwing him to the floor. He tried to break his fall with both arms but only one of them worked. He struggled to his feet, only to find one of them had—

—he pressed his weight against the side of the bed and reached out for the light

"No!" she cried.

He knew, of course, what he would see even before light flooded the room.

Still . . .

He spoke as clearly as he could, the words coming out slowly because of the facial cleft and hare lip. "I knew it would have to be soon."

She stared at him. "I knew it that night you met Danny."

He looked down at his deformed leg and its club foot. "Do you suppose he's happier now?"

She looked out the window. "I know he is. You took away the thing that drove him to search for me in the first place. Don't you remember the newspaper clipping I showed you a few days ago? Dan and Lori got married. Because of what you did for him, because you assumed his affliction, he found the strength to pursue happiness. With no afflictions, how could he fail? How could *any* of them?"

He smiled. "But we have each other. And I love you so very, very much."

"And I love you, my dear Wayne."

"Then would you smile for me? That's all I need now, just a smile."

"I can't," she said.

"Why?" She seemed thinner to him, but it was probably the bad eye playing tricks. He shuffled slowly to her side and took her hand, looked up into her eyes. "Aren't you happy?"

She bent low and kissed him gently on the lips. "Do you remember when I told you that I didn't care about physical beauty?"

"Yes."

A tear crept to the surface of her eyes. "I lied." She broke away and crossed to the other side of the room, hugging herself and shuddering. "I don't know what happened, Wayne, but knowing that you would

112

become . . . like you are, the thought began to eat at me, annoy me, sicken me." She faced her own reflection in the mirror.

"When I think of all the pain you took away from the others, all the happiness you gave them a chance to obtain after such lonely lives, I can't help but love you with all my heart and soul. And when I look at myself, and see how alive I am, when I touch my flesh and *feel* it and know that, because of you, I have an existence that I can at last call my own, I feel such tenderness toward you I could just . . .

"But I have my own mind now, and something has awakened there, something that sees and acknowledges my own beauty yet at the same time is repulsed by the sight of you. And I hate it, Wayne. I hate it so much because it will only get worse. I can see a morning very soon where I won't even be able to look at you and that's the last thing I want."

"This is all new to you," he said, feeling his heart lodge in his throat. "So many feelings denied you for so long, so many thoughts you've never experienced—"

"No, it's more than that. Don't you see? Is your soul so naïve that you can't understand that this woman, me, this thing that I now am because of you . . . I love you so very much, but I don't want you."

He remembered the lyrics to some stupid song from the 1970s, something about how imaginary lovers never turn you down, and laughed at himself and his reflection, imagining how he was going to explain his condition to the people he worked with. He touched the hideous mound of flesh that he called a face and said, "So what do we do now?"

She came toward him. "Dream me away."

"I can't. You're all I've got."

She took a deep breath. "Then I have to leave." She dressed and started toward the door.

"Don't I at least get a smile?" asked Wayne.

She paused by the door, her shoulders tensing as if she were making an unpleasant decision, then turned to him with contempt in her eyes and said, "I don't waste my smiles on freaks, Wayne, and that's what you are, it's what you've always been and always will be. You were beyond saving the day I came to you at lunch. You were worse than those zombies I pointed out to you; at least they had something to strive for in life."

He knew what she was doing, that she was trying to make him angry enough to *tell* her to leave—the noble lover sparing the other's feelings—but even though he knew it was simply a ploy, it nonetheless struck at something in his core, breaking apart his feelings of godliness and purpose, and despite his best efforts to dismiss her words and actions, his chest tightened in fury. "You were what my life was for, you were always the thing I most wanted to achieve."

"Not only a freak but a fool as well. God, how you disgust me."

"Don't say that, please."

"Freak."

"Don't."

"Monstrosity."

". . . *please* . . ."

'You're nothing more than a hideous malignancy, Wayne, and I curse the day you found me."

He felt his hand wrap tightly around the lamp. "Don't."

"I hope you die of loneliness. I hope they find you in a heap on the floor, wallowing in your own filth and beyond help. Then maybe they'll shoot you and put you out of your misery."

He pulled the lamp off the table and rushed at her, swinging it with all his strength and caving in half her skull. She crumpled to the floor, bleeding and whimpering. Wayne dropped the lamp and fell to his knees, cradling her in his arms as best he could.

"I'm so sorry," he pleaded. "I just couldn't live without you."

She reached up and touched him, her eyes fading. "Isn't this how your dreams always end? In longing and grand, romantic tragedy?"

". . . yes . . ."

"Well, then . . ."

He held her until the life faded from her eyes and her limbs went stiff and cold. He held her until her flesh became dried and rotted and gray and began to flake off. He held her until his own strength began to dissolve, and then he kept her close to him, pressing her against his chest until she was little more than bones and at long last—he had no idea how long they had lain together this way—she became nothing more than particles of a diamond that swirled into the air, becoming dust and then nothing, nothing at all. He lay there in silence and loneliness, the cramps in his stomach worsening, his body dwindling away. The sun seemed to rise and fall within seconds, entire years passing in the space of an hour.

Come, and I will teach you the disillusionment of the body as it perishes in the rain of grief.

He gathered the dust that once was her close to him.

Come, and I will teach you the death in fading roses never sent to one you admire from afar.

He gathered her dust into his hands and pressed them against his face.

Come, and I will teach you the emptiness of lonely orgasms in night-flooded, loveless rooms.

He lay very, very still, his heart breaking as he willed his body to become dust so they could be as one.

Come . . .

It was weeks before they found him.

No one could ever figure out why he'd been smiling.

True Love never dies.

FIREFLIES

by Bradley H. Sinor

Bradley H. Sinor has seen his work appear in the *Merovingen Nights* anthologies, *Time of the Vampires, Lord of the Fantastic*, and other places. He lives in Oklahoma with his wife Sue and two strange cats.

SEEKING SOMEONE SPECIAL for a 5 foot tall, dark-haired SWF. Enjoys long walks and runs in moonlight. Environmentalist and protector of endangered species who loves to get close to nature, the closer the better. ISO open-minded M. Stamina & imagination a plus. If the night is your time of day and the full moon calls you, give me a howl.

Fireflies.

Yes, fireflies. That was what the lights of Manhattan reminded Miranda of, the fireflies in the bushes outside her father's house so very long ago.

She had watched them from her bedroom window on summer evenings from the time she was a little girl. They drifted in clouds across the lawn, flanked by single outriders cutting through the darkness. So far away and yet so tantalizingly close.

You thought you could touch them, but when you reached out, they were gone. If you caught one, it was gone in a moment, as well, leaving only a tiny dark husk on the palm of your hand.

Standing in Washington Square Park it felt like they were just a heartbeat away from starting their nightly dance, yet seemingly impossible to capture or even touch. *So very long ago.*

Miranda drew a long drag off her unfiltered cigarette, savoring the taste of the smoke deep in her lungs. A moment later she snuffed it out in the dirt and loose pieces of wood that covered the rough surface of the waist-high brick wall where she had been standing for a half hour. The dead stub disintegrated into ashes and paper in her hand.

She had arrived half an hour early, just so she could watch the people, watch the fireflies begin their dance. Around her, people gathered in twos and threes, music and conversation mixing together as the lights of the Manhattan skyline grew brighter with the vanishing sun.

Fireflies.

For perhaps the hundredth time Miranda found herself questioning her own judgment. The day she had placed the ad in the Personals column of the East Village weekly, this moment had been the farthest thing from her mind. Miranda had stared at the small personals ad form for only a moment before beginning to write.

No, that day it had been anger, anger at her family in general and the Elders in particular. The day before, and the day after, the whole idea of the ad seemed silly and even a bit pathetic. Even more so when the recorded sounds in the voice mailbox supplied by the newspaper began to accumulate.

Then there had been his voice.

Kyle.

Her original plan in dating a human was to do something to enrage the sanctimonious Elders of the Pack. *"Humans are Prey, nothing more, nothing less!"* Not that she really disagreed; it was more their attitude, their demands of controlling every single aspect of her life.

She looked around her, at the street performers, the singers, the punks, the lovers, all the figures that filled the night in Washington Square. It was a scene she was quite familiar with. Even so her stomach was churning with uncertainty.

In full lupine form she could prowl in any of the five boroughs, easily taking her prey from the most deserted sections of the city. The Elders had long preached that the Pack should hunt only along the edge of humanity, through broken buildings and into the shadows of forgotten lives.

That was no challenge, no fun, and Miranda enjoyed a challenge. So, taking partially human, partially wolf form, *she* sought out *her* prey in places like Times Square, or even on Broadway itself. During the Hunt was when Miranda felt fully alive.

The tales told by the occasional survivor, the ones she *allowed* to get away, were too fantastic for even the most lurid of tabloids to print, although some had. Miranda had kept a few clippings, headlines blazing out in 100-point bold letters:

MONSTER PREYS ON MANHATTAN

KILLER RIPS THROATS FROM VICTIMS

12-FOOT-TALL BEAST
PROWLS CENTRAL PARK

The last one amused Miranda, considering the fact that even in her highest heels she stood only five foot three. Besides, she rarely went anywhere near Central Park. Someone else was responsible for that little rumor.

No, it was not fear that set her stomach churning. It dawned on her that ever since she had made the date to meet Kyle, she had been worried whether she would actually like him, and vice versa.

"How . . . human," she said softly.

The big clock on the bank switched its display over to read 9:00. Miranda felt *his* presence, a gentle shifting in the air, a change in the lights around her.

Kyle.

A tall figure, in dark gray that seemed to flow out of light and darkness at the same time approached her. His straw-colored hair seemed to glow in the reflected lamplight that filled the park. As he passed them, people stepped away, like fireflies darting away from the light.

"Good evening, Miranda, I'm Kyle," he said.

Miranda straightened her leather jacket, pushing it open to reveal her purple blouse and silver wave-shaped belt buckle at her waist.

"And how can you be sure that I'm this Miranda you're looking for?" she said.

Kyle reached out and took her hand.

"The same way you know that I am who you are waiting for," he said.

The funny thing was, if one of her cousins had described this situation to her, Miranda would have been certain they had OD'd on too many designer drugs or far too many romance novels.

Miranda had the sudden feeling that this was going to be a very interesting evening. Okay, he wasn't exactly what she had expected when she placed the ad, and they had spoken. He was better. Showing up with him at Pack functions would be sure to enrage the Elders; she could almost hear most of the females in the Pack drooling over him now. All this was going to really help twist the knife in the Elders' collective craw.

But there as something *different* about him. Different, but familiar. Miranda couldn't quite put her finger on just what it was, but there was something. Deep inside her the Beast recognized that difference in Kyle, and was howling in agitation. It would be so simple to let herself go, let the Beast have its freedom. But no, not now, not now!

"You can still walk away," he said, as if sensing her uncertainty.

"True. But so can you. And given the circumstances, I wouldn't blame you in the slightest," she said.

"I wouldn't dream of it," he said.

"Neither would I."

From beyond the borders of light formed by the flickering tiki torches that marked the edge of Kyle's rooftop balcony she could hear the screeching of police sirens. Rescue trucks and ambulances filled the night, all seemingly headed in the same direction. She wondered what was going on. First one sound, then two, then three, until there were too many to pick out individual ones. Miranda followed the sounds, listening to them merge, separate, and then fade away.

Disappearing, like fireflies with the coming of light. *Fireflies.*

"Here we are," said Kyle.

The sound of his voice gave Miranda a start. He moved quietly toward her, carrying two brandy glasses. It bothered her that she had not heard him approach. There was that damned feeling again, *something* that she could almost put her finger on, but not quite. If it were something Kyle was deliberately hiding, she had to admit he was good.

She savored the aroma of the amber liquid for a long moment before letting a tiny amount slip across her lips. The taste was a thick, heady one that both burned and exhilarated as it rolled down her throat.

"This is old and very good," she said. "I'd say it was not from this century."

"And I would say that you are quite right," said Kyle. "You have an exceptional palate for one so young. It was laid down for one of Napoleon's Marshals."

"Marshal Davout, or perhaps Soulet? I doubt it was Massena, he was too much of a teetotaler."

Kyle arched an eyebrow at her. He was startled, and that was exactly what Miranda wanted. After all, you don't expect a blind date to be able to spout off the names of some of the Marshals of France under Napoleon Bonaparte.

"So, did you slip an aphrodisiac in it?"

"Do I need one?"

Miranda laughed.

This evening had definitely *not* been the sort of thing she had expected. For a few hours she had been able to relax, to forget who she was, and to be just Miranda. She realized that it had been a long, long time since she had been able to do that. Just be Miranda. Not Miranda du Shane, daughter of Conrad and Esther du Shane; not Miranda, a daughter of the Pack; not Miranda, a were who stood outside of humanity. Just Miranda.

They had walked and talked for what seemed like hours. Eventually, Kyle had led them to a small club in the East Village, Greely's Pub.

"I think you are going to like this place," said Kyle. It was decorated in the style of any number of pubs that Miranda had seen in Ireland and Scotland, but without the veneer of faux-Celtic that far too many of these places in New York had.

They laughed and drank and danced. At one point, Miranda was pulled on stage with the band and handed an Irish drum to join in their rendition of "Gypsy Rover." The musicians seemed pleased with the result, as was Miranda.

"Is there anything you aren't good at?" Kyle asked.

"Many things."

"Perhaps we can discuss this over brandy somewhere else?"

"And where would that be?"

"At my apartment."

They sat and sipped their drinks, listening to the sounds of the city around them, feeling the breeze as it moved across the patio. Their eyes locked and everything around them faded away. Then, between one heartbeat and the next, lips, tongues, and hands began to probe every inch of their bodies, moving faster and faster across clothing and then bare skin.

Kyle lifted Miranda, holding her in the air, her long legs wrapped around him. Miranda's nails shifted to claws, carving deep paths across Kyle's back, trails of blood marking the places she had touched.

"Oh, don't they just look so purrrrty!"

"Yes, its just pure dee romantic like, like one of those movies with Tommy Hanks playing him, and she'll be played by little Meggie Ryan."

"Yeah, the gigolo and the bitch!"

Miranda had come awake a moment before the first one spoke. She and Kyle had fallen asleep on the futon. It was just after 2:00 AM. They were no longer alone.

Three figures stood near them, relaxed and watching. She didn't even have to see them clearly to know they were there and who they were, their scents were quite familiar. *Pack!* Gregory, Dean, and Michael Ray; her cousins.

She opened her eyes, muscles tense and ready to react, and slowly rose on one elbow. Her relatives had not chosen to come in full wolf form; instead, they wore the part human, part lupine appearance that had occasionally graced the covers of such intellectual publications as the *Weekly World News*.

Deep inside her the Beast screeched, demanding to

challenge them. Miranda smiled. This wouldn't be the first time that she had had to put them in their places. It wouldn't be the last, she knew that much.

"Should I ask something stupid, like 'What do you want?'" said Kyle.

Miranda looked down at her lover. He had not moved a muscle, his breathing hadn't changed, nothing to alert her to the fact that he was awake. His voice was calm and unemotional.

"I suppose you could," said Gregory. His small narrow figure was half hidden behind a large container-grown tree.

"If it makes you feel better," said Dean. "You can say any damn thing that you want and I certainly won't stop you."

"Of course," said Miranda's other cousin, "that doesn't mean we might not do something after you've had your say."

"Thank you. I wondered when you three idiots were going to show yourselves. I've known you were following us since just outside of Washington Square. You might as well have been carrying signs."

Before the last word was completely said, Kyle was on his feet. He moved with a speed that surprised Miranda, grabbing Dean and throwing him hard against the balcony wall. He stood there, stunned, a moment and then slid to his knees, surprised and disoriented, the breath knocked out of him, but otherwise unharmed.

Kyle turned on one foot to face the nearest one, Gregory. Then, suddenly Kyle was gone. He had leaped ten feet straight into the air and came smashing down into the other man's back, sending him into a heap on the floor.

"Good, you're good!" said Michael Ray. "But I'm better!"

"Fight, don't talk, puppy," said Kyle.

That was when Miranda caught sight of Kyle's fangs. The incisors had shifted down into place, weapons as deadly as Kyle's hands. She realized now what that *something* she had sensed about him had been. He was *Family, vampiri!*

"Stop this! Stop it now!" said Miranda.

The Beast flowed over her, seizing her and beginning the change with a speed that startled even Miranda. Like her cousins, she did not take full wolf form. A fine reddish-blonde fur covered her bare skin in only seconds; the Beast voice echoed from her lips.

"I said stop it, before I tear you all apart!"

Kyle and Michael Ray did not break eye contact for nearly a minute. The other two were getting stiffly to their feet, uncertain of what to do now.

"Pack?" Kyle said politely to Miranda. Though from the tone of his voice and the look of amusement on his face, she knew he had known her for what she was from the beginning.

"Well, duh! You were expecting maybe Martha Stewart? Now, all four of you back off. I'm never one to stop a fight, but this is nonsense!"

"It's 'is fault," said Gregory " 'e started it!"

"Gregory," said Miranda. "We'll have none of that phony British accent of yours. Everybody knows you were born in Talequah, Oklahoma."

"Look, man," said Dean. "We just wanted to put a

scare into you and our little cousin. Anything else she had planned was all her idea."

"We didn't know you were Family," said Gregory.

"Look, puppy, you invaded my aerie, my home. I have every right to beat the daylights out of all three of you and tack your worthless hides up over the mantle," said Kyle.

His voice was cold and as menacing as anything Miranda had ever heard. Far different than the man she had met a few hours ago in Washington Square. That man seemed gone now, like a firefly vanishing in the darkness.

Fireflies.

"Any time, any place," said Gregory.

"No! If you try anything, he won't have to do any more than watch," said Miranda. "I will kick your collective keesters from here to Crabapple Cove, Maine! And you know I can do it. Just remember last July fourth, if you don't think so!"

Miranda's three cousins looked at each other, then at her. One at a time they shifted back to human form.

"All right," said Dean. "Will you be coming with us, Miranda?"

"No," she said.

A look of confusion crossed Gregory's face. "You aren't thinking of . . . I don't think a member of the Family qualifies as proper Prey."

"No, he doesn't. But I'll be staying here for a while, anyway," she said.

"You know the Law. Pack and Family do not mix. The Elders will not be happy," said Gregory.

"I don't care. I've never cared what the Elders had

to say," she said. "I'll be staying. That is, if Kyle wants me to."

Kyle answered by taking her hand in his.

"You know that the Elders, both of Pack and Family, are not going to approve," said Kyle.

Miranda nodded. "That's what I had in mind from the beginning, gaining their disapproval. I hardly intended to involve you or the Family in my little strategy," she said.

Kyle smiled, then said in a high nasal voice, with just a touch of faux-Bostonian accent. *"A vampire and a werewolf. Oh, no! Simply will not do! Not at all, at all! After all, what would the other Families say?"*

That about summed things up, although her parents and cousins of the Pack would, no doubt, be a lot more vitriolic about the idea of a relationship with Kyle. It was as serious as if he were a human, aka Prey, but a different type of serious. She could hear her father's voice quoting the Law: *"Pack and Family do not mix, save under the most extraordinary of circumstances. They go their way, we go ours, and these are not extraordinary circumstances."*

"You realize that we could be Outcast."

Being Outcast was a threat as dire as any that could be made to vampire or were, short of a *Dark Hunt*, where one of their own was Prey, and which could only end in the Final Death. The Pack was the center of the universe to a were. The Pack took care of its own, as did the Family. If you were Outcast, no longer part of the Pack of the Family, then you were Prey, as surely as if you were a mortal born.

Miranda had never seen it happen. She had heard

tales of the Dark Hunt. But there had never been one in her lifetime. They were things told around campfires in the depths of the night. The very idea of being cut off was nearly impossible to conceive.

"I know, and I don't care," she said. "Do you?"

"Not particularly," he said. "Uncle Xavier has always said that I would come to a bad end."

"A bad end! That's a nice thing to say to a girl!" Miranda threw her head back in mock indignation. Out of the corner of her eye Miranda thought she spied a firefly, but when she turned toward the insect, she found an owl perched on the wall, watching the whole tableau.

Without a word, she angled her head toward Kyle, offering her bare neck.

Kyle's fangs touched her like a whisper, leaving a sensation in their wake as intense as their lovemaking had been. He barely took a spoonful of blood, but she would not have begrudged him more. Freely given, there was a strength in it that did not come otherwise.

"I hope we're not interrupted by any more of your gate-crashing relatives," said Kyle.

Miranda let out a long sigh. This was a moment that she knew would come, it was time to lay her cards on the table.

"I'm afraid that that was my fault. I sort of wanted someone to find out that I was dating outside of . . ."

"The Pack? Your species?" he said.

"Ah . . . yeah. I knew it would drive the Elders crazy. So after we made our date for tonight, I made sure I let it slip to one of my blabbermouth sisters, Linda, what I had in mind. You should have seen the look on her face when I said you weren't to be Prey," she said.

"So when did *you* pick up on the Rover Boys?"

"Practically from the time I got to Washington Square. You may have noticed they are about as subtle as a train wreck. I figured they would follow us and report back, not try to stage a rumble on your balcony. By now the Elders know about us. I would say they will be furious, which is exactly the way I wanted them."

"Does it matter to you, how they feel?" asked Kyle.

"Yes, but not nearly as much as it did before I placed that ad, before I came to the park."

"So what are you going to say to them, now, about us?"

"Probably the same thing you'll be saying to your Uncle Xavier and the rest."

"Deal with it?"

"Exactly. I like the way you think, mister."

"Oh, really. Do you just want me for my mind?"

"No, your body as well," Miranda said as she padded softly back to the futon, motioning for Kyle to join her. He moved soundlessly to her side, cupping her face in his hands and bending his head down to kiss her. The thrill his touch sent through her body was indescribable. Even so, she knew there would be trouble ahead. But all of her concerns and worries melted away in Kyle's presence. *Our time may be brief*, she thought as her lips met his, *but like the fireflies, it will burn just as bright.*

BERNARD BOYCE BENNINGTON AND THE AMERICAN DREAM

by Peter Crowther

Since the early 1990s, more than ninety of Peter Crowther's short stories (plus a few poems) have appeared in a wide range of magazines and anthologies—and as individual chapbooks—on both sides of the Atlantic: two collections of these stories appeared in 1999. In addition, he is the editor or co-editor of sixteen anthologies and the co-author (with James Lovegrove) of the novel *Escardy Gap*. He has served as a Trustee of the Horror Writers' Association and as a Judge for the World Fantasy Awards, and his review columns and critical essays on the fields of fantasy, horror, and science fiction still appear. He lives in Harrogate, England with his wife, Nicky and their two sons.

SWS Seeks Soulmate
Tired of the same old humdrum?
Is one day just like the next and the one before

it? Do you see less in front of you than what's gone before? Take a break and enjoy a relationship you will never forget.
But be warned:

Once you've decided, there's no turning back.

In a seemingly ever-changing and uncertain life that constantly veers dangerously close to the cliffside of loneliness, we cherish those few things that remain constant. And one of those is the neighborhood bar.

You always know where you are with a neighborhood bar, even when that neighborhood is the sprawling metropolis of New York City.

Chairs are for relaxing, beds for sleeping but there's no place better than a bar for dreaming. And the best of them all is Jack Fedogan's place, a two-flight walkdown on the corner of 23rd and Fifth.

The Land at the End of the Working Day—for that's what it's called, this bar—could just as easily have been called the Land at the *Beginning* of the Working Day, but it wasn't. The truth is, apart from the Great Unknown, Jack Fedogan's bar—for a lot of folks—is all there is outside of the working day . . . like a small way station situated at Civilization's End, a final resting place before plunging off into who knows what, the huge sea of uncertainty that stretches, sweeping across time zones, to infinity in any direction.

The clientele of the Working Day stand or sit on that island, on the welcoming boards and stools beneath the pleasantly calming lighting, listening to the music wafting from Jack's CD player beneath the counter, catching sound-glimpses of the sea of humanity that roils outside the doorway upstairs, kind of like listening to the sound of the real sea caught in a shell washed up on a lonely beach, thinking every so often of its mystery, the never-ending swells and the currents, sometimes playful, sometimes harmful, wondering whether their course at the end of this night or the next night or some night soon should be straight on out, beyond the lights and on into the shadows. But they rarely choose that course.

Mostly they go back, these folks, back into that which they know, at least secure in the knowledge that they can return another night and face the same decision, with a glass of beer in one hand or a malt or a highball, and maybe a cigarette in the other or a stogie, with perhaps Chet Baker singing a soft refrain from the speakers, thinking that maybe—just maybe— maybe tonight they'll head off to something new, something different. Because the opportunity is there and that's all that's really needed: the thought that the situation can be changed and so it's not so bad.

A few of those almost-intrepid adventurers are here now, not exactly considering their options—at least, not consciously—but they're here and they wouldn't know how to answer a question that asked why. They're just here. And though they don't know it, they're dreaming.

These are the chosen few, these patrons momentarily lost on the road of life. These are the few who have the potential to question. Some—though not many in *this* establishment—question too deeply when they get around to biting the bullet, and find they've submerged themselves and lost the way . . . find that the asking, so *much* asking, has left no room for answers. They only know, these terminally lost souls, that they took a drink, or maybe a couple of drinks, over maybe a couple of nights, maybe more, to get here . . . so maybe taking a few more drinks might help them to get back. And if it doesn't work tonight, then maybe it'll work tomorrow night. Or the night after that one. Then the trick is getting through the long parched wilderness that exists between those nights.

And that's when the dreaming becomes a nightmare.

But the people in the Working Day know the ropes, know how to read the liquor . . . how to make it work *for* them and not *against* them. These people are the healthy ones; they still have questions, sure, but they keep a tight rein on them, keep them from building up so much strength that the questions turn on them and consume them until all there is is the liquor. And still more liquor. Liquor that they don't use to work up the strength to ask any more . . . now they use it to drown out the noise of their asking.

For as we all know, no sound ever truly dies— particularly the sound of an unanswered question; it just keeps on getting softer, drifting up with the smoke around the top of a room or amidst the branches of the trees in the park or nestled with the pigeons on the narrow ledges a couple of stories up above the city, looking down on the streets and whispering its insistent refrain to you time and again . . . because that's all it knows how to do.

And then, all there *is* is the streets . . . and most everyone knows that, for most folks other than the hardened store-doorway-dwellers and the troglodytes that live in the labyrinthine tunnels that crisscross beneath the city, there are precious few answers to anything out there.

For the people gathered tonight in the Working Day, some answers have been found and the questions still remaining don't have quite the same degree of urgency any more.

There will be a half-dozen people here for the little drama that will unfold tonight, and that's counting Jack who's always here, tending bar and playing music and passing the time of day—or night—with folks who want a few words with their liquor. Four of the half-dozen are regulars and two of them new folks. One of the new faces is still to arrive.

Over in one of the booths along the back wall, a tall man sits with his coat collar pulled up around his neck. His is the one new face that's already here in Jack Fedogan's bar—one of those faces that blow in off the streets, sometimes just the once and sometimes on a few more occasions—and so Jack and the other regulars have paid maybe a little more attention to watching him than they might do otherwise.

They've noticed, for example, that the coat the man's wearing is a thick coat, navy blue, in a heavy serge weave, with dark pants showing creases you could cut paper with, and heavy black shoes, laced up and double tied. Beneath the coat collar he sports a thick woolen scarf, still knotted, and on his head he wears a wide-brimmed hat, navy blue again—covering tufts of hair sticking out from beneath like sagebrush clumps—the hat's brim snapped down rakishly over his eyes, even here inside the Working Day where Jack Fedogan keeps the atmosphere warm and cozy. And they've noticed the black hold-all bag on the floor next to his feet, a scuffed bag, one that has seen a lot of wear and tear, years of being carried or thrown in the back of a car, in the trunk maybe, bouncing side to side as the car goes from here to there, or maybe many plane rides and numerous adventures on carts to and from airplanes and many trips along moving baggage claim lines, going round and round until its owner spotted it and retrieved it from the monotony. The bag looks full on this outing, though the eyes watching it can't exactly figure out what it contains.

To the three regulars at the table in the center of the floor, their regular table, the man appears to be lost in thought, nursing a bottle of beer which he keeps on moving around from side to side, slouched back in his chair, apparently watching the condensation patterns it makes on the table. The watching doesn't seem to contain much in the way of interest. The man looks sickly, the regulars have agreed in hushed conspiratorial tones, coming down with a head cold or maybe the flu . . . or maybe he's got a more exotic ailment in these days of ailments so exotic that even their names are acronym codes of letters and symbols, because the implications of the words they hide are just too terrible to contemplate . . . wasting diseases that take away a man's dignity as well as his strength and his looks and his mind.

They figure he's here to forget something or to find it, looking for answers the way so many are. But most of all, he looks lonely.

In the small trio of regulars locked in a round of their customary joke-telling, Jim Leafman knows all about loneliness and about trying to find answers outside of the Working Day. Jim, who collects garbage for a living and carries the smell of carbolic soap with him wherever he goes, remembers sitting in his '74 Olds outside an apartment building on 23rd waiting for his wife to set off for home just a block away, watching her run-walk along the sidewalk, her hair newly tidied and her hose pulled up straight and the feel of another man's hands still fresh in her body's memory. He remembers watching her and trying to sense her shame, watching her until she isn't there any more.

And he remembers coming back another night or maybe later that same one, the inside of the Olds an olfactory trinity of JDs, betrayal, and a red-tinged fury that licks at the insides of his eyes and makes them dry, makes his eye sockets hurt—though maybe that was just the JDs—sitting there watching the door to the apartment building once more, this time with his old .38 cradled in his lap, with nothing making any sense at all in his life and so what does it matter what he does. This, Jim recalls now, must be how it starts for these folks who just walk out one day and blow people away in fast food outlets or movie house lines.

But now Jim sits at a table in the Working Day, nursing a glass of warm Bud instead of a cold automatic, listening to Miles Davis and Herbie Hancock trade licks on "Little One" from the Davis quintet's ground-breaking ESP studio set from the mid-sixties while he, Jim, trades similar licks, but conversational instead of instrumental, with his friends.

Jim's wife has been moved out for almost a year now, living with the same guy—who says monogamy is a thing of the past?—a man who sells office furniture, living in the same apartment block that he watched all those months ago.

He sees them sometimes, one or the other of them—never the two of them together—and he pretends to himself that it's just a coincidence that he should see them, neatly forgetting that he's been driving or walking up and down 23rd for maybe an hour, even though he has no reason to be there, convincing himself that it's just serendipity, ducking back into store doorways or turning quickly to stare at window displays so they don't see him. He only does this when he's feeling wistful, hankering for something he was hankering for back then, something in which he no longer sees any intrinsic value but something he feels cheated out of achieving.

And he's feeling wistful tonight. Wistful and lonely, thinking about a movie he saw a couple nights ago on cable, Al Pacino as a short-order cook falling in love with some starlet—he doesn't remember her name, maybe Michelle something . . . funny name?—and he wonders if he'll ever share his life with another woman.

Then he hears the footsteps on the stairs leading down from the street and he turns around, eyebrows half raised like he's being casual.

A younger man sitting at the same table, a man with a thick thatch of blond hair, a working man's Robert Redford, also looks around while he nods to the music and glances aside at Jim. He leans forward and lifts the pitcher, pours beer into his glass and then shouts across to Jack Fedogan—Jack polishing glasses behind the long counter . . . always looking like he's polishing glasses but in reality thinking about his wife

Phyllis, which fact McCoy, like everyone who's fortu-
nate enough to be a regular imbiber in this Watering
Hole Mecca for Dreamers, knows only too well—to
bring another pitcher and this time make it one that
doesn't leak. And he turns to Jim and chuckles, takes
a drink and chuckles some more when Jim's face
breaks open around the mouth and he, too, takes a
drink through an easy but contrived smile, like they're
both acting . . . regulars here in this wonderful place,
pretending loneliness is something other people suffer
from while they carry on establishing and marking
their territory against all newcomers.

And that particular catchall could well have been
written with one man in mind, the man who has just
come down the stairs. For this man is a newcomer in
every sense of the word, looking like he wouldn't be
much at home anywhere that would have him, an out-
sider, lost and alone in the night and the city it
shrouds.

McCoy, who some folks call Mac—but only those
folks he likes or who know him really well—feels his
smile fade a little at that thought. He has just got
himself a new job, his fourth since leaving Midtown &
Western Trust & Loan around about the same time
as Jim was coming to terms with his wife cheating
on him, and McCoy feels it's cause for some kind of
celebration . . . so the fading smile is a little disconcerting, if not downright annoying.

But then it's also cause for some kind of reflection,
and right now, tonight in the Working Day, he's thinking back to his time with the Saving & Loan company, still
the only company in the city with two ampersands in
its name, thinking back to wall-to-wall meetings where

nothing ever seemed to get decided but where he felt whole, the way all men feel when they're in regular work, work they feel counts for something even when they know it doesn't, measuring achievement by their pay packet instead of by the inner glow that comes with a job well done, well appreciated, and somehow meaningful.

So, McCoy's job working at a Midtown agency as a copywriter on the annual accounts for a company that produces some kind of ball bearings up in Schenectady seems like both a step forward and a step back, in that paradoxical way everything seems some nights, when the darkness seems a little deeper and a little longer than usual. But there's a girl there that he likes and a couple days ago he built up the nerve to speak to her, over by the photocopier, asking her if maybe she'd like to do something sometime. The girl just looked at him like she was seeing him for the first time, wondering what rock did this guy crawl out from under, and she said to him that she was busy that night. Someone at one of the desks over by the water dispenser let out a snigger that sounded like a duck's fart and the girl walked off away from the photocopier leaving McCoy standing there, feeling like he was buck naked in the middle of Grand Central at 8:30 in the morning. He took the response as a clear sign of disinterest on her part.

Coming home on the subway these past few nights, with the autumn turning into winter and people all around kind of snuggling up against each other, McCoy has been wondering where he can go to meet somebody, and that thought occurs to him again right now, with the entrance of the new arrival . . . McCoy wondering where in hell this guy would go to find someone he could be happy with.

Jack walks across from the bar, eyeing the man who has just stepped out of the real world and into his private domain, and places a fresh pitcher on the table, takes the other one away with a grunt that to some might seem rude but to others not that way at all, and around the grunt he's *tum-tumming* in tune with Wayne Shorter's tenor break on "Agitation" like he's got no worries in the world . . . like he's still got a wife in the apartment upstairs, a wife who's still alive and well and waiting for him when he closes up.

The third man at the table, the "Holy Ghost" of this particular trio, reaches for the new beer and fills his glass, shaking his head and smiling at Jack Fedogan's back, thinking all the time about the checkup he's got day after tomorrow, thinking about the seeing-eye pipe the doctor's going to run down his dick and into his body, twirling it around to get a good look at his prostate—my, will you just look at that!—and wondering whether it's going to be followed by meaningful stares as the doc tries to find the words to tell him, tell him not to start any long books or get too engrossed in any TV serials.

Then he notices the man standing over at the foot of the stairs, in the bar but looking like he's still a little bit outside, like he's wondering whether he's done the right thing coming in here, looking around at the empty tables and at the one where the three friends are sitting—all of them now watching this new addition—and the booth over on the back wall, where a pasty-faced man makes tabletop mosaics out of beer puddles, seemingly oblivious to anything . . . except his eyes are watching intently.

This man, the third of the three friends, is Edgar Nornhoevan, a big man, big and bearded, a big bearded man whose toes never curl and who never grimaces in pain except when the doctor runs that pipe down his dick every six months. The next time is just two days away, and Edgar is not looking forward to it one bit.

Edgar knows diddly about loneliness but he knows all there is to know about cancer. The way Edgar figures it, you're never lonely with a tumor.

It's been almost a year now since the cancer that Edgar expected turned out to be just a slight enlargement, and the pills have been working just fine, so fine that Edgar can once again hold his own—*pardon my French, ma'am!* as Jack might say, Jack who speaks no language other than English-American—when he takes a pee, sometimes feeling like it's the best sensation in the world that meaningful expulsion, so all seems okay it would be just fine and dandy if Edgar were not going for his checkup day after tomorrow. But the fact that he is has brought back the memories and the uncertainty, like he's never going to get rid of this feeling even if he really is okay, never going to get rid of the feeling that maybe something's happening that just shouldn't be happening. Something inside his body. Someplace where he can't see, can't get at.

And this is why Edgar Nornhoevan never feels lonely, except when it's late and he slips between the sheets, turns out the light, and listens to the sirens caterwauling in the nighttime streets. *Hey*, a little voice says to him then, faint in the darkness, *I sure am lonely.*

Jack gives a flourish with his ever-present cloth, sweeping it across a bar top that's already clean enough to eat your food straight off of without so much as a plate or a napkin, and he nods to the newcomer.

"Get you something?" Jack asks.

The man looks at Jack and then around at the rest of the bar, frowning, like he's considering this strange language . . . wondering whatever could it mean, this bizarre singsong of grunts and wind. Then, without so much as a word, he sidles up to the bar and onto a stool. Dutifully, Jack wipes the portion of counter right in front of him. "Beer?" he suggests.

The man rubs a hand over his face, allowing it to linger a little on his mouth, pulling it down some and letting the bottom lip flap up into place like it's one of those exaggerated lips on the cartoon cat in Tom and Jerry— the lip makes a *flapatapatap* sound in Jack's head and for a moment he fights off a smile.

The man wears his hair long, unfashionably long by today's standards even if he were a twenty-something—which he is clearly not . . . unless one could stretch the "something" element into another three decades—and it hangs over his ears and his forehead and his collar in black curls that look like they haven't seen soap and water in a long time. Meanwhile, what there is of it on top is a little thin, combed or brushed back across a balding pate.

"My name is Bernard Boyce Bennington," the man says, the first word of which he pronounces with an emphasis on the "ard" syllable, stretching the vowel out like taffy, while the first comes out as "buh," like he's just been gut-punched. He holds out a hand to Jack.

"Jack Fedogan," says Jack Fedogan, shaking the proffered hand.

"This your bar, or are you just tending it?"

"It's my bar."

For a few seconds, they both seem to be satisfied with the exchange of information, even Jack . . . who now regards the man with a squint, wondering if he needs to reach under the counter to retrieve his pacifier—a smooth-handled baseball that he keeps there to quiet down troublemakers—or make an excuse to go to the cash register where he keeps the Saturday Night Special Phyllis used to rag him about. But the man seem harmless enough—if a little on the flaky side—and the ever-patient Jack is prepared to give him the benefit of the doubt, at least until he hears what he's after.

'I have a story for you," Bernard Boyce Bennington tells Jack, "if you want to hear it," he adds.

Jack waves his hands magnanimously. "That's what bars are for," he says, "telling stories. But they're also for buying drinks. So I'll make a deal with you." He leans on the counter. "You buy one of my beers and I'll listen to your story. How's that sound to you?"

The man looks around again, does his lip thing— *flapatapatap*—once more, and then nods. "That sounds fair to me," he says, and he scans the refrigerated shelves at the back of the bar, the ones with all the bottles on them. "Give me . . . I'll have a Michelob," he says after some deliberation, his eyes scanning the brightly-colored labels first one way and then the other.

"Coming right up." Jack produces the bottle, flips the cap off with the bartop opener, and pours about half of it into a glass he's pulled from the back shelf. He puts the glass on a coaster right in front of the new customer, and the bottle next to it, then polishes the counter around it, even though he hasn't spilled any beer. Jack Fedogan never spills beer.

The man takes a sip, more like it's meant to pacify the bartender than to relieve any inner thirst, and then sets the glass back down on the bar, making sure it sits squarely on the coaster. "I'm looking for someone," he announces out of the blue. "A woman."

"And it's a big Amen to that one, friend," Edgar Nornhoevan observes. Edgar is halfway across to the washrooms and well within earshot of the man's conversation with Jack Fedogan. He turns back to the table, toward Jim Leafman and McCoy Brewer and says, "Fella here looking for a woman. Do we have any we can spare?" And he lets out a deep throaty laugh.

McCoy shakes his head. "Don't think we can help with that one," he says, and the wistfulness of his tone overrides the self-deprecating humor by around a hundred to one.

"She come in here, this woman?" Jack asks, his mind already running through the images of the various women who occasionally sit on the stools at his bar or over in one of the booths along the back wall, nursing Manhattans and screwdrivers as they reflect on the barren ground that their life has become, Jack trying to match up one of the images with the man sitting right in front of him now.

Jim Leafman and McCoy Brewer pick up their glasses and the pitcher and stroll over to the bar, Jim taking the stool a couple over from the newcomer and McCoy standing a few feet away from the counter. Edgar goes off in search of the restroom.

"Truth is, I don't know," Bernard Boyce Bennington says.

Although Bernard Boyce Bennington is indeed the man's name, it is not the one he has most often been called these past forty-five of his fifty-one years. It's Daisy, which, he explains to Jack and Jim and McCoy in a tired voice, comes from the fact that his two first names—and his last, for that matter—begin with the letter B, hence "Daisy," the stock-in-trade BB gun that graced a million homes at around the same time as Forry Ackerman kicked off *Famous Monsters of Filmland*, and you could earn extra money by delivering *Grit* door-to-door which you could then spend buying hundreds of toy soldiers for a couple of bucks or packets of seed to grow your own underwater monkeys.

The 1960s were wonderful times for him, the man continues, times during which he read comic books voraciously before going on to spend inordinate amounts of money buying up back issues from dealers who stretched out the once acceptable grading system of "Mint," "Fine," and "Good," into myriad subcategories which involved buyer and seller alike studying, with magnifying glass and plastic gloves, the item under dispute—a comic book, for goodness' sake!—while haggling over such heinous deformities as "small crease on back cover" and "small chip from bottom of spine." By this time, school had given way to college, and college then emptied BB out into a world for which he was wholly unprepared.

Jack glances across at Jim and McCoy—and Edgar, who has returned from his safari to the restroom, retrieved his glass from the table and sat down next to Jim—and gives a quick raise of his eyebrows that says *So when does this story get interesting?* although nobody seems to be taking any notice. Jack gives the counter a quick wipe and looks back at the man.

"My first job was as a computer operator, handling the mainframe for a small Savings and Loan outfit in Jersey City," he says, taking a sip of Michelob that wouldn't have quenched a fly's thirst. "It was a machine whose numerous metal boxes and whirling tape- and disk-drives filled a room the size of an entire floor of a plush apartment out on Riverside Drive. Of course," he says, turning to his audience, "this same long-ago machine had but a fraction of the processing capacity of the word processor that now sits on my cluttered desk, but then that's progress."

Progress, the newcomer explains, moves life on with casual disregard for the Bernard Boyce Benningtons of the world, but he didn't let this bother him too much. He moved into programming, which meant he could spend his life even further away from other human beings . . . filling his days with printouts as tall as the small boy he once was, and which he would scrutinize for long hours to find the misplaced or juxtaposed numbers that had caused a particular program to fail, and his evenings surrounded by his beloved comic books.

And, oh, how Bernard loved his comic books.

"I had full runs of most of the Marvel titles that had turned the industry on its head in the early 1960s, and I'd bought back and filled out DC tittles such as *House of Mystery* and *House of Secrets*, all of which I just adored." Here he stops for a few seconds and glances around the bar—which is still empty save for the man in the booth, still wearing his hat and coat and scarf—like he's checking to make sure nobody sneaked in while he was talking. Apparently satisfied that he's in control of the situation, the man called Daisy continues with his story . . . which even Jack, who has long held a secret fascination for the old comic books of his youth—things like *Sad Sack* and *Mutt and Jeff* and, his favorite, *Archie*—is beginning to enjoy.

"Trouble was, I found it annoying that, in order to protect my investment—because these things are damned expensive," he says, frowning, "I was reduced to reading some of the books wearing a mouth mask and skintight gloves. And that took away much of the sensation of reading.

"To me, comic book reading is a multisensory experience, and full enjoyment can only truly be achieved with as many of the senses in contact with the actual book—the smell of the primitive ink mixes and the feel of the resilient paper stocks used in the old Sparta, Illinois, printing plants coupled with the almost primal feeling of holding a genuine artifact were considered by many to be as important (and by some to be *more* important) than the occasionally infantile drawing techniques and frequently infantile plotting employed in the sweatshop creative bullpens of the 1930s and '40s."

Edgar's eyes are wide as saucers. This guy sure knows a lot of two-dollar words, he's thinking, but Edgar is glued just the same.

"How does all this tie into the woman you're looking for?" Jack asks.

"I'm getting to that," the man says, and he takes another sip. McCoy gives Jack a sneaky frown to back off and let the guy talk . . . so Jack gives the counter another wipe and waits.

"Those were the days, the days before Frederick Wertham declared war on what he considered to be the sadistic and evil manipulation of kids' minds carried out by the pre-Comics Code Authority comic books, when horror truly was horror." Bernard Boyce Bennington stops and his eyes go all dreamy. "My, but I loved them all, those ridiculous books, despite the predictable denouements and the scrawky pen and pencil work. I loved the monsters and the dragons, adored the animated rotting corpses seeking vengeance; I delighted in the alien horrors stalking far-off worlds . . . but, most of all, I loved vampires, particularly those in the old EC comic books, before Bill Gaines fell foul of Doctor Wetham and was forced to anesthetize the stories in *Crypt of Terror, Haunt of Fear*, and *Vault of Horror* to the point of virtual emasculation. Long-toothed creatures of the night drawn by Jack Davis and which owed more to Nosferatu than to Bela Lugosi's tuxedo-clad Euproean Count . . . and paved the way for the TV adaptation of Stephen King's *'Salem's Lot* and the almost animal-like Mr. Barlow.

"But this lifelong fascination with horror comic books and, in particular, with the undead made me a difficult man with whom to strike up a casual conversation. I accept that without question. And this, in turn, meant that my chances of companionship were slight at best, what with the vast majority of the fairer sex's staunch ignorance of such fundamentally important matters. Sure," he went on, shrugging his shoulders, "I had passed time in comic convention bar areas chewing the fat with like-minded souls—most of whom could recount exact dialogue and page numbers of 'key' stories in the favorite books—but these brief liaisons were ill-fated and amounted to nothing even approaching stability. But then something happened that was to change my life."

The man stopped and took anther drink, this time a bigger one which almost drained the glass. Without even asking, Jack Fedogan pulled another Michelob off the shelf, flipped the cap, and placed it on the bar.

"Eventually, earlier this year, just as the summer was giving way again to autumn's moods of melancholia, the lure of settling down coupled with a suddenly looming mortality persuaded me to actively look for a mate. But the question was, how should I do it?

"Singles bars were out. They were filled with folks that I could scarcely identify with, sharp dressers all, driving sleek continental cars and wearing the latest colognes and playing the latest CDs. Sex was what those folks were after and it wasn't—at least not primarily—what I was after. What I was after was the American Dream . . . a wife, a house, Norman Rockwell-style picket fences, and the smell of meat loaf coming from the oven."

"That's quite a dream," Jack says, his mind drifting back to his life with Phyllis.

"You know," Jim ventures, "I had a dream once . . . dreamed I won the Lottery."

Edgar nods. He's thinking of informing the others that sex would be pretty high up on the list of things he wants right now, but instead he says, "Yeah?"

Jim carries right on the way Jim can do when his mind isn't fully on what his mouth is doing. "Bought a car."

"Why'd you need a car in New York?" McCoy asks.

Jim gives a shrug, shuffles his glass around on his coaster. "I don't."

"But what was the first thing you did?"

"I didn't say it was the first thing. Just that I bought a car."

"What else did you buy?" Edgar says, a smile tugging at the corners of his mouth, taking a rise out of Jim.

"Don't remember. Just remember the car."

McCoy says, "What kind of car was it?"

"A Mustang." In Jim Leafman's mouth the word sounds like a mantra— *mussssstannnng*—or a sibilant call for rain by an old Apache or Shawnee, staring up into the sky looking for water-bearing clouds.

"Now *that* was the American Dream," says Edgar. "That's what they called it. By the 1950s, young couples marrying, heading out to the suburbs, buying houses and cars, starting families. It must've seemed like we had it all."

"Ah had a dream!" McCoy says, trying to capture the milky rounded tones of Martin Luther King.

"I was six in 1950," Edgar says. "Didn't know nothing about no American Dream. My folks lived—"

"You want to let the guy finish his story or what?" Jack asks, frustration spread thick in his words.

Edgar nods and waves for the newcomer to go on with his tale.

"Dating agencies were the next consideration, but even those made for a short-lived solution, the problem being that I just couldn't cope with the intrusive questioning of the patronizing proprietors."

And so it was, Bernard Boyce Bennington explains, on a cloudy and cold October day, with the leaves in Central Park blowing across the street in crinkly brown flurries, that he hit upon the idea of checking the "want ads."

"It sounds a lot easier than it really is," he tells them. "Most of what was available fell either into the outre style of the *Village Voice*, which failed to deliver any solutions, apart from providing lurid photographs of 'college girls just minutes away,' 'outcall Asian bodywork,' and 'hot and horny local girls'—most of whose names seemed to be Cherri or Jade or even Strawberry, and all of whom insured complete satisfaction and discreet billing . . . not to mention 'All Major CCs, ATM & Debit Cards Accepted'"—in amidst the usual three- or four-line enigmas such as 'Bottom in need of Top' and 'Romantic SBF Seeks Big Dipper' . . . or the traditional of *New York* magazine, whose 'Strictly Personals' section offered 'matchmaking' and 'marriage' in amongst advertisements placed, purportedly, by 'professionals,' a select band with which I did not, in all honesty, believe I had much if anything in common.

"In a moment of rare desperation, I even called up an ad which promised 'A Hot Line to My Wildest Dreams' only to find that the sultry-voiced girl—who actually sounded as though she was expiring—"

"Expiring?" says Jim. "You mean, like . . . sweating? How can you sound like you're—"

"That's *per*spiring," Edgar points out.

Jim grunts something by way of an apology and visibly shrinks on his stool.

"Anyway, this girl," the man continues, "offered only Tarot readings, phrenology sessions, numerology classes, palm reading, and my future as prophesied by the stars . . . and, as I assumed Michael Keaton—my favorite actor, by the way, since Tim Burton's Batman movies—didn't know me from Adam or Zachary, that had to be something to do with astrology."

Bernard Boyce Bennington drains his glass and, with a quick salute to Jack, pours the new bottle.

"Then came the big break, a small ad in the *New York Press* 'variations' section." He reaches into the inside pocket of his jacket and removes a folded piece of newspaper, its print smudged in places and the folds starting to tear. He holds it out to Jack. "Here, read it yourself."

Jack takes the paper and unfolds it, holding it so Jim and Edgar and McCoy can lean over and read it at the same time. The paper reads:

Single White Succubus Seeks Soul Mate
Tired of the same old humdrum?
Is one day just like the next and the one before it? Do you see less in front of you than what's gone before? Take a break and enjoy a relation-

ship you will never forget
But be warned:

once you've decided, there's no turning back.

The ad finishes with a cell phone number.

"What's a sucker-bus?" Jim Leafman asks.

"A Greyhound headed for Las Vegas," says Jack, who has never held with gambling.

"A succubus is a female demon," Bernard Boyce Bennington answers. "Legend has it that they have sex with sleeping men . . . and," he adds, "they steal their souls."

Jim Leafman sits up from the bar, wondering if it's his imagination or has it suddenly gotten cold in the last couple of minutes. "She the woman you're looking for?"

The man nods and takes a drink of beer.

"Couldn't you just call her?" McCoy says.

The newcomer shakes his head. "I tried that, many times since. Just get a solid tone. But the first time, I got straight through," he says, setting his glass back on the bar. "It was a little before two AM on a particularly black night during which the wind buffeted my apartment windows and rattled the glass in the casements. A woman's voice answers—in the background I could hear soft music, and glasses clinking and muted conversation—and, so help me, she says my name. 'Good evening, Mister Bennington,' she says to me. 'Where do you want us to meet?'"

McCoy gives out a low whistle. "How'd she know your name?"

"I have absolutely no idea . . . but, if she was a

succubus then one can only presume that she had abilities far beyond our understanding."

Jack pushes his cloth to one side and leans more heavily on the bar. "Did you go meet her?"

"I regret that I did."

"You *regret?* What? Was she a dog?"

"No," the man says to the bartender with a sad smile. "No, far from it. She was the most beautiful woman I have ever seen.

"Long story short, I met up with her, corner of 23rd and 3rd, and we walked into Gramercy Park, hand in hand. I remember how cold her hand felt to the touch, but I didn't think anything of it . . . at least not then. It was late at night and it was a cool night and I just put it down to bad circulation. Anyway, unusually for me, I became quite . . . shall we say, stimulated by her—there was something about her, some aura, some intoxicating scent . . . a mixture of fresh flowers and musk or patchouli, something sweet-smelling and yet old and musty . . . hard to explain. And I stopped, just inside the park, and suggested that perhaps we could go back to my apartment, but she declined. Or perhaps hers, I suggested . . . and she laughed. She didn't have an apartment. She lived out in the city, she told me, in the bars and drinking holes, the hotel lounges and the nightclubs, a different one every evening. She said that she got all the custom she needed from these places and that the newspaper advertisement was simply an experiment. Mine had been the only call, she told me, and she would not be repeating the experiment.

"We carried on into the park and—" He stops and looks at his beer for a few seconds. "This is a little difficult for me." He takes a deep sigh and a long gulp of beer, draining the glass. "She was very attentive to me. So attentive in fact that by the time we had gone but a few yards into the park, barely out of the glow of the lamps by the street, she had fully removed her clothes, pulling them off in bravura sweeps of crinoline and lace, whisking them up into the night air to expose white flesh which seemed to exude some kind of aroma all of its own. The grass around us became quickly littered with her clothes, a skirt, then her blouse, followed by a satin vest and a brassiere, and finally by her panties.

"Then I removed my own clothes."

"Jesus H. Christ," Edgar mutters.

Jim Leafman twists awkwardly on his seat.

McCoy says, "That kind of thing can get you locked up."

Jack Fedogan agrees.

"Believe me," B. B. Bennington says imploringly, "this is not something I normally do. I was . . . I was drunk with her, I felt the heavens coming down to meet me and me crashing upward to meet them; I felt that I could lift a mountain and live forever, I felt so happy I wanted to weep. But that was only the beginning." He looks up at Jack. "Could I have another of those beers?"

In a flash, Jack reaches behind and pulls a Michelob across, flips the cap, and stands it next to the newcomer's empty glass. Then he shifts his weight to his other leg and says, "Then what happened?"

The man pours the beer, takes a sip, and continues with his story. As he does so, he takes something out of his jacket pocket—something in a brown paper bag,

folded in a rectangular shape like maybe it's a book—
and he sets it on the counter. All eyes watch the
stranger's hand place the object but no eyes move
away with the hand: they stay on the object, four
minds wondering what on Earth it could be and what
significance it could have to the story now unfolding.

Bernard Boyce Bennington shrugs. "Then the inevitable happened, of course. Right there on the grass in
Gramercy Park. I . . . I won't go into the details here,
gentlemen; it is sufficient to say that I have never felt
such a feeling before. More than that, I truly never
believed such a feeling was possible. She moved with
a slow grace, her body lithe and supple, and her
mouth . . . well, it was everywhere. As was her voice."

It is Jack Fedogan, suddenly aware that there is no
music playing, who responds first. He pulls out a Char-
lie Mingus CD and slips it into the player, keying in
track numbers and hitting the play button. As the first
strains of music drift into the air, he says, "Her
voice?"

"I had my eyes closed, so great was the feeling of
elation and spiritual contentment, but all the time we
were making love she was speaking to me."

"What was she saying?" McCoy asks.

"All kinds of things . . . things about my past, that
nobody else could know, and things about comic book
stories, all of which she appeared to have read. She
knew everything about me and everything about what
I had done or read or hoped for. And she told me
that this night, right then and there, lying on the grass
in Gramercy Park, was the pinnacle of my life. She
told me I would never be lonely again."

Then he stops speaking.

Jim looks at Edgar and then at McCoy and McCoy looks at Jack and then at Edgar, and then everyone turns to look at the stranger, waiting for him to say something more. Eventually it's Edgar who breaks the silence.

"And then what?"

"And then she was gone," comes the answer.

"Gone?" It's a single word delivered by four voices.

Bernard Boyce Bennington reaches for the brown paper package and all eyes follow his hand. "I must have . . . I must have, blacked out or something. But when I came to and opened my eyes, she had left me . . . no clothes, no note, nothing except this." And he pulls open the bag and removes a small battery-operated cassette player.

"Listen," he says, and he presses the play button.

At the same time, Jack Fedogan turns down the volume button on the CD system hidden below the bar, forcing the familiar strains of 'Good-bye Porkpie Hat'—in particular John Handy's flutter-tonguing alto duel with Mingus' tremolo basswork—off into some ethereal background, like in a party scene in a movie, when the opening pan shot with the loud soundtrack has finished and now the characters have something to say.

And it's fitting. For as one melody—Mingus' eternal paean to Lester Young, who died less than two months before this legendary 1959 recording—stops, another melody filters into the Land at the End of the Working Day . . . a melody without notes or words, but rather one with the sound of the wind in the trees, and the distant hum of traffic and occasional muted shouts.

Suddenly, somewhere deep inside the recesses of the newcomer's cassette player, the far-off wail of a siren hums like a fly, disappearing before it's hardly got started. And then, closer, there's a grunt. It's a man's grunt.

The grunt is followed by another, deeper this time, more drawn out.

Then a sigh, also deep, again unquestionably a man's sigh.

For several minutes the quartet of regulars sits or stands entranced by the sounds coming from the machine sitting on the counter.

They hear trees rustling and they hear the sounds of movement, interspersed with sighs and soft kisses and even an occasional word, always in a man's voice, an *Oh!* or an *Ah!*, and then an *Oh, God!*, the word "God" drawn right out, long and thin and deep.

They feel they're intruding, Jim and Jack, and Edgar and McCoy, feel like they're peeping at another man's keyhole in the dead of night, and deep within them they feel, to a man, the stirrings of desire and companionship, the feelings forcing away the blight of loneliness that affects so many people in cities and towns and desolate truck cabs lit only by the orange or green glow of the dashboard dials and the waft of cigarette smoke.

And then it stops.

The stranger reaches out and presses the button, cutting off the silence.

Jim Leafman takes a drink and shakes his head.

Jack Fedogan stands up from the bar, thinks about reaching for his cloth and then decides against it. Instead, he turns up the volume again on his CD player,

Peter Crowther

turns it up without hardly realizing he's doing it, and the opening strains of "Self Portrait in Three Colors," a song with no solos, the very same haunting music that graced John Cassevetes' directorial debut movie, *Shadows*, fills the bar.

Edgar Nornhoevan looks at Jim and then at McCoy, whose eyes are closed, his hands thrust deep into his pants pockets.

And then Bernard Boyce Bennington speaks.

"You didn't hear her, did you?"

The four men exchange glances and, silently, elect a spokesman.

Shaking his head, the Working Day's bartender says, "No, there was only you . . . only your voice we heard."

"*I* heard her," a new voice says.

They turn around and come face-to-face with the old man from the booth along the back wall. He must have come across while they were listening to the tape, come across real quiet so that nobody noticed him. And now here he is, sitting propped against the table right behind them, his battered valise by his feet. "*I* heard her," he says, shaking his head, a smile playing across his mouth.

"She did me, too," the man says, and he reaches into his pocket, pulls out a small cardboard strip. "Did me in a train station down in Philly, late at night, in one of those booths where you can get four photographs for a dollar, behind a floor-length curtain oblivious to the world and the night. I fell asleep afterward—right there in the booth, which was the only place we could find that offered any kind of privacy—and when I woke up, curled up on the floor like an abandoned child, there on top of my clothes was this."

He hands the strip across to McCoy who accepts it and takes a look.

The strip has four photographs on it, each one with a man in the foreground, his back to the camera. The man appears to be naked, though the camera has only caught him to the small of his back, and his face, though it only appears in profile in just one of the shots, looks enraptured.

But more than that, tufts of his hair are sticking up no matter which way he moves his head . . . like someone is holding them, tugging them. Only there's nobody else in the photographs.

Bernard Boyce Bennington lets out a stifled moan. "That's her," he says, "Oh, my God, that is *her*."

As McCoy Brewer hands the strip across to Jack Fedogan, the old man says, "But *you* don't see her, do you? *You* see only me."

"There isn't anyone else on this except for you," Jack says. "If it *is* you. Fella here looks a lot younger and, well . . . in a mite better shape than you look right now. No offense," Jack says as he hands the strip across to Jim Leafman.

"None taken," the old man says. "It was a long time ago, almost twenty years. She left me with—" he pauses and nods at the strip of photos, "—with that, and she took everything else that I had. My job, my home . . . and my sanity.

"I was getting a late train, going home after an all-day meeting that had gone on into one of those corporate dinners that offer only headaches and indigestion. I wasn't looking for excitement, wasn't looking for adventure—at least not right then, though I'd been getting a bit down, you know . . . lonely . . . wondering what life was all about. Maybe that was it: maybe I'd gotten the scent of vulnerability about me . . . because that's what loneliness is, isn't it? Being vulnerable.

"Then, out of the shadows, she came up to me. There was hardly anyone else in the station, just a couple of bums sleeping off the booze, and a guy sweeping up the concourse way down away from me. And she says to me, 'Mister Yordeau, where can we go to be private?' "

"She knew your name, too?"

The man nods to McCoy. "Knew everything about me. Said she usually hung out in bars and clubs and so on—here in New York—same thing she told him." He nods to Bernard Boyce Bennington. "And that was it. I went with her, may God have mercy on my soul . . . I went with her, looked around for someplace we could be alone, my heart thumping in my chest, and I saw the photo booth. We went inside and clothes started coming off right away, no questions asked, no conversation, no nothing." The man stopped and shook his head. "I had never felt anything like that before in my life and I've never felt anything like it since."

"So what did you do?" Jack asks, passing the old guy a beer and handing bottles out to everyone . . . like it's a private party.

"Well, everything went to hell . . . like I said. I left everything behind me—and I mean *every*thing. And I started hanging around in bars trying to find her . . . to get her back . . . to—" He shrugged. "I don't know

162

what I wanted—wanted her back, I guess . . . wanted to do it again.

"And I had conversations with bartenders and their regulars, showed them the photographs. And nobody could see her. Pretty soon, I realized she'd done something to my head. And after a few years, I changed."

"Changed?" says Edgar. "Changed how?"

"Oh, I still looked for her—and I still do, even now—but not with the idea of getting her back again. I stopped showing people the photographs. Now I just go to a few bars every night . . . and I watch. And when I find her . . ." He turns and glances down at his bag, then stoops and picks it up, runs the zipper along and pulls it open.

"Jesus Christ!" says Jack Fedogan.

The man pulls out a wooden-headed mallet and a fistful of sharpened stakes, each one about a foot long.

"I mean to end her power," the old man says, dumping the mallet and the stakes back into the bag. "I mean to free myself, free others—like him—and I mean to make the world safe from her, whatever she is."

Bernard Boyce Bennington lifts the brown paper bag from the counter, having returned the player into it, and slips it into his pocket.

Jim Leafman says, "So how come you both end up in here . . . tonight?"

The man shrugs. "Coincidence. Nothing more. I guess it had to happen one day in one bar . . . two of the people she's tainted coming together in the same place at the same time."

"You followed me," says Bernard Boyce Bennington, backing away now, backing toward the stairs.

The old man shakes his head, eyes closed.

Jack, also shaking his head . . . and waving his arms around, says, "Hey, hold on now . . . this guy was in here bef—"

"You followed me, and you want me to lead you to her."

And right about now, there's a sound from up the stairs . . . maybe even from out on the street, and Jack feels a breath of fresh air on his face.

The four men facing the stairs look up at the first footstep, then Jack looks, too, and Horace Parlan lets his fingers drift along the piano keys in Jack's CD player, lost in that long ago impossibly wonderful session with Mingus. They look up the stairs, suddenly aware of the silence contributed to the scene in classic western style, the way any good honky-tonk ivories man would do when someone walked in through the saloon doors . . . aware of that and the foot on the wooden stairs, hearing another step, leaning over to try to get a glimpse of whoever's coming down into the bar, but they can't see anything.

Then Bernard Boyce Bennington stops right where he is, his heels jammed up against the bottom stair, his brown paper bag clasped in his hand, and he breathes in deeply.

McCoy Brewer notices that there are tears running down B. B. Bennington's cheeks, and he breathes in again, savoring the smell of the outside must be, McCoy thinks and he takes a step forward.

The man turns and looks up the stairs.

The others lean still farther, like vaudevillian stuntmen or Keystone Kop fall abouts, still trying to see up the stairs. The feet have stopped, and all they want to see is an ankle . . . a shapely ankle, maybe . . . in a high-heeled pump, standing in that narrow right-angle triangle of a gap between the upstairs floor and the banister rail leading downstairs . . . but then whatever made that foot-stepping kind of noise turns right around before they can see anything at all, never mind put a leg to the imagined ankle, and a waist to the leg, and a torso to the waist, a neck to the torso and, most desired of all, a head to crown off their creation. It turns and moves back up the few stairs it's come down, back to the outside world and the mischievous air that waits there.

And for a few seconds right now . . . and even more seconds and minutes and maybe hours in the times to come and all the times that these men have left to them to think their midnight thoughts, the four men watching the stairs and the stranger called Bernard Boyce Bennington think maybe they imagined it, the footsteps . . . that maybe the night and the hour and the stories have gotten the best of them . . . that maybe it was the wind blowing down the New York City streets the way it does, a lonesome wind looking for a little late-night company, blowing the door so it clanged a little, nothing more: because, hey . . . it was late for a woman to be walking down into a bar by herself, wasn't it?

But not all of them harbor such doubts.

Without so much as a word, B. B. Bennington takes the stairs out of the Land at the End of the Working Day, a low deep sad moan building in his throat as he flings himself up the stairs two and even three at a time, putting distance between himself and the people still standing watching him . . . McCoy's hands partly outstretched in a mixture of defense and reasoning, Jim Leafman holding onto Edgar Nornhoevan's arm, and the old man with the black valise already starting for the stairs. Jack Fedogan watches it all in dumbfounded amazement.

"Hey!" Edgar calls, sliding off of his stool, though nobody is sure whether Edgar's calling out to Bennington or to the old man with the valise.

And then there's the sound of a car horn, squealing brakes, raised voices . . . and the unmistakable dull *crump!* of something being hit out on the street.

Already, the old man is nearing the top of the stairs.

Edgar Nornhoevan is halfway up.

McCoy and Jim are on the first couple of steps, and Jack is stepping from behind the bar.

They arrive in that order out on the rainy windswept street.

It's late at night on the corner of 23rd and Fifth, and there's nobody to be seen. Nobody except a small man with what might be the beginnings of a beard or just stubble from laziness. He's wearing a small peaked cap, a sleeveless cardigan sweater, and his rolled-up shirtsleeves are already soaked. He's standing by the side of a yellow cab, its motor still running, the driver's door wide open and the strains of rap music drifting out into the night, savoring a freedom of sorts. The man is looking down at a bundle in the road, partly covered by his cab, and every few seconds he looks around, his arms spread in confusion . . . and just once in a while he glances across the street at the empty sidewalk which carries on along 23rd in the direction of Park Avenue South and, beyond that,

Lexington, which, of course, gives onto Gramercy Park.

"Not my fault," the man is explaining to anyone who will listen. "Not my fault, man," he says again, waving a hand whose fingers are kind of pointed and kind of curled in, waving it at the people who have suddenly gathered on the sidewalk. "Guy comes up out of—" The man looks around and sees the sign, THE LAND AT THE END OF THE WORKING DAY, and his eyebrows flick up, just for a second or two, and everyone knows there's a voice in the back of his head asking *What the hell kind of a place is that, man?* but immediately dismissing it because he's a New Yorker and he's seen many strange names on the buildings around town and many strange people coming out of them. "Guy comes up out of there, man, runnin', and he gets to the curb and he looks around and then it's like he sees somethin' across the street and he just steps off, man . . . I mean—" He does the wave with his pointy-curly hand again and then smacks both hands together. "—and *Blammo!*, you know what I'm sayin', man? I couldn't do nothin', I mean I couldn't do nothin' at all. Dude just steps out and *Blammo!* Shit," he concludes, dragging the word out so that it's two syllables, "shee" and "itt." He shakes his head and pushed his cap back. "I ain't never hit nobody, man, and I been drivin' cabs for eighteen years." His voice is a little high-pitched and he sounds close to tears. He turns to the others and says, "Any of you guys a doctor or somethin'?" He looks down at the bundle again. "Shit," he says, "you think maybe he's dead?"

Jack steps across and leans over Bernard Boyce

Bennington and looks into the man's open eyes, watching the raindrops fall on the pupils without so much as a blink. There's a thin trail of darkness at the corner of his mouth—his *smiling* mouth, Jack notices—which washes away every three or four seconds and then reappears, and there's a wide stain of blackness on the man's shirtfront.

The cab driver has turned away and is now looking down 23rd. "You know," he says, over his shoulder, "there was somebody across the street, you know what I'm sayin' here? Some woman, looked like. She must've seen it wasn't my fault, man but she just up and went. Where the hell did she go?"

The old man with the black valise steps forward and places a hand on the driver's shoulder. "Where'd she go?"

"Huh?" The cab driver looks like someone's just asked him an arcane algebraic formula known only to Harvard lawyers.

"The woman. You see what she looked like? Where she went?"

The driver shrugs. "She looked like . . . I don't know what she looked like, man," he says. "She was . . . she was just a woman." Then he shakes his head. "Maybe there wasn't any—"

"You see where she went?"

"I think it was a woman, man," the driver says, looking around at the street and trying to piece it all together again because everything has happened just so fast. "Too dark and too wet to tell for sure. But seems to me she was standin' right there, like she was makin' to cross but standin' well back from the curb." He shakes his head again, trying to shake free the sight of a woman's face—oh, such a *sweet* face—looking up at him, speaking silently to him about the loneliness of the streets and the night . . . telling him, deep down in his head, down where everything mattered and nothing mattered . . . telling him that she understood and that one day she would take that loneliness away from him . . . and that all he had to do was wait, wait and keep silent . . . because one day they would meet again. And she reached down to the man on the roadway and lifted a brown paper package from his hand.

"She saw it, man. She saw it wasn't my fault."

From his crouched position next to the bundle in the road, Jack Fedogan says, "He's dead." Jack feels around the body, beneath the jacket, and then leans over to look beneath the cab. Then he stands up and looks out into the street, shielding his eyes.

"What is it?" McCoy Brewer asks.

Jack shrugs. "The cassette player. It's not here."

"It must be there," McCoy says, crouching down.

The old man spins the driver around. "Which way?"

"What?"

"Which way did the woman go?"

"Hey, man, I didn't see her go no way, man."

"How far is Gramercy Park?" the old man asks.

"Huh? You want to go to Gramercy in *this?*"

"How far?"

The cabbie points down 23rd. "Couple blocks down to Lexin'ton and then one block down, man."

The old man pulled his coat collar up and started across the street, his arms wrapped tightly around his battered valise and its cargo of release. He's already across the street before the shouts but he doesn't respond, just keeps on jogging along 23rd, passing beneath overhead lights, growing smaller and smaller, his footsteps growing fainter and fainter.

"I'd better call 911," Jack says. He removes the apron he always wears and drapes it across Bernard Boyce Bennington's face and chest. The rain immediately pastes it down and the first telltale signs of darkness start to show amidst the apron's stripes. "You want to come inside?" he says to the cabbie, who is still staring down 23rd, staring and frowning, although there's nobody to be seen anymore.

"What's he want in Gramercy Park?" the driver asks.

It's Edgar Nornhoevan who answers. "He wants what we all want," he says. "A little companionship to keep out the cold."

The driver reaches into the car and switches on his hazard flashers, slams the door. Then he joins the others and, as one, they go back down into the Land at the End of the Working Day, prolonging the dream and putting off that dreadful. moment when they, like all of us, must be alone again.

WEROTICA

By Esther M. Friesner

Esther Friesner has written over twenty novels and coedited four fantasy collections, including the *Chicks in Chainmail* series, the most recent of which, *The Chick is in the Mail,* was published in 2000. Her short fiction appears in *Excalibur, The Book of Kings, Black Cats and Broken Mirrors,* and numerous appearances in *Fantasy and Science Fiction* and other prose magazines. She lives in Madison, Connecticut.

Likely lad seeks lassie. SWM, athletic, outdoorsy, successful, faithful, wants to share moonlit strolls, fireside snuggles, warm fuzzies, and the occasional walk on the wild side. Looks unimportant, good taste very. Put an end to my solitary days and lone wolf nights. No smokers, drug users, or vegans, please.

It was a first date to remember.

Weylin Maclain lay back in a strange bed, exhausted and so thoroughly sated that the few remaining brain cells still flickering feebly amid the ashes of unparalleled erotic pleasure began demanding that he show them some ID. As a rule, sensual banquets like last night's marathon did not happen to him. Absolutely nothing in his previous love life could compare to what he had just experienced, unless first augmented by a factor of twenty-five in the least, and even then the result would fall short. Or in other words:

"Wow. That felt really . . . *good.*" He rolled onto his side and threw one arm over the slim, pale body beside him. "I mean, that was just— It was so— And when you wouldn't stop doing that thing with the— Jesus, Chanetta, I was so totally— *Wow.*"

The recipient of Weylin's fumbling attempts at grateful acclamation smiled lazily up at him, her eyes two slits of burning green beneath long, black lashes. She and he had been going at it for the better part of the night, yet time had not smeared nor custom streaked her carefully kohl-lined lids and white-powdered face. Perhaps she appeared untouched by her recent sexual athletics because the untrained eye could not perceive where the chalky makeup left off and the sun-starved skin began. Then again, maybe the untrained eye was too busy staring at the intricately tattooed circle of miniature ankhs playing ring-around-the-nipple on her right breast to bother looking at anything else.

"Are you happy, my beloved?" Chanetta murmured. "I'm so glad. I was worried that I wouldn't be . . . wild enough to please you."

"Are you kidding?" Weylin blurted. "You were so— I was almost— We nearly broke the— And what you did with the wasabi and the— I think I've lost all feeling in my— Owooo-*eee!*" It was only a minor

variation on the theme of *Wow,* but it had a most unexpected effect.

The lady threw her arms around Weylin's neck, brought his head down sharply, and demanded, "Do that again."

"Do—?"

"Howl. Howl for me, my love." She pressed her lips to his ear, her breath scorching skin already rubbed more than a little raw, and fervidly whispered, "I know it won't be as good as it's going to be, when the change overtakes you, but I still want to hear you howl now."

"Change?" said Weylin. "What change?"

Chanetta didn't care for questions. She took matters into her own hands and soon had him howling till dawn.

That was when she told him *what change.*

In a downtown coffeehouse called Piccini's where the tiny mosaic-topped tables were nearly as colorful and twice as stable as the customers, Weylin laid his case before his best friend, George Perrine. If he was hoping that George would confirm his own prefabricated convictions in the matter at hand, he was promptly, bluntly disappointed.

"There!" said George, jabbing his finger at Weylin's much-refolded copy of the *Village Voice.* "And there and there and *there!* Oh, and there, too. I can count at least seven separate places in your ad where she damn well *could* get the idea she'd be dating a werewolf. And that's without including the 'lad' part. Clever reference, totally wasted, wasted, *wasted.* No one reads Albert Payson Terhune these days, more's the pity."

Weylin frowned as his friend's fastidiously manicured nail underscored almost every part of the personal ad he'd spent so many anxious hours composing while clients clamored for his ear and back issues of the *Wall Street Journal* piled up on his desk unheeded. "You're kidding," he said, leaning back in his chair and taking a long, nervous pull at his double chocolate latte. "I don't see it at all. You're nuts."

"Your new breeder-chick gets hot for the Wolfman and *I'm* nuts? Sweetheart, why do you insist on acting so bloody surprised by what happened? You did everything in that ad but say 'Be my bitch.' " George had a wicked grin, part bawdy choirboy, part barracuda.

"Now just one damn minu—!"

"Tsk-tsk. You're foaming at the mouth again, Fido. Literally." George leaned across the table and dabbed the streak of steamed milk from Weylin's upper lip, then dropped back into his own seat. "No need to be so touchy. You asked for my opinion and I gave it: You use worms, you catch fish; you leave cheese, you get mice; you wave lottery tickets, you get my mother—don't I wish. The right bait for the right job, and that ad is definitely, positively, utterly the *perfect* bait for attracting a werewolf groupie."

Several heads turned and the whole coffeehouse went quiet. George was an unemployed actor with a fine set of equally unemployed lungs and no interest in volume control.

"Jesus, George, you want to lower your voice?" Weylin hissed, cringing behind his steaming cup.

"No," George replied amiably. "I read that Piccini's is *the* newest hot spot for theater people. As we speak, the next table over might be hosting a producer, a casting director, an agent fairly *palpitating* to possess my talents. Can I deny him the supreme joy of discovering me just because *you* hopped into bed quick-and-stupid? Again." He sipped his mochaccino demurely.

"Dating Chanetta is *not* stupid." Weylin's teeth gritted. "She's the best thing that ever happened to me since I moved to the godforsaken city."

George was skeptical. "The best thing that happened to you after six whole years of living in Manhattan is scaring up a reject from the Addams Family? A tuppeny-ha'penny halfwit Gothette who is under the impression that she's dating Lyle Talbott's ugly brother? Your upper East Side apartment, your bigass Wall Street salary, your subscription to the Metrofuckingpolitan Opera all wither and die by comparison to *that*? Why don't you just tell me to totz on down to the IRT local and see if my tongue will stick to the third rail on a cold morning? Maybe I'm credulous enough to believe that, too."

Weylin paid him no mind, conning his own Personals ad for the hundredth time. "Okay, I admit that the part about 'warm fuzzies' might be open to several interpretations, but I still say there's no way anyone could conclude I'm a werewolf based on *this*. Chanetta's an artist, she's got a wonderful imagination and a great sense of humor. This whole werewolf thing is probably just a big joke on her part, an original way to break the ice."

"Break the *ice*?" George sighed. "Weylin, friend of

my incredibly squandered Terre Haute boyhood, I saw what your apartment looked like the day after she slept over the first time. She broke *everything*. Enthusiastic little minx, isn't she? I admit she's rather fetching, and if she had a brother, I'd probably be all over him like a bad Swedish massage, but wake up and smell the— Well, I suppose you can't smell much of anything else in *this* place. This is a relationship with no future. It began with a misunderstanding, it's rolling along on a logjam of lies, and it's going to end in disaster, heartbreak, and maybe just a *soupçon* of bloodshed if you're not lucky. Which you're not; trust Auntie George on this one."

"And the voice of the stay-at-home-Saturday-night romance expert is heard in the land," Weylin grumbled.

George snapped his fingers at a passing waiter. "*Garçon!* Another mochaccino *pour moi* and a bowl of milk for my catty friend! Or is there another feline term I ought to be applying to you, hm?" He looked at Weylin and raised one eyebrow. The waiter and Weylin both chose to ignore him.

George was accustomed to being ignored, which did not mean he ever accepted it. With one elegant move he swept his cup and Weylin's from the tabletop. "Oops," he said, with comic-strip word-balloon distinctness. "Clumsy me. Full cups are *so* much harder to knock over. Especially when they're brought by someone who isn't a Mister Poutyface." He stared at the waiter meaningly.

Two fresh drinks hit the tabletop with alacrity, though George's landed more in his lap than in the cup.

"Oops," said the waiter, no easy thing to say while maintaining a wide, fake smile.

"He wants me," George confided as he dabbed mochaccino from his khakis.

"Oh, great." Weylin slumped back, gazing into the depths of his new latte in dejection. "A man spills coffee on you, and you read it as a come-on. Why the hell did I ever ask *you* to vet my ad for hidden meanings? Which are *not* there, by the way. *You* live in a fantasyland where subtext grows like fungus!"

"Bullshit. I never went to Harvard." George drank what was left of his coffee. "Look, angel, you've got the unmistakable air of a crippled vole that's just been dropped into a rattlesnake mosh pit. You're trying to escape, but you know you can't, so you're going to grab out wildly in every direction except the right one. The question is *not* whether your ad led Jezebel o'Bedlam to believe you turn hairy at the full moon. Somewhere *other* than your palms, I mean. The question *is*: When are you going to tell her the truth?"

It might have been the right question, but it got no answer out of Weylin. As the silence between them deepened, George tapped his fingers on the tabletop impatiently.

"I see," he said at length. "That good in bed, is she? Or are you just glad to be getting any at all?"

"There's more to our relationship than sex," Weylin said with a small snort of indignation.

"Yes, there's also lycanthropy. Dear boy, sooner or later there'll be a full moon scheduled to make an appearance. You'll have to tell her before then because frankly, as soon as the moon's up and you're still the same-old-same-old, I can't picture her patting you on the back and telling you it's okay, it doesn't matter, it happens to a lot of werewolves."

"Dammit, George! I don't know why I even bothered talking to you about this. You are not only wrong about Chanetta, you are so unbelievably wrong about everything else even *vaguely* related to interpersonal relationships that—"

Just then the waiter placed the bill on the table. Weylin interrupted his diatribe to reach for it, knowing as he did the usual state of George's wallet. There was a phone number scribbled on the detachable receipt at the bottom along with the words *I know some fun ways to get out coffee stains. Call me.*

Weylin passed the check across the table. "Tell me what to do, George," he said.

"Step One: Knock on her head, see if anyone's home, and tell the lady of the house that there are no such things as werewolves. If, as you claim, she's just been kidding about that, you can both enjoy a good laugh followed by a good— But I shall spare my blushes. If she has *not* been pulling your leg, or whatever, proceed to Step Two: Tell her that you, in particular, are not a werewolf. Mind you, this is *not* the time to hit her with the fact that what you *are* is a financial analyst. She'll be in enough pain as it is. And for God's sake, don't get *cute* and do your Nixon imitation when you say 'I am not a werewolf.' If she disagrees, refer her to Step One, all the while bearing in mind that no one likes to have her illusions shattered. Be kind, be gentle, and be sure to lock up any household implements sharper than a plum."

"What if she gets mad? What if she—" he swallowed hard and spoke the unthinkable "—leaves me?"

"Very hard to leave anyone when you're naked," said George, helpful to the end.

Step One did not work. Even when two people have reached that stage in the night's activities when all their clothing is puddled on the floor, there is still no room in the bed for the naked truth.

Amazing, Weylin thought as he bought himself a much needed time-out in the bathroom. *She* wasn't *joking. She* does *believe in werewolves. Man, the look on her face when I said they don't really exist—!* He shook his head as if trying to dislodge just one bit of their recent heart-to-heart that might make sense.

Chanetta's face rose before him, her eyes wide with anguish. *How can you say such hurtful things to me, Weylin? I thought you loved me! Oh! I see how it is: I've displeased you, somehow. You don't think I'm worthy to behold you in your full magnificence. I'm just a silly little girl to you, good enough to screw when you're in* this *form—* (She couldn't keep the note of contempt out of her voice) *—but when you feel the moon's power in your bones you want a* real *woman.*

It didn't seem to bother her that she was arguing against the as yet unproffered premise of Step Two. She believed in lycanthropy with the irrational passion of a Cubs fan. Nothing he said could change her convictions concerning werewolves *per se* either. Neither the "it's just a story" nor the "it's just a B-movie" nor the "it's just a role-playing game" assertions worked.

I suppose next you'll be telling me that there are no such things as vampires either! she sobbed. And like a fool, he'd tried to do just that.

Bad move. Bad, bad move.

"How was I supposed to know her roommates were all dating weirdos who—who—" He couldn't say it. It was bad enough listening to Chanetta tell him about the various . . . libidinal idiosyncrasies in which her friends and their Sanguinary Others indulged.

But I care nothing for the weak world of the blood-ghoul, Chanetta had told him proudly. *The vampire stalks the night, yet flees and cowers from the sun. Ah, but the werewolf commands the hours of both night and day! Unsensed, he passes through our midst while we, his natural prey, go about our mediocre little lives like the sheep we truly are. He is the true master! He, and not the vampire, is the true lord of the night! Besides—* and she'd given his earlobe a kittenish nibble *—screwing vampires is so over.*

Oh, yes, Anne Rice had plenty to answer for and no mistake.

Weylin's solitude was broken by a timid knocking at the bathroom door. "Weylin?" Chanetta's voice sounded small and fragile, like a sick child's. "Weylin, I'm dressed and I'm going now. Forever. Good-bye."

He threw open the door and grabbed her roughly, without restraint or apology. Three strands of skull-shaped ivory beads and the miniature bronze canopic jar that she wore around her neck dug craters into his bare chest. "Don't go, Chanetta!" he cried. "I'm sorry, I didn't mean to hurt your feelings, I—I—I was just fooling. I was so afraid that you—that you were only toying with me, that you couldn't accept me for what I am."

"Oh, Weylin!" Chanetta's whole face lit up so brightly with unconstrained joy that it was only a matter of time before the Melancholia Police arrived to revoke her Goth license. She embraced him ardently. "I understand, my beloved: So many years of dwelling with the curse of the wolf upon you, never knowing that you would someday find a kindred soul who would not see it as a curse but a blessing! No wonder you lashed out at me. Other lovers have hurt you too many times in the past, so now you seek to wound before you are wounded. Trust does not come easily to you. Ah, my precious one, but in time you *will* trust me fully, I know it. And when you do, it is the one hope of my heart that you will then deign to grant me the *ultimate* intimacy."

Weylin was confused on the same scale that the Atlantic Ocean was mildly damp.

"I thought we already *had* the, um, ultimate intimacy."

Chanetta laughed. "You still tease. But *you* know what I mean. And until then . . ."

If there was a land speed record for shedding one's clothes, Chanetta broke that, too.

"Bite me," said George. He said it in his usual, carrying voice, but no one in Piccini's so much as raised an eyebrow. In this venue it was a phrase as hackneyed to the regular patrons' ears as *aloha* to Hawaiian tour guides.

"Say what?" asked Weylin.

"That's what *you* have to say to a werewolf if you want him to bring you over to the fangs-and-fur side of the Force. Of course that's provided you can *find* a werewolf to start with. I suppose you could always place an ad in the Personals." He was joking, but Weylin was clearly not in a receptive mood. George rolled his eyes and forged on: "Hey, you've seen *Dracula,* right? Well, people become werewolves the same way they become vampires: The bite of one creates another. That's how the system works. There are some minor variations to the rule in both cases, otherwise we'd be up to our butts in bloodsuckers and lycanthropes, but who gives a rat's ass? At least I know rats' asses *exist.*"

Weylin only sighed.

George clucked his tongue. "Poor baby. You've got it bad, don't you? If they ever need a poster child for Terminal Desperation, the tiara is yours. I mean, have mercy, but are you even *listening* to yourself? You know there's no such thing as a werewolf, but here you are, asking me how you can become one. *Me!* What in hell ever gave you the idea that *I'd* know something like that?"

"Well . . . you do. You just told me."

"Oh, for—!" George rolled his eyes dramatically. "It's *folklore.* If I could tell you the story of Rumpelstiltskin, would you assume I knew how to spin straw into gold?"

Weylin set both elbows on the table and bowed his head into his hands, beaten. "You're right, George: I am desperate. I can't help it. I love her. I don't care if she's a little . . . eccentric about this whole werewolf thing, I still can't picture myself living without her."

"This is a conspiracy, right?" George drew away from his friend, his face a mask of suspicion. "It's all part of the great Hetero Agenda to make sweet, innocent queers like me so damn curious about what this woman can possibly be doing to you in bed that we betray our own kind and come over to sample the breeder goodies. Well, it won't work! And neither will I!"

The waiter came over with a plate of chocolate biscotti. "George, darling, shut up," he said calmly. "I didn't even get around to asking my boss if there were any job openings here." He turned to Weylin. "I couldn't help overhearing—" he began.

"No surprise." Weylin nodded at George. He and the waiter exchanged sympathetic looks. George used one of the biscotti to give them the finger.

"Anyway, I think I can help you. *Maybe.* My name is Lorant Petofi—"

"Oh, *that* name's going to be all over *Playbill.*"

"Shut up, George. —and I still remember my grandma Kari telling stories about werewolves and stuff like that from the Old Country. Now according to her, if you had the curse of the wolf on you and you wanted to be cured, you had to seek out a wise old Gypsy woman. I figure it ought to work both ways. I mean, a doctor has to know how to give you a disease if he's going to know how to cure it, right? And there has to be a way to turn you into a werewolf without another werewolf's bite, otherwise where did the first werewolf come from?"

"I am taking a strictly Creationist stance on that one," said George.

Lorant gave him the fish-eye, then bent over the table and scrawled a phone number on Weylin's napkin. "Here," he said, shoving it at him.

"He's a *breeder,* you little slut." George glared.

Lorant shook his head wearily. "Third time's the charm: Shut *up,* George." To Weylin he said: "This is the number of a family friend-of-a-friend, someone

Mom always mentions when she talks about the old stories Grandma used to tell. Her name's Ilona Nagy and I think she might be able to help you."

"She's a wise old Gypsy woman?" Weylin asked, picking up the napkin.

"Sort of."

It was a good thing that Lorant had the presence of mind to call ahead and brief the aforementioned family friend-of-a-friend as to Weylin's little "problem." Otherwise, when Weylin first crossed the threshold of the Gypsy's lair, he might have taken one look, fallen into a flurry of confusion, and bolted. As it was, he had no time to do so much as stammer out his name or his business. The Gypsy already knew all, and she proved it by plunging right to the heart of the matter before he could force out a word.

"Werewolves," said Ilona, a faint smile playing about her full lips. "Most people choose to run *away* from them. What's the matter with your little playmate, Mr. Maclain? Rugby players aren't wild enough for her?"

"What little playmate?" Weylin asked, mesmerized by the dark young beauty just within arm's reach across a neat oak desk. This was not the stereotypical Gypsy hag of his preconceptions. "Um, that is, yeah, right, Chanetta and the whole werewolf thing, uh . . ."

"Chanetta." Ilona repeated as if savoring a mouthful of dark red wine. "Such a pretty name. For a pretty lady, eh? Pretty enough for you to come to me seeking the curse rather than the cure."

"Then there *is* a curse of the werewolf? A real one?" Weylin could scarcely believe his fortune, although for a moment he couldn't say whether it was good fortune or bad. "So that means . . . you can help me?"

"I could." Ilona steepled her fingers and tilted her chair back. Like everything in the office including herself it radiated style, good taste, and piles of money. "The question is: Should I?"

"I'd be willing to pay." He realized how lame the offer sounded as soon as he made it. Lorant's "wise old Gypsy woman" didn't inhabit an abandoned storefront or a side street walkup down in the Village. No, her haunt was a glass-and-chrome castle in the heart of the Financial District, within broker-hurling distance of his own corporation. (When she'd given him the address over the phone and told him to meet her there well past normal business hours, he simply assumed she worked as a cleaning woman.) She wore neither garish patchwork skirt nor fringed paisley shawl nor bright bandanna knotted 'round her head. She *did* sport gold earrings to accessorize her Ralph Lauren suit, but not in the flashy hula-hoops-for-hamsters size. Rather, a caterpillar would find it a bit of a tight squeeze to pass through their tasteful circumference.

Ilona picked up a Mark Cross gold pen and twirled it like a miniature helicopter blade. "We can discuss remuneration for services after we have settled the question of whether there will be any services provided at all."

"I knew it." Weylin sagged. "Lorant told you I was nuts and now you're just trying to let me down easy. I know I must *sound* crazy, looking for the curse of the werewolf, but if you only understood how I feel about—"

"What makes you think I don't?" Ilona countered. "You are not the first person to risk all for love, including any claims to sanity. Others besides you have done as much, and then not even for love, merely sex. I know I have. I remember the first time I enjoyed the attentions of a superlative lover. It was as if I were a starving man who stumbles across a laden apple tree. He has never tasted anything so exquisite in his life and so he devours the fruit and clings frantically to the one tree, all the time not realizing that an entire orchard awaits him just beyond the horizon." She looked him right in the eye.

Weylin fidgeted. Ilona was sharp, and like most sharp things, she had the power to inflict swift and painful damage. "Not exactly a proponent of monogamy, are you?" he asked, trying to blunt her edge with a feeble joke.

"But I am," she countered. "I distinguish between love and raw desire even if . . . others do not. If I'd been speaking about love just now, I still would have placed that lone apple tree in sight of an orchard, only it would be an orchard thick with lemons."

Ilona stood up and walked around her desk until she was towering above him. "I am not trying to turn you from your course, Mr. Maclain," she continued. "If becoming a werewolf is what you want, I can give it to you. Just because I work on Wall Street doesn't mean I've lost the craft that was passed down to me from my mother and my mother's mother and all our female line. Magic is my heritage, but it's got a lousy dental plan. All I ask is that you think the matter through thoroughly, rationally. A curse is not like a cold or a bad haircut; you do not get over it with the passage of time. A true curse lasts forever. Knowing this, do you still wish to be a werewolf?"

"Of course I want to be a werewolf!" Weylin exclaimed. "That's the whole reason I'm here."

She shook her head, still smiling. "You answer too quickly. Often a glib *Yes* is a flimsy mask for *No, I've changed my mind, but I've come this far and I'll look like a fool if I back out now.*"

She was right, of course, but that didn't mean Weylin was about to admit as much. He didn't think bluster would work on Ilona, so he opted for wounded dignity instead: "I don't believe you grasp my situation fully, Ms. Nagy," he said. "A man in my line of work doesn't have either the time or the opportunity to meet women—not outside of the office. I've been too lonely for too long. Now that I've found someone who lo— who cares for me deeply, I'll do whatever it takes to keep her."

"What makes you insist that I don't empathized with you completely, Mr. Maclain?" Ilona inquired. "You are not so alien to me. Lorant informs me that we are colleagues. In case you haven't noticed, I, too, work in a field where I find a crystal ball almost as helpful as a pair of brass ones. So tell me: What is a nice financial analyst like you doing, placing personal ads in the *Voice?* There are other means of meeting people available to those of our kind. Some matchmaking agencies specialize in young professionals and Ivy League graduates. And you're not exactly a gargoyle. Far, far from it." Her fingertips stroked his cheek lightly, casually. It was all he could do to keep from trembling. "Are you too shy, too cheap to pay the agency fee, or is it just that you knew exactly what you were doing, that you *wanted* to find someone who is not quite so . . . vanilla?"

Hearing the uncomfortable truth never failed to embarrass Weylin, and being embarrassed never failed to make him mad. He shot out of his chair and growled at Ilona. " 'Our kind?' " he mocked. "Pretty strange to hear exclusionist talk coming from a Gypsy. If you are a Gypsy. There's a big difference between dealing in poultry futures and stealing chickens."

She slapped his face. Then she seized it and brought her mouth to his so hard that her teeth drew blood from his lower lip. "*That* was what I meant by 'our kind,' Mr. Maclain," she said, panting. "The kind of people who play by the rules and wear the uniform, but who also choose when and where we'll play the game." She drew his face to hers again, only more gently, and licked the blood from his lip with a few quick darts of her tongue. Then she sauntered back to the far side of the desk and reapplied her lipstick as if nothing had happened. "Two points, my favor. Your turn." She smiled into the mirror in her little gold compact.

Weylin's head spun. Without thinking he strode around the desk, lifted her out of her chair as if she were a child, and kissed her with a hunger he'd never known. She responded eagerly, only breaking free from his embrace long enough to shut her office door. As she returned to his arms she whispered, "I promise not to confuse this with love if you won't, Mr. Maclain," and pulled him down onto the carpet.

Later, when he tried to tell her how much he loved

her, she laughed. "What about our promise? Perhaps you *will* love me, in time; perhaps you won't. Few can. Love demands that we understand much, accept much, and forgive more. Baring our bodies is nothing—anyone can do that—but it is when we bare our true selves that we learn the difference between love and lust."

Weylin recalled Chanetta's reaction when he'd tried to tell her that he wasn't the man—or beast—of her fantasies.

"A lie's a lousy basis for an adult relationship," he said, as if he'd just discovered a hitherto unknown Revealed Truth of Western Civilization.

"Unless you're planning on a political career."

"No, I mean it. I *see* it, now. It's time I told Chanetta who—what—I really am, and this time I won't back down, no matter how upset she gets. This time I'm going to put some teeth into it."

Ilona laced her arms around his neck. "Now I *can* help you, Mr. Maclain," she said.

The trees of Central Park whispered in a chill evening breeze, their crowns black and lifeless, waiting for moonrise. Chanetta snuggled closer to Weylin, her arms around his waist, her chin resting firmly on his shoulder and demanded, "Does *she* have to be here?"

"I do." Ilona settled herself more comfortably on the blanket the three of them shared, impervious to the other woman's baneful glare. "I'm his therapist and we are on the cusp of a major breakthrough moment. Even werewolves can benefit from analysis, you know, as long as it's not that Jungian crap."

"She *knows?*" Chanetta switched her stare of outrage from Ilona to Weylin.

"I—I couldn't very well keep something like that from my therapist," he replied. "Counterproductive. Anyway, she's a Gypsy; they're used to this kind of . . . syndrome."

"Dear child." Ilona stretched across Weylin's lap to pat Chanetta's hand. The three of them sat in a row on a tatty old quilt that Chanetta had brought to the park with the frank intention of using it for a make-do mattress once her beloved went through his Change. "Dear, *sweet* child, I can't express how happy I was when Weylin told me all about you. *At last,* he said, *I have found someone who loves me for myself, for what I really am!* Oh, have you any idea how wretched it must be to have to conceal one's true nature from the beloved? To put on a false front at all times for fear of losing him? We in the profession refer to it as 'courting' behavior. Everyone does it, to some degree. When we finally drop the mask, we prove the durability of the relationship. For one man, it happens when he picks his nose in the presence of his inamorata, for another, the moment comes when he dares to fart in her company without blaming it on the cat. For Weylin it will be . . . something a little more dramatic. The danger of rejection is very imminent, very real, potentially very devastating. I could not in good conscience allow him to face that possibility alone."

"Well, if that is the case, you can go home right now." Chanetta looked smug. "*I* won't reject him for what he really is. It's the whole reason that I love him!"

"Mmm. Perhaps you are right, child." Ilona got to

her feet and brushed bits of dead leaves from her dress. "Just hearing you swear that you love him for himself is enough for me. I wish you both well." She vanished into the surrounding foliage like smoke just as the first light of a full moon trickled through the leaves.

Chanetta sat there, gazing expectantly at Weylin for about ten minutes before she asked, "Well? When does it start? How long does it take? Do we have to wait until the moon is at its height or—?"

"No," said Weylin. "I think I've kept you waiting long enough." And that was when, at long last, he told her the truth.

"Ah, *there* you are, Weylin." Ilona's voice reached his ears as if from a great distance. Figuratively speaking, it *was* a long haul from the realms of insensibility to the waking world. "For a while I was afraid I would have to leave you here and fetch some smelling salts. I don't like to fetch anything." She sounded in high spirits, positively buoyant, possessed by that breed of gaiety which implies that cheerfulness is a team sport: Be there or be square.

Easy for her *to be so chipper*, Weylin thought with bitterness of heart. *It's not like* she *was the one Chanetta knocked cold.* Still groggy, he sat up and touched the side of his head gently. *Whoever said that the truth hurts must've had moments like this in mind.*

"My poor darling, how you have suffered," Ilona cooed from the shadows. "Soon I will make you feel *much* better, I promise."

"Uh . . ." Weylin peered in the direction of the voice, straining his eyes to the utmost. "That sounds very nice, but . . . where are you?" He saw no one, not even the outline of Ilona's body against the bushes. It wasn't as if he were sitting in complete blackness, lost in the heart of some murky wildwood straight out of the Brothers Grimm. The full moon was now halfway up the sky, showering the park with icy silver radiance. If that weren't enough, there were plenty of street-lamps illuminating the paths, and the milky wash of New York's clustered neon in the distance, leeching darkness from the night.

Ilona gave a throaty laugh. "Where am I? Right here. Waiting."

"For what?" Weylin was miffed. "For Chanetta to clobber me a second time while you just stand by and watch?"

"There will be no second time," Ilona said sweetly. "Clouting the beloved with a rock is hardly a tasteful way of ending an adult relationship. That was rude. I made her realize this. She won't do it again."

"With a *rock?*" Weylin might have been clobbered only once, but he was stunned twice. "I could've been lying here, bleeding to death, while you were trying to teach her *good manners?*" He tried getting to his feet, but his legs felt as if they belonged to someone else. He sat down hard and remarked: "Ow."

Except it came out as "OwooOOOoooh!"

Ilona trotted out of the bushes just as Weylin got his first clear look at the thick brown fur covering his hands. Even as a she-wolf Ilona was still lovely, though he found the crimson stains on her muzzle very disquieting. When she burped up one of Chanetta's old rings right at his feet, he was fit to be tied and wholly reduced to pronouns:

192

"I— You— She—"

Ilona wagged her tail. *"Us,"* she said complacently. "Do not be afraid, my pet: Soon your metamorphosis will be complete. It always takes longer, the first time."

"Why is this happening to me? *Why?*" he moaned. He tried to cover his face with his hands and wound up bopping himself in the muzzle with huge, powerful paws. Although he now lacked the fingers for the job, he could still feel the spot on his lower lip where Ilona's teeth had drawn blood in that first, fierce kiss.

"Bite me," he whispered, recalling George's impishly-phrased instructions for achieving lycanthropy.

"Maybe later," said Ilona. She nuzzled him playfully. "I never *meant* to bite you. It was an accident of passion. Are you angry?"

Weylin didn't answer immediately. He was still adjusting to his changed state. As his transformation neared completion, all of his senses tingled, enhanced beyond his wildest imaginings. The night called to him with a hundred fresh, tantalizing voices, and he realized that for the first time since he'd moved to New York City he was actually hoping he'd run into a mugger.

Finally he said: "I never said I *didn't* want to be a werewolf. Not in so many words." His ears drooped slightly. "Poor Chanetta. She could've had what she wanted, if only she'd really loved me, if she'd stood by me, stuck around instead of doing a bash-and-run."

"She didn't run too far," Ilona reminded him. "But you are right, my love: Had she only waited, had she been patient instead of willful, things would have gone differently for you. And *much* differently for her. I regret her death deeply." She burped again. "But a Pepto ought to fix that."

"You know, this won't be so bad after all," Weylin said, tongue lolling in a doggy grin. "It could even be a good career move for me. On Wall Street it pays to have the inside track when it's dog-eat-dog. And hey, it's only once a month. I can use it as a symbolic way to get in touch with my feminine si—"

Ilona nipped his ear, hard. "Go New Age nerd on me again and there's more where that came from." She bounded off, then back, frisking her tail. "Goth always goes straight to my hips. Come on, let's get some exercise!" She dashed away and Weylin followed, joyously baying at the moon.

SOMEONE TO SHARE THE NIGHT

by Tanya Huff

Born in the Maritimes, Tanya Huff now lives and writes in rural Ontario. On her way there, she spent three years in the Canadian Naval Reserve and got a degree in Radio and Television Arts which the cat threw up on. Recent books include the novels *The Quartered Sea* and *Valor's Choice,* and a single author collection entitled *What Ho, Magic!*

You write for a living, Henry reminded himself, staring at the form on the monitor. *A hundred and fifty thousand publishable words a year. How hard can this be?* Red-gold brows drawn in, he began to type.

"Single white male seeks . . . no . . ." The cursor danced back. "Single white male, mid-twenties, seeks . . ." That wasn't exactly his age, but he rather suspected that personals ads were like taxes, everybody lied. "Seeks . . ."

He paused, fingers frozen over the keyboard. *Seeks what?* he wondered, staring at the five words that, so far, made up the entire fax. Then he sighed and removed a word. He had no real interest in spending time with those who used race as a criteria for friendship. Life was too short. Even his.

"Single male, mid-twenties, seeks . . ." He glanced down at the tabloid page spread out on his desk searching for inspiration. Unfortunately, he found wishful thinking, macho posturing, and, reading between the lines, a quiet desperation that made the hair rise off the back of his neck.

"What am I doing?" Rolling his eyes, he shoved his chair away from the desk. "I could walk out that door and have anyone I wanted."

Which was true.

But it wouldn't *be* what he wanted.

This is not an act of desperation, he reminded himself. Impatient, perhaps. Desperate, no.

"Single male, mid-twenties, not into the bar scene . . ." The phrase *meat market* was singularly apt in his case. ". . . seeks . . ."

What he'd had.

But Vicki was three thousand odd miles away with a man who loved her in spite of changes.

And Tony, freed from a life of mere survival on the streets, had defined himself and moved on.

They'd left a surprising hole in his life. Surprising and painful. Surprisingly painful. He found himself unwilling to wait for time and fate to fill it.

"Single male, mid-twenties, not into the bar scene, out of the habit of being alone, seeks someone strong, intelligent, and adaptable."

Frowning, he added, "Must be able to laugh at life."
Then he sent the fax before he could change his mind.
The paper would add the electronic mailbox number
when they ran it on Thursday.

Late Thursday or early Friday depending how the
remaining hours of darkness were to be defined,
Henry picked a copy of the paper out of a box on
Davie Street and checked his ad. In spite of the horror
stories he'd heard to the contrary, they'd not only gotten it right but placed it at the bottom of the first
column of Alternative Lifestyles where it had significantly more punch than if it had been buried higher
up on the page.

Deadlines kept him from checking the mailbox until
Sunday evening.

There were thirty-two messages. Thirty-two.

He felt flattered until he actually listened to them
and then, even though no one else knew, he felt embarrassed about feeling flattered.

Twenty, he dismissed out of hand. A couple of the
instant rejects had clearly been responding to the
wrong mailbox. A few sounded interesting but had a
change of heart in the middle of the message and left
no actual contact information. The rest seemed to be
laughing just a little *too* hard at life.

But at the end of a discouraging half an hour, he
still had a dozen messages to choose from; seven
women, five men. It wasn't thirty-two, but it wasn't bad.

Eleven of them had left him e-mail addresses.

One had left him a phone number.

He listened again to the last voice in the mailbox,

the only one of the twelve who believed he wouldn't abuse the privilege offered by the phone company.

"Hi. My name is Lilah. I'm also in my mid-twenties—although which side of the midpoint I'd rather not say."

Henry could hear the smile in her voice. It was a half smile, a crooked smile, the kind of smile that could appreciate irony. He found himself smiling in response.

"Although I can quite happily be into the bar scene, I do think they're the worst possible place to meet someone for the first time. How about a coffee? I can probably be free any evening this week."

And then she left her phone number.

Still smiling, he called it.

If American troops had invaded Canada during the War of 1812 with half the enthusiasm Starbucks had exhibited when crossing the border, the outcome of the war would have been entirely different. While Henry had nothing actually against the chain of coffee shops, he found their client base to be just a little too broad. In the café on Denman that he preferred, there were never any children, rushing junior executives, or spandex shorts. Almost everyone wore black and, in spite of multiple piercing and overuse of profanity, the younger patrons were clearly imitating their elders.

Their elders were generally the kind of artists and writers who seldom made sales but knew how to look the part. They were among the very few in Vancouver without tans.

Using the condensation on a three dollar bottle of water to make rings on the scarred tabletop, Henry watched the door and worried about recognizing Lilah when she arrived. Then he worried a bit that she wasn't going to arrive. Then he went back to worrying about recognizing her.

You are way too old for this nonsense, he told himself sternly. *Get a . . .*

The woman standing in the doorway was short, vaguely Mediterranean with thick dark hair that spilled halfway down her back in ebony ripples. If she'd passed her mid-twenties it wasn't by more than a year or two. She'd clearly ignored the modern notion that a woman should be so thin she looked like an adolescent boy with breasts. Not exactly beautiful, something about her drew the eye. Noting Henry's regard, she smiled, red lips parting over very white teeth and it was exactly the expression that Henry had imagined. He stood as she walked to his table, enjoying the sensual way she moved her body across the room and aware that everyone else in the room was enjoying it, too.

"Henry?" Her voice was throatier in person, almost a purr.

"Lilah." He gave her name back to her as confirmation.

She raised her head and locked her dark gaze to his. They blinked in unison.

"Vampire."

Henry Fitzroy, bastard son of Henry VIII, once Duke of Richmond and Somerset, dropped back into his chair with an exhalation halfway between a sigh and a snort. "Succubus."

*   *   *

"So are you saying you *weren't* planning to feed off whoever answered your ad?"

"No, I'm saying it wasn't the primary reason I placed it."

The overt sexual attraction turned off, Lilah swirled a finger through a bit of spilled latté and rolled her eyes. "So you're a better man than I am, Gunga Din, but I personally don't see the difference between us. You don't kill anymore, I don't kill anymore."

"I don't devour years off my . . ." He paused and frowned, uncertain of how to go on.

"Victims? Prey? Quarry? Dates?" The succubus sighed. "We've got to come up with a new word for it."

Recognizing she had a point, Henry settled for the lesser of four evils. "I don't devour years off my date's life."

"Oh, please. So they spend less time having their diapers changed by strangers in a nursing home, less time drooling in their pureed mac and cheese. If they knew, they'd thank me. At least I don't violate their structural integrity."

"I hardly think a discreet puncture counts as a violation."

"Hey, you said puncture, not me. But . . ." She raised a hand to stop his protest. ". . . I'm willing to let it go."

"Gracious of you."

"Always."

In spite of himself, Henry smiled.

"You know, hon, you're very attractive when you do that."

"Do what?"

"When you stop looking so irritated about things

not turning out the way you expected. Blind dates *never* turn out the way you expect." Dropping her chin she looked up at him through the thick fringe of her lashes. "Trust me, I've been on a million of them."

"A million?"

"Give or take."

"So you're a pro . . ."

A sardonic eyebrow rose. "A gentleman wouldn't mention that."

"True." He inclined his head in apology and took the opportunity to glance at his watch. "*Run Lola Run* is playing at the Caprice in ninety minutes; did you want to go?"

For the first time since entering the café, Lilah looked startled. "With you?"

A little startled himself, Henry shrugged, offering the only reason that explained the unusually impulsive invitation. "I'd enjoy spending some time just being myself, without all the implicit lies."

Dark brows drew in and she studied him speculatively. "I can understand that."

An almost comfortable silence filled the space between them.

"Well?" Henry asked at last.

"My German's a little rusty. I haven't used it for almost a century."

Henry stood and held out his hand. "There're subtitles."

Shaking her head, she pushed her chair out from the table and laid her hand in his. "Why not."

Sunset. A slow return to awareness. The feel of cotton sheets against his skin. The pulse of the city outside the walls of his sanctuary. The realization he was smiling.

After the movie, they'd walked for hours in a soft mist, talking about the places they'd seen and when they'd seen them. A primal demon, the succubus had been around for millennia but politely restricted her observations to the four and a half centuries Henry could claim. Their nights had been remarkably similar.

When they parted as friends about an hour before dawn, they parted as friends although it would never be a sexual relationship; sex was too tied to feeding for them both.

"World's full of warm bodies," Lilah had pointed out, *"but how many of them saw Mrs. Simmons play Lady Macbeth at Covent Garden Theater on opening night* and *felt the hand washing scene was way, way over the top?"*

How many indeed, Henry thought, throwing back the covers and swinging his legs out of bed. Rather than deal with the balcony doors in the master suite, he'd sealed the smallest room in the three bedroom condo against the light. He'd done the crypt thing, once, and didn't see the attraction.

After his shower, he wandered into the living room and picked up the remote. With any luck he could catch the end of the news. He didn't often watch it but last night's . . . date? . . . had left him feeling reconnected to the world.

". . . when southbound travelers waited up to three hours to cross the border at the Peace Arch as US customs officials tightened security checks as a precaution against terrorism."

"Canadian terrorists." Henry frowned as he toweled

his hair. "Excuse me while I politely blow up your building?"

"Embarrassed Surrey officials had to shut down the city's Web site after a computer hacker broke into the system and rewrote the greeting, using less-than-flattering language. The hacker remains unknown and unapprehended.

"And in a repeat of our top story, police have identi-fied the body found this morning on Wreck Beach as Taylor Johnston, thirty-two, of Haro Street. They still have no explanation for the condition of the body al-though an unidentified constable commented that 'it looked like he had his life sucked out of him.'

"And now to Rajeet Singh with our new product report."

Jabbing at the remote, Henry cut Rajeet off in the middle of an animated description of a battery-operated cappuccino frother. Plastic cracked as his fingers tightened. A man found with the life sucked out of him. He didn't want to believe. . . .

As part of an ongoing criminal investigation, the body was at the City Morgue in the basement of Van-couver General Hospital. The previous time Henry'd made an after hours visit, he'd been searching for in-formation to help identify the victim. This time, he needed to identify the murderer.

He walked silently across the dark room to the drawer labeled Taylor Johnston, pulled it open, and flipped back the sheet. LEDs on various pieces of ma-chinery and the exit sign over the door provided more than enough light to see tendons and ligaments stand-ing out in sharp relief under desiccated parchment-colored skin. Hands and feet looked like claws and the features of the skull had overwhelmed the features of the face. The unnamed constable had made an accurate observation; the body did, indeed, look as if all the life had been sucked out of it.

Henry snarled softly and closed the drawer.

"You don't kill anymore, I don't kill anymore . . ."

He found the dad man's personal effects in a manila envelope in the outer office. A Post-it note suggested that the police should have picked the envelope up by six PM. The watch was an imitation Rolex—but not a cheap one. There were eight keys on his key ring. The genuine cowhide wallet held four high end credit cards, eighty-seven dollars in cash, a picture of a golden retriever, and half a dozen receipts. Three were out of bank machines. Two were store receipts. The sixth was for a credit card transaction.

Henry had faxed in both his personal ad and his credit information. It looked as though Taylor Johnston had dropped his off in person.

"Blind dates never turn out the way you expect. Trust me, I've been on a million of them."

In a city the size of Vancouver, a phone number and a first name provided no identification at all. Had Lilah answered when he called, Henry thought he'd be able to control his anger enough to arrange another meeting but she didn't and when he found himself snarling at her voice mail, he decided not to leave a message.

"Although I can quite happily be into the bar scene . . ."

She'd told him she liked jazz. It was a place to start.

*   *   *

She wasn't at O'Doul's although one of the waiters recognized her description. From the strength of his reaction, Henry assumed she'd fed—but not killed. Why kill Johnston and yet leave this victim with only pleasant memories? Henry added it to the list of questions he intended to have answered.

A few moments later, he parked his BMW, illegally, on Abbot Street and walked around the corner to Water Street, heading for The Purple Onion Cabaret. There were very few people on the sidewalks—a couple, closely entwined, a small clump of older teens, and a familiar form just about to enter the club.

Henry could move quickly when he needed to and he was in no mood for subtlety. He was in front of her before she knew he was behind her.

An ebony brow rose, but that was the only movement she made. "What brings you here, hon? I seem to recall you saying that jazz made your head ache."

He snarled softly, not amused.

The brow lowered, slowly. "Are you Hunting me, Nightwalker? Should I scream? Maybe that nice young man down the block will disentangle himself from his lady long enough to save me."

Henry's lips drew up off his teeth. "And who will save him as you add another death to your total?"

Lilah blinked, and the formal cadences left her voice. "What the hell are you talking about?"

Demons seldom bothered lying; the truth caused more trouble.

She honestly didn't know what he meant.

"You actually saw this body?" When Henry nodded, Lilah took a long swallow of mocha latte, carefully put the cup down on its saucer, and said, "Why do you care? I mean, I know why you cared when you thought it was me," she added before he could speak. "You thought I'd lied to you and you didn't like feeling dicked around. I can understand that. But it's not me. So why do you care?"

Henry let the final mask fall, the one he maintained even for the succubus. "Someone, something, is hunting in my territory."

Across the café, a mug slid from nerveless fingers and hit the Italian tile floor, exploding into a hundred shards of primary-colored porcelain. There was nervous laughter, scattered applause, and all eyes thankfully left the golden-haired man with the night in his voice.

Lilah shrugged. "There's millions of people in the Greater Vancouver area, hon. Enough for all of us."

"It's the principle of the thing," he muttered, a little piqued by her lack of reaction.

"It's not another vampire."

It was almost a question so he answered it. "No. The condition of the corpse was classic succubus."

"Or incubus," she pointed out. "You don't know for certain those men weren't gay, and I sincerely doubt that you and I alone were shopping from the personals."

"I wasn't looking to feed," Henry ground out through clenched teeth.

"That's right. You were looking for a victimless relationship and . . ." Lilah spread her hands, fingernails drawing glistening scarlet lines in the air. ". . . ta dah, you found me. And if I'm not what you were looking for, then you were clearly planning to feed—if not sooner, then later—so you can just stop being so 'more ethical than thou' about it." She half turned in her chair, turning her gesture into a wave at the counter staff. "Sweetie, could I have another of these and a chocolate croissant? Thanks."

The café didn't actually have table service. Her smile created it.

Henry's smile sent the young man scurrying back behind the counter.

"Is there another succubus in the city?" he demanded.

"How should I know? I've never run into one, but that just means I've never run into one." The pointed tip of a pink tongue slowly licked foam off her upper lip.

Another mug shattered.

"Incubus?"

She sighed and stopped trying to provoke a reaction from the vampire. "I honestly don't know, Henry. We're not territorial like your lot, we pretty much keep racking up those frequent flyer miles—town to town, party to party . . ." Eyebrows flicked up then down. ". . . man to man. If this is your territory, can't *you* tell?"

"No. I can recognize a demon if I see one, regardless of form, but you have no part in the lives I Hunt or the blood I feed from." He shrugged. "A large enough demon might cause some sort of dissonance, but . . ."

"But you haven't felt any such disturbance in the Force."

"What?"

"You've got to get out to more movies without subtitles, hon." She pushed her chair out from the table and stood, lowering her voice dramatically. "Since you've been to the morgue, there's only one thing left for us to do."

"Us?" Henry interrupted, glancing around with an expression designed to discourage eavesdroppers. "This isn't your problem."

"Sweetie, it became my problem when you showed me your Prince of Darkness face."

He stood as well; she had a point. Since he'd been responsible for involving her, he couldn't then tell her she wasn't involved. "All right, what's left for us to do?"

Her smile suggested that a moonless romp on a deserted beach would be the perfect way to spend the heart of the night. "Why, visit the scene of the crime, of course."

Traffic on the bridge slowed them a little and it was almost two AM. by the time they got to Wreck Beach. Taylor Johnston's body had been found on the north side of the breakwater at Point Grey. Henry parked the car on one of the remaining sections of Old Marine Drive but didn't look too happy about it.

"Campus security," he replied when Lilah inquired. "This whole area is part of the University of British Columbia's endowment lands and they've really been cracking down on people parking by the side of the road."

"*You're* worried about Campus Security?" The succubus shook her head in disbelief as they walked away from the car. "You know, hon, there are times when you're entirely too human for a vampire."

He supposed he deserved that. "The police have been all over this area, what are we likely to find that they missed?"

"Something they weren't looking for."

"Ghoulies and ghosties and things that go bump in the night?"

"Takes one to know one." She stepped around the tattered end of a piece of yellow police tape. "Or in this case, takes two."

For a moment, Henry had the weirdest sense of déjà vu. It could have been Vicki he was following down to the sand, their partnership renewed. Then Lilah half turned, laughingly telling him to hurry, and she couldn't have been more different than his tall, blonde ex-lover.

Single male, mid-twenties, seeks someone to share the night.

So what if it was a different someone. . . .

He knew when he stood on the exact spot the body had been found, the stink of the dying man's terror was so distinct that it had clearly been neither a fast nor a painless death.

"Not an incubus, then," Lilah declared dumping sand out of an expensive Italian pump. "We may like to take our time, but no one ever complains about the process."

Henry frowned and turned his face into the breeze coming in off the Pacific. There was no moon and except for the white lines of breakers at the seawall, the waves were very dark. "Can you smell the rot?"

"Sweetie, there's a great big dead fish not fifteen

feet away. I'd have to be in the same shape as Mr. Johnston not to smell it."

"Not the fish." It smelled of the crypt. Of bones left to lie in the dark and damp. "There." He pointed toward the seawall. "It's in there."

Lilah looked up at Henry's pale face, then over at the massive mound of rock jutting out into the sea. "What is?"

"I don't know yet." Half a dozen paces toward the rock, he turned back toward the succubus. "Are you coming?"

"No, just breathing hard."

"Pardon?"

He looked so completely confused, she laughed as she caught up. "You really don't get out much, do you, hon?"

The night was no impediment to either of them, but the entrance was well hidden. If it hadn't been for the smell, they'd never have found it.

Dropping to her knees beside him, Lilah handed Henry a lighter. He stretched his arm to its full length under a massive block of stone, the tiny flame shifting all the shadows but one.

"You can take the lighter with you." Lilah rocked back onto her heels, shaking her head. "I, personally, am not going in there."

Henry understood. Succubi were only slightly harder to kill than the humans they resembled. "I don't think it's home," he muttered dropping onto his stomach and inching forward into the black line of the narrow crevasse.

Lilah's voice drifted down to him. "Not a problem,

hon, but I'd absolutely ruin this dress. Not to mention my manicure."

"Not to mention," Henry repeated, smiling in spite of the conditions. There was an innate honesty in the succubus he liked. A lot.

Twice his body-length under the stone, after creeping through a puddle of salt water at least an inch deep, the way opened up and, although he had to keep turning his shoulders, he could move forward in a crouch. The smell reminded him of the catacombs under St. Mark's Square in Venice where the sea had permeated both the rock and the ancient dead.

Three or four minutes later, he straightened cautiously as the roof rose away and drew Lilah's lighter out of his pocket, expecting to see bones piled in every corner. He saw, instead, a large crab scuttling away, a filthy nest of clothing, and a dark corner where the sucking sound of water moving up and down in a confined space overlaid the omnipresent roar of the sea. A closer inspection showed an almost circular hole down into the rock and about ten or twelve feet away, the moving water of the Pacific Ocean. A line of moisture showed the high tide mark and another large crab peered out of a crevice just below it. It was obvious where the drained bodies were dumped and what happened to them after dumping.

The scent of death, of rot, hadn't come from the expected cache of corpses so it had to have come from the creature who laired here.

Which narrows it down considerably, Henry thought grimly as he closed the almost unbearably hot lighter with a snap.

* * *

Lilah and a young man were arranging their clothes as he crawled out from under the seawall. The succubus, almost luminescent by starlight, waved when she saw him.

"Hey, Sweetie, you might want to hear this."

"Hear what?" The smell of sex and a familiar pungent smoke overlaid the smell of death.

The young man smiled in what Henry could only describe as a satiated way and said, "Like you know the dead guy they found here this morning, eh? I sort of like saw it happen."

Henry snarled. "Saw what?"

"Whoa, like what big teeth you have, Grandma. Anyway, I've been crashing on the beach when the weather's good, you know, and like last night I'm asleep and I hear this whimpering sort of noise and I think it's a dog in trouble, eh? But, it's not. It's like two guys. I can't see them too good but I think, 'hey, go for the gusto, guys,' but one of them seems really pissed 'cause like the tide's really high and I guess he can't go to his regular nooky place in the rocks and he sort of throws himself on the other guy so I stop looking, you know."

"Why didn't you tell this to the police?"

The young man giggled. "Well, some mornings you don't want to talk to the police, you know. And I was like gone before they arrived anyhow. So, like, is this your old lady, 'cause she's one prime piece of . . . OW!"

Henry tightened his grip on the unshaven chin enough to dimple the flesh. He let the Hunter rise, and when the dilated pupils finally responded by dilating further, he growled, "Forget you ever saw us."

"Dude . . ."

*   *   *

"It's a wight," Henry said when they were back in the car. "From the pile of clothing, it looks like it's been there for a while. It probably lives on small animals most of the time, but every now and then people like your friend go missing off the beach or students disappear from the campus, but since they never find a body, no one ever goes looking for a killer.

"Last night, it went hunting a little farther from home only to get back and find the tide in and over the doorway. Which answers the question of why it left the body on the beach. It must've had to race the dawn to shelter."

"Wait a minute." Lilah protested, pausing in her dusting of sand from crevices. "A wight wouldn't care about going through salt water. Salted holy water, yes, but not just the sea."

"If it tried to drag its victim the rest of the way, he'd drown."

"And no more than the rest of us, wights don't feed from the dead," Lilah finished. "And all the pieces but one fall neatly into place. You don't honestly think a wight would pick its victim from the personal ads, do you, hon?"

Unclean creature of darkness seeks life essence to suck.

"I don't honestly think it can read," Henry admitted. "That whole personals thing had to have been a coincidence."

"And now that we've answered that question, why don't we head for this great after-hours club I know?"

"I don't have time for that, Lilah. I have a silver letter opener at home I can use for a weapon."

"Against?"

She sounded so honestly confused he turned to look at her. "Against the wight. I can't let it keep killing."

"Why not? Why should you care? Curiosity is satisfied, move on."

Traffic on Fourth Avenue turned his attention back to the road. "Is that the only reason you came tonight? Curiosity?"

"Of course. When a life gets sucked and it's not me doing the sucking, I like to know what is. You're not really . . . ?" He could feel the weight of her gaze as she studied him. "You're not seriously . . . ? You are, aren't you?"

"Yes, I am. It's getting careless."

"Good. Someday, it'll get caught by the dawn, problem solved."

"And when some forensic pathologist does an autopsy on the remains, what then?"

"I'm not a fortune-teller, hon. The only future I can predict is who's going to get lucky."

"Modern forensics will find something that shouldn't exist. Most people will deny it, but some will start thinking."

"You do know that they moved *The X-Files* out of Vancouver?"

Henry kept his eyes locked on the taillights in front of him. The depth of his disappointment in her reaction surprised him. "Our best defense is that no one believes we exist so they don't look for us. If they start looking . . ." His voice trailed off into mobs with torches and laboratory dissection tables.

They drove in silence until they crossed the Burrard Bridge, then Lilah reached over and laid her fingers on Henry's arm. "That's a nice pragmatic reason you've got there," she murmured, "but I don't believe you for a moment. You're going to destroy this thing because it's killing in your territory. But it has nothing to do with the territorial imperatives of a vampire," she added before he could speak. "Your territory. Your people. Your responsibility." She dropped her hand back onto her lap. "Let me out here, hon. I try to keep my distance from the overly ethical."

His fingers tightened on the steering wheel as he guided the BMW to the curb. "You *weren't* what I was looking for when I placed that ad," he said as she opened the door. "But I thought we . . ." Suddenly at a loss for words, he fell back on the trite. ". . . had a connection."

Leaning over she kissed his cheek. "We did." Stepping out onto the sidewalk, she smiled back in through the open door. "You'll find your Robin, Batman. It just isn't me."

Henry returned to the beach just before high tide, fairly certain the wight hadn't survived so long by making the same mistake twice. He blocked the entrance to the lair with a silver chain and waited.

The fight didn't last long. Henry felt mildly embarrassed by taking his frustrations out on the pitiful creature, but he'd pretty much gotten over it by the time he fed the desiccated body to the crabs.

He broke a number of traffic laws getting home before dawn. Collapsing inside the door to his sanctuary, he woke at sunset stiff and sore from a day spent crumpled on a hardwood floor. He tried to call Lilah and tell her it was over, but whatever connection there'd been between them was well and truly broken. Her phone number was no longer in service.

The brief, aborted companionship made it even harder to be alone.

For two nights, he Hunted and fed and wondered if Lilah had been right and he should have been more specific.

Overly ethical creature of the night seeks sidekick.

The thought of who'd answer something like that frightened him the way nothing else had frightened him over the last four and a half centuries.

Finally, he picked up the list of e-mail addresses and started alphabetically.

The man who came in the door of the café was tall and dark and muscular. Shoulder-length hair had been caught back in a gold clasp. Gold rings flashed on every finger and dangled from both ears. He caught Henry's eye and strode across the café toward him, smiling broadly.

Stopped on the other side of the table.

Stopped smiling.

"Henry?"

"Abdula?"

They blinked in unison.

"Vampire."

Henry dropped back into his chair. "Djinn."

Perhaps he ought to have his ad placed somewhere *other* than Alternative Lifestyles.

FIXER-UPPER

by Tim Waggoner

Tim Waggoner has published more than fifty stories of fantasy and horror. His most current stories can be found in the anthologies *Civil War Fantastic*, *Warrior Fantastic*, and *Bruce Coville's UFOs*. His first novel, *The Harmony Society*, will soon be available. He teaches creative writing at Sinclair Community College in Dayton, Ohio.

I'M NOT LOOKING FOR PERFECTION. I'm looking for you! SWF, 25, slim, attractive. Are you ready to reach your full potential? If so, I'm waiting.

As Brad walked into the bookstore café, he felt like he was going to die. His skin was slick and hot as frying bacon, and it felt as if needles were jabbing the backs of his eyeballs. His head throbbed, his stomach roiled, and he couldn't decide which he needed more: a stiff drink or a hit off a joint. Maybe both. No, scratch that. *Definitely* both.

This was a mistake. He never should have agreed to come here, but a bookstore had seemed safe enough. It was one of the few places outside his cramped apartment where he almost felt at ease— emphasis on *almost.* And while he'd never stopped at the café before, he'd passed by it plenty of times as he was browsing. His therapist had said the familiarity would make him more comfortable, help him follow through with meeting . . .

"Brad?"

He almost turned and fled as she rose from a table: a pretty blonde with long straight hair for whom the adjective *willowy* had surely been invented. She approached, moving easily and with a relaxed confidence that he both envied and found intimidating. He was suddenly too conscious of the extra ten pounds he carried around his middle, wished he'd trimmed his beard, worried that his mouthwash wasn't strong enough, mentally kicked himself for not going out and buying new clothes. Not that she was spectacularly dressed—a simple pullover blouse and jeans. But on her, the outfit became *haute couture.*

She didn't wait for him to acknowledge her question. "I'm Connie." She smiled and held out a long-fingered hand, the nails cut short, unpainted, skin creamy with a hint of pink in the creases of her joints. Brad had a thing (one among many) about touching and being touched, but he wasn't stupid. He took her hand, hoping his wasn't too clammy, and shook. Was it his imagination, or did she hold onto his hand longer than strictly necessary? Did she let her flesh slide against his as she withdrew her hand? Or was he obsessing, paying too much attention to detail, reading too much into things?

Connie looked at him, continuing to smile a slightly

lopsided smile that Brad found instantly endearing, its slight imperfection only adding to her beauty. He knew he should say something, had mentally run through a dozen different opening lines on the bus on the way over here, but each one had been more lame than the last. Besides, now that he was really here, really with her, he couldn't remember any of them.

"You want to sit down? Since I got here first, I ordered coffee for both of us." Again, she didn't wait for him to respond. She took his hand and led him over to her table, where two mugs of coffee sat cooling. He found himself sitting down, though whether he had accomplished this maneuver of his own volition or whether she had steered him into the chair, he couldn't have said.

As she sat opposite him, Brad dug into his pants for his wallet. "How much do I owe you for the coffee?"

She smiled again. "How about you get the next round?"

There was something about that smile, about her tone of voice. It was obvious that she recognized how nervous he was, but it didn't seem to matter to her that he was coming off as a complete spaz. There was something about her that made him feel safe, accepted.

He smiled back, the tension in his shoulders draining away, the nausea in his gut subsiding. "I'm Brad. But I guess you already figured that out."

"It wasn't hard. You did leave a description of yourself on my voice mail, remember? Though I'm not sure I agree that you look like . . . how did you put it? 'Like the bastard love child of Jerry Garcia and

Andy Warhol.' " She grinned. "So tell me, is this your first time responding to an ad?"

He nodded, wishing he'd never come up with that stupid Jerry Garcia line. He thought about taking a sip of coffee, decided against it. His luck, he'd end up spilling it all over both of them and sending them straight to the burn unit. "I've read the personals for years . . . always wondered about the people who wrote them, what they were like, why they chose to reach out like that. It seems so . . . I don't know. Anonymous." He realized how that sounded and hurried to add, "Not that there's anything wrong with taking out an ad. I mean, I answered yours, right?"

If Connie was upset by his answer, she didn't show it. Instead, she leaned forward, green eyes suddenly intense—forest green, emerald green, dancing green flame, hot and cool at the same time. "Why *did* you respond to my ad? Why did you pick mine out of so many others?"

Brad thought for a moment. "Honestly? Because it sounded as if you weren't expecting too much." And because he was so damned tired of being alone, but he decided not to add that part, not this early.

She smiled again, and he sensed she was sizing him up with those green eyes, coldly appraising him. He felt exposed, vulnerable, as if she were shining twin klieg lights on him that revealed every flaw, both outer and inner.

"Why don't you tell me something about yourself?" she asked. "Something . . . interesting."

Forty-five minutes and two cups of coffee later, Brad had finished telling her his life story, or at least the bare outline of it.

"You know something, Connie? You're really easy to talk to. Easier than my . . ." He'd been about to say *therapist,* and even though she knew all about that now, he instead said, "than anyone else I know."

"Why don't you tell me one more thing about yourself, something that you'd change if you could. Just one thing."

Brad hesitated. He wasn't sure why; he'd told her plenty already, too much, probably.

"It's just for fun," she urged. "Kind of like a little personality test, a way to get to know you better. But if you don't want to . . ."

He wanted to, God how he wanted to! He had never met a woman like Connie before, one who seemed to accept who he was, warts and all, unconditionally. He'd told her all about his screwed-up life, and she hadn't blasted him with pepper spray and run screaming into the night. If she wanted to play a little Q&A game, that was just fine by him.

"I don't know. I've got more than enough bad traits to choose from." He chuckled uneasily. Connie continued smiling, but her eyes bored into him, their intensity more than a little disturbing. "I guess if I had to pick just one thing about myself to change, I'd like to stop smoking. I had an uncle who smoked two packs a day for nearly thirty years and died of congestive heart failure before he was fifty. I'd like to keep from going the same route, you know?"

Connie nodded. "That's a good place to start." Before he could ask what she meant, she looked at her watch. "It's getting late; I have to go."

Here it comes, he told himself. *Here's where she says*

she had a nice time talking with me, but she doesn't think it's going to work out. Have a nice life, Brad.

"I had a good time talking with you, Brad."

He groaned inwardly. He was about to tell her that he understood, no hard feelings, when she added, "Let's do it again. Maybe tomorrow night? Same place, same time?"

Brad was so surprised that for a moment all he could do was stare. Finally, he managed to make his head bob up and down in a fair approximation of a nod.

She gave him one last smile. "I'll look forward to it." She stood, started to go, then paused and rested a hand on his shoulder. Her touch made him shiver. "I like you, Brad. I think you have a lot of potential." Then she removed her hand and walked away. His gaze tracked her as she wended between the bookshelves and out the door.

Brad sat for several minutes, unable to believe how well things had worked out. He felt like a man who had won the lottery, been told by his doctor that the test results were negative, and received a telegram from heaven stating that his sins had been forgiven— all on the same day.

It wasn't until he was on the bus heading home that he realized Connie hadn't told him anything about herself.

Later that night, at three in the morning, Brad sat before his computer, working on a Web page for a client and thinking about his meeting with Connie. He couldn't believe that he had told her so much. He had babbled on and on, practically telling her his entire life story—such as it was. He was twenty-nine, and until last summer he had lived with his alcoholic dad and his agoraphobic mom. He was a recovering alcoholic himself, as well as a recovering drug addict. Along with a host of other neuroses, he was prone to panic attacks and obsessive-compulsive behavior. Physically, he wasn't in great shape either. He was plagued by allergies, migraines, and irritable bowel syndrome. His face was pockmarked by the severe acne he'd suffered during his teenage years, and due to his atrocious diet—consisting primarily of Taco Bell and Dunkin Donuts—his cholesterol level was sky-high. Because of his various psychological and physiological problems, his medicine cabinet was a mini-pharmacy of prescription drugs whose various and often conflicting side effects only added to the sum total of misery in his life.

He wasn't a complete loser, though. Thanks to his skill with computers and an inherent sense of design and composition, he was able to support himself, more or less. He barely made enough money as a Web designer to cover the cost of his medicine and the rent on his one-bedroom hovel, but at least he didn't have to live in the spiritually toxic dump that was his parents' house anymore.

Best of all, tonight he had met a beautiful, intriguing woman who seemed to accept him for what he was and who—wonder of wonders, miracle of miracles—wanted to see him again!

Brad decided to mark his good fortune with a celebratory cigarette, realizing as he made this decision that he hadn't felt the urge to light up since leaving the bookstore. Which was kind of weird, since he usually smoked a pack-and-a-half a day. He told himself that he'd probably just been so jazzed about meeting Connie that he hadn't really needed a jolt of nicotine until now. He reached for the pack of Camels next to his mouse, and as his fingers wrapped around the plastic, fire blossomed in his gut, as if some invisible assailant had rammed a white-hot knife blade into his stomach. Hissing in pain, he released the cigarettes and fell out of his chair onto the wooden floor. He lay on his side, dripping sweat and panting like a wounded animal, until the pain subsided.

He managed to get on his feet and stay there, though his legs felt as if their bones had been replaced by pipe cleaners. He'd had reactions to his medicines before, but none this severe. He'd have to call his doctor in the morning. He reached for the cigarettes again, fully intending to get back on the carcinogenic horse that had thrown him, but he hesitated. He knew it was foolish, knew that the cigarettes had had nothing to do with his attack, but in his mind, he couldn't help but associate them with the agony that had ripped through his insides.

He withdrew his hand. Maybe he'd try again later, when the memory of the attack wasn't so fresh.

It wasn't until close to dawn, when he finally crawled onto his bare mattress and settled down to sleep that he remembered the last question Connie had asked him in the café, about which aspect of his personality he'd like to change. He remembered how she'd responded when he'd told her he'd like to quit smoking.

That's a good place to start.

* * *

"Hold it a little higher."

Brad obeyed, lifting the sheaf of wallpaper up and trying to press it flat against the wall. "Well?"

Connie frowned. "I don't know. What do you think?"

"I like Miro." Some people might have found the surrealist artist's trademark lines and squiggly shapes an odd choice for a wallpaper design, but Brad thought it would go well with the ultra-modern, ultra-hip furnishings Connie and he had picked out.

"Me, too. I'll get someone in here the first of the week to put it up for us."

"Couldn't we do it ourselves?" Brad asked.

Connie put a hand on his forearm. "You make too much money to be hanging your own wallpaper, sweetie. Besides, you need to save your artistic energies for work."

"I suppose." He dropped the sheaf of wallpaper and walked across the polished hardwood floor of their loft apartment. His footsteps echoed in the generous space of the living room, though it was so large Brad had come to think of it as the living auditorium.

Connie came up behind him, wrapped her arms around his waist, stopping him. She laid her chin on his shoulder and said, "Is something wrong?"

"No . . . yes. I don't know." He sighed, gently pulled free of Connie's embrace and turned to face her.

"Aren't you happy with your life?" she asked. "Eight months ago you were living in a one-bedroom roach farm. And now—"

"Now I'm the boss of my own Web design company, and I live in one of the most ridiculously overpriced apartments in town. I don't smoke anymore, don't feel a need to drink or do drugs. I'm not nervous anymore . . . at least, not much, and I said good-bye to my therapist two months ago. The strongest medicine I take these days is an occasional decongestant."

"You forgot to mention that you're in love with a beautiful, exciting woman."

Brad smiled. "There's that, too."

"I can see why you might be unhappy," Connie said in a teasing tone. Your life sounds like a living hell."

Brad chuckled. "I don't mean to complain. My life's wonderful, like a dream come true. Better than a dream, because it's real. It's just . . ."

"What?"

"I can't shake the feeling that I don't really deserve all of this." He gestured at the apartment around them, though he was talking about so much more than merely their quarters. "It feels as if everything is somehow your doing."

Connie's eyes narrowed, and her lips pursed slightly. "What makes you say that?"

He took her hand and led her over the white leather and chrome futon, and they sat. He continued holding her hand as he spoke. "The first night we met, when you asked what one thing I'd like to change about myself, and I told you I wanted to quit smoking?"

She nodded for him to continue.

"I stopped that very night. After that, whenever I tried to pick up a pack of cigarettes, I became violently ill. I couldn't smoke now if I wanted to."

"Honey, that's just—"

"And it's not only the cigarettes," he hurried to add. "It's booze and drugs and being afraid to talk to people and not having enough confidence in myself, and a dozen other things. All problems that I used to have . . . problems that you somehow fixed."

Connie's smile seemed forced. "Maybe the love of a good woman—"

He shook his head. "It's more than that. Every once in a while—not every day because that would be too obvious, wouldn't it?—you ask me about something in my life that I'd like to change. Not always in those words, but that's what it boils down to. And whatever I tell you I want to change, whether it's something big, like I don't want to drink anymore, or something small, like I don't want to feel awkward riding elevators with strangers, the next day or so, it's fixed. I no longer have the desire to drink; just the thought of it makes me want to vomit, and suddenly I'm no longer intimidated by people on elevators, I'm striking up conversations with them. And it all happens after I've talked with you."

Brad felt foolish for bringing this up, hoped that she would pat him on the hand, tell him it was all his artist's imagination at work, suggest that he consider seeing his therapist again, maybe just once or twice more, to dispel this silly fantasy.

Instead, Connie looked at him a long time, her expression unreadable. Finally, she took in a deep breath and let out a noiseless sigh. "All right. It's true. I have been . . . helping you."

Brad felt as if his spinal fluid had been replaced with freon. He wanted to yank his hand away from Connie's, wanted to get off the futon, put as much distance between them as he could. That's exactly what the old Brad would have done. But the new, improved Brad was no longer ruled by his fears, so he remained sitting, and continued holding her hand while he listened.

"You know the old cliché about how behind every good man there's a good woman? About how a president or king often has an influential adviser that's called the power behind the throne? Well, that's what I am. Or rather, what my people are. We can . . . *inspire* changes in humans. Help them become more than they are, reach their full potential."

Brad remembered something Connie had said to him at their first meeting, just before she left. *I like you, Brad. I think you have a lot of potential.*

"My people don't have a name for ourselves, at least, not one that matters. Over the millennia, some humans came to realize what we can do. We've been called everything from muses to witches, demons to angels, genies to gods, and I suppose there's some truth in all those terms. But we think of ourselves merely as artists whose chosen media are human lives."

Brad wanted to laugh, to congratulate her on coming up with such an inventive joke. But he knew from her tone and facial expressions that she wasn't putting him on. More, he could sense the truth of her words deep in the core of his own being, and why not? If she truly had been somehow rearranging his life, his very personality, why wouldn't he be aware of it on some level? What else would have prompted him to raise the subject in the first place?

"So the ad you placed . . ."

"Was my way of finding new men to work with. Some of my people are drawn to those already in fields of power and influence—business, politics, entertainment. But I prefer working with more modest material."

He recalled the first line of her ad: I'M NOT LOOKING FOR PERFECTION.

"Thanks for the compliment." Now he did stand and walk away. Connie rose to her feet and followed.

"It's not what you think," she said.

"Isn't it?" He walked over to the picture window, looked out at the city lights glowing in the dark. "You talk about humans as if we're some separate species, a particularly clever animal that you can teach amusing tricks to."

She stepped beside him, slipped her hand into his. He surprised himself by not drawing away. "It's not like that," she said. "At least not with me. I need to fall in love with my subjects before I can fully commit to working with them. And I fell in love with you that first night in the café. You were so sweet, so vulnerable . . ." He didn't turn to look at her, but he could hear the smile in her voice as she added, "I couldn't resist you."

"Subjects, plural. There've been others." It wasn't a question."

"Yes. My people live much longer than hum—than yours. Would you hold it against me if I had other lovers before you, perhaps a husband or two?"

He thought for a moment. "No, I wouldn't."

She shrugged. "This is no different."

He turned to her then. "But it *is*. You've used whatever powers you possess to change me, to make me into something different than I was."

She reached up to touch his cheek. "Love always

changes the one who feels it. My power is just somewhat more direct. Tell me: are you happy?"

"Yes." He couldn't deny it.

"And do you love me?"

Softer, almost a whisper. "Yes."

She leaned forward, kissed him gently. "Then what's to worry?"

He put his arm around her and together they looked out into the night.

After a time, he said, "You know, I've been thinking lately that business is pretty good, but it would be nice if I had the opportunity to develop my artistic side more."

Connie smiled.

Swirling images—a barking Doberman, a man sleeping, furry-meaty roadkill, a baby crying—backed by a nearly subliminal susurration of voices. A large mirrored panel rotated slowly in the middle of the featureless room, reflecting the images onto the smooth, white walls, as well as onto any viewers who might be present.

"The mirror's rotation needs to be speeded up a bit," Brad said. He listened for a moment. "The audio should be louder, too."

Connie keyed a note into her palm-held computer. "If you had flown in to oversee the installation of the exhibits yourself . . ."

He waved her comment away as a mass of scuttling beetles moved across his chest. "I was busy finishing that new piece for the Tamika corporation. Besides, I sent detailed instructions which, evidently, were too difficult for the idiots who run this museum to read. C'mon, let's go check the next one."

They exited the room, walked down a short unlit corridor and entered another chamber. Here, four large screens surrounded the viewer with blurred still images whose details were impossible to make out. At random intervals, the images simultaneously exploded into roaring, rushing movement lasting only a few seconds before once more falling still. All the while, a voice whispered a continuous chant about losing one's individuality, one's very identity to the monster called Love.

"This one seems pretty good." Brad had to speak loudly to be heard over the chant and the periodic outbursts of roaring sound. "The screens could be moved back a little, though, and angled so they aren't quite as symmetrical."

Connie made a note, and they walked to the next room.

"So, how does it feel to have your very own retrospective?" she asked as they entered the next exhibit. Here, two giant screens faced each other, lines of numbers scrolling across their surfaces so rapidly that the eye could barely make them out. The screens were hooked to twin computers which constantly struggled to infect each other with a virus while defending themselves against the other's attack.

"It's flattering, of course, but premature, I think. After all, I'm only forty-three." He examined the screens for a moment, then nodded. "This one looks good." He started for the next room without waiting to see if Connie followed.

No one else was in the museum tonight, except a

security guard or two somewhere. Brad had asked the museum's directors to allow him to check the exhibits by himself, after hours, and of course they had acquiesced. After all, he was Brad Sutphin, wasn't he? *The* Brad Sutphin, internationally acclaimed avant-garde video and computer artist. No one said no to him.

In this room, the floor was covered by a sheet of Plexiglas. Beneath it were rows of monitors which displayed computer-generated images of baby animals being crushed by hobnailed boots. A busy signal, occasionally punctuated with, "If you'd like to make a call, please hang up and dial again," echoed through the air.

Brad frowned as he gazed downward. "The colors don't look quite right. I hope those cheap bastards that run this place didn't chintz on the monitors. I told them my pieces need top-of-the-line equipment—not that the submorons who'll tromp through here would ever notice the difference. Make a note, Connie."

"Brad, I think we should—"

He whirled on her, eyes blazing, voice tight. "I said take a goddamned note."

Connie lowered the palm computer to her side. "And what if I don't? Will you hit me . . . again?"

Brad glared at her. "You think I'm afraid of you? Afraid of the big, bad *goddess?*"

Connie didn't retreat before Brad's anger. She stood calmly, coolly. "No."

"What will you do to me, Samantha? Wiggle your nose and make me—gasp—bite my nails?"

"You can't stand it, can you? Can't stand the thought that all your fame, that your very talent, was given to you by me. It's eating you up, gnawing away at your heart and soul."

"Bullshit. Truth is, I never really believed in your so-called powers. Yes, you helped me get where I am today, no argument there. If it wasn't for you, I'd still be a total feeb. But that was then, and this is now, baby. You want to stick with me, that's fine. If you don't, that's fine, too. There are hundreds of women who'd kill for a chance to be with a guy like me."

"You should know. You've sampled enough of them, haven't you?"

Brad became suddenly uncomfortable. "I don't know what you mean."

"I mean you've been screwing around for a while now with every fringe art groupie who flings her pierced and tattooed little body at you."

Brad fell silent, and the two of them listened to the nagging drone of the busy signal, the blandly helpful tones of the obsequious operator. *If you'd like to make a call . . .*

"Look, we've been together for a while, and I'm grateful for everything that you've done for me. Like I said, I don't buy any of that supernatural crap, but you pulled me out of my shell, gave me confidence, helped make me who I am today, and I'll always love you for that."

"But?"

"But it's time to move on. For both of us." He forced a smile. "Nothing lasts forever, right?"

Connie slowly smiled. It was a smile without warmth, without any semblance of human emotion, the sort of smile that might cross a serpent's lips. "Too true." Her eyes began to glow with a soft green light. Brad told himself it was just a reflection from the monitors, but deep down he knew better.

"My people always face a dilemma when it comes to putting the finishing touches on a project. How best to end it? Some prefer to let their subjects expire peacefully of old age, while others— like Jackie O, Yoko, and Colonel Parker—follow the 'better to burn out than fade away' school." She glided forward, placed hands that were no longer quite human on his shoulders, gazed up at him with eyes that had become tiny video screens. "Myself, I favor a somewhat more aesthetic approach."

Brad tried to tear himself away, but her grip was like iron, and the illumination from her eyes was drawing him closer . . . closer . . . Brad Sutphin—*the* Brad Sutphin—screamed.

"Hush, sweetie. It'll all be over in a minute."

And it was.

". . . an interesting piece . . ."

". . . weird . . ."

". . . man's a genius . . ."

". . . heard he missed the opening reception. Guess he thinks he's too good to . . ."

". . . called again?"

"Breaking Up is Hard to Do."

"Not very original . . ."

Beneath the Plexiglas covering, displayed on dozens of top-of-the-line monitors, Brad Sutphin's face looked up at the museum-goers as they filed through the exhibit. His forehead was dotted with sweat, his eyes haunted, feverish. He was speaking, but the only audio in the room was the insistent drone of a busy signal followed by an operator's admonition to hang up if you wanted to make a call. Still, it wasn't all that hard to read Brad's lips, and many people did. He was saying, "I'm sorry," over and over and over and . . .

SECRET IDENTITIES

by Nina Kiriki Hoffman

Nina Kiriki Hoffman has been pursuing a writing career for nineteen years and has sold more than 150 stories, two short story collections, and several novels, including *The Thread that Binds the Bones,* winner of the Bram Stoker Award for first novel, and *The Silent Strength of Stones.* She has also written a collaborative young adult novel with Tad Williams, *Child of an Ancient City.* Her most recent novel is *A Red Heart of Memories.* Its sequel, *Past the Size of Dreaming,* will come out in March 2001.

WIZARD SEEKS WITCH. Tired of slaving over a hot cauldron all alone? Let's make beautiful magic together. NA, ND, NS. Herbs and healing potions OK.

The whole point of personals in the *Weekly* is to sit around after high school on Fridays in the mall food court with my friends and read the ads aloud and laugh. It's one of our many rituals, part of the cement that holds us together.

This wizard ad looked as hokey and lonely and sad as all the others, but something about it spoke to me. I couldn't quite put my finger on it.

Well, there now. I was lying to myself again. It was the way the words sparkled silver while I read them.

"Hey, Brenda, why'd you stop?" asked my friend Marshall. He slouched in his chair; these days, he always slouched. He had shot up to six foot four over the last summer, and he couldn't seem to get used to it. His blond hedgehog hair hung half over his eyes. He opened his McBurger and pulled out the pickle slice, glanced at me through his fringe.

Julie, my other best friend, togged out in a truly tacky Hawaiian-print Goodwill shirt, a black miniskirt, and knee-high Doc Martens, put down her forkful of salad and gave me a green-eyed glare.

At tables all around us, mothers tried to shush screaming children. People ate and talked, or sipped fancy coffee drinks and talked, or watched TVs that dangled from the ceiling. Closed captioning was on, which was good, because you couldn't hear the TVs over the noise. Eight different countries' Americanized food smells mixed in the air.

I always read the personals aloud to the others because I can eat faster than anyone else I've ever met. I'd finished my french fries five minutes earlier and picked up the paper.

I said slowly, "You guys ever think about answering one of these ads?"

"Eww. No," Julie said. "Short trip to Loserland!"

"What if Fate is waiting in the paper for you?"

"Why are you even thinking about this?" Marshall asked me. He flipped the pickle slice toward a trash can. It flopped onto the floor. He shrugged. "Something catch your eye?"

Feeling stupid, I read them the wizard ad.

"Eww, eww, let's experiment!" Julie said. "Brenda, you're up for this one. It's not like we haven't noticed you're the Witch of the Western World."

"Excuuuse me," I said. "But that's your title."

Julie gave a little grin that showed her fangs. Her canines came down kind of in front of the rest of her teeth, and she was self-conscious about her smiles, so most people thought she was always sullen. Half the time they were right. She added distance by hiding half her face behind her long straight black hair.

"Marshall?" Julie said. "Tiebreaker? Vote for which of us is witchier."

"No way." He shoved the rest of his hamburger into his mouth so he wouldn't have to take sides.

"Stop cheating. I'll do it," I said. I wanted to anyway, even though I didn't think I should. "Only, what is it we do?"

Julie checked the beginning of the personals. "Jeeze," she said. "You can call a 900 number and pay two bucks a minute to listen or respond. What a racket. You're supposed to be eighteen at least. Sha, like we haven't called 900 numbers before, but I still say no! It took me two months to get back my private line after last time. Or you can write, if there's a symbol at the end that has a little hand holding a pen."

We turned the paper over and looked at the wizard ad again. Yep, there was a hand holding a pen.

Marshall rummaged through his backpack and pulled out a spiral-bound notebook and a black Bic ballpoint. He chewed and swallowed the rest of his hamburger and rejoined the world of the potentially vocal. "Okay," he said. "What do we want our answer to say?"

"Hey, big strong wizard, I'm your witch," Julie said. "Show me some new tricks!"

"Sucks," I said.

Julie's eyes clouded. She looked at Marshall.

"As a wizardly kind of guy, I think it's cute," said Marshall. "And it kind of fits the profile."

"Let's see you come up with something better," Julie said to me in her snottiest voice.

I put my finger on the ad in the paper. The words flashed silver. I licked my lips and said, "I have been keeping my true identity a secret from my family and friends for years. Are you the one I can finally talk to?"

Marshall transcribed what I said. He and Julie looked at me, not smiling, not frowning. Julie said, "But that's not funny at all. It's nonresponsive. It's totally lame. Besides, it's a big honking lie. What's the matter with you, Brenda?"

"Nothing. I say we both send in our replies, and let's just see who gets an answer."

Julie likes to think she can't resist a dare. Actually, this is sad but true. Nobody should have such an easy button to push. But then, I picked my friends for qualities besides their ability to do mental gymnastics.

Still, you want your friends to have free will. Sometimes.

"You're on," she said, predictably.

"Do we send photos?" I wondered.

"No. That's icky," Julie said. "Well, this whole idea

is icky. Hey, how about we cut some model pictures out of magazines and include them?"

"Don't you think the guy will be able to tell they're from a magazine? And if two different answers have the same kind of pictures in them he'll suspect some kind of trick. I wonder if our letters should be longer. Shouldn't we be writing about all our good qualities or something?"

"How much information did the guy give us? Not much. Why should we give him more?"

"Yeah, but he's the fisherman and we're the suckers."

"I'm leaving mine just the way it is," Julie said.

I held out a hand to Marshall, and he passed over his notebook. I studied what I'd said and what Julie had said. Marshall had written every word legibly, and even spelled everything correctly. He'd make a heck of a secretary.

Something to contemplate when I set up my world empire.

I touched my words with an index finger. For an instant, black ballpoint writing flashed silver.

"Mine's fine, too," I said.

"Should we type them?" Marshall asked.

If we didn't want to appear babyish, we should probably type them. It would be more businesswomanlike.

I chewed my lower lip and studied my letter. "I'm going to write it longhand," I said. "Can I have a piece of paper and borrow your pen?"

"Sure. I live to serve," Marshall said.

Sometimes I suspected him of higher awareness. It was kind of intriguing, in a risky way.

I ripped paper from Marshall's notebook and took his pen, then wrote my letter and signed it Brenda. "Geeze, where should I tell him to reply? I don't want him to have my address."

"Put your phone number," Julie said. "In fact, I'm going to use your phone number, too, okay? I think sometimes my parents monitor my answering machine messages."

"All right." I'd trained my parents not to touch my answering machine. I wrote my private number. Touched my letter, watched silver flash from the words. All set.

"I'm so sure he can tell how old we are by our handwriting," Julie said. "I'm going to type mine."

"They have demo typewriters at Sears," said Marshall. "Let's do it now. I want to see you guys actually mail these things."

Marshall was getting frisky! On the other hand, he had a point. If I didn't mail this letter soon and in the presence of my friends, I might drop it in one of the food court trash cans. Who needed to take a chance? My life was perfect just the way it was. I had perfect parents, a perfect room in a perfect house, perfect friends, a perfect school career, not too much success and not too little. All my plans had worked out.

So, naturally, I was perfectly bored.

We went to Sears and typed Julie's letter, then went to a stationery store and bought envelopes and stamps. There was a mail drop-off right at the mall. Julie and I watched each other as we simultaneously dropped our envelopes into the mailbox. She looked more serious than sullen.

Then I had a really weird thought. I wished I had

touched her letter with my finger and checked for silver flashes.

Too late now.

"Probably nothing will happen," Julie said.

Monday, Julie and Marshall came to my house after school.

The answering machine in my room blinked at us. Three messages.

Marshall settled on my pastel pink bedspread, and Julie and I sat near my desk on wire-backed ice-cream-parlor chairs with pink cushions. I got out my phone log and a pen with a parrot at the top and pressed the playback button.

"Brenda, please, please, I know you said no in school today, but please, please, please, change your mind and say yes. Please come to the Friday night dance with me, please?"

Julie favored me with her canine-flashing grin. "Gee, Bob's got it bad for you, doesn't he?"

I hissed at her. I had not planned Bob. He and his obsession with me were ugly intrusions into my otherwise perfect life. Yet he never gave up. Usually I just didn't let my friends know how he pestered me. Maybe I'd have to make some kind of plan re: Bob.

The answering machine's flat voice timestamped the message. The tape clicked into the next message.

"Secret identity. Call me," said a deep chilling voice, and he left a number, which I wrote down. I shivered.

"Guess Brenda wins this one," Marshall said.

Time-stamp. Next message.

"Tricky witch. Call me," said the same voice, and left the number again.

He had left the messages within a minute of each other. Had he noticed they both went to the same phone number? How could he not?

"Or Julie," said Marshall. "Naw, Brenda came first." He bounced to his feet. "Now that that's settled, let's actually talk about the Friday dance. One of you is going to put me out of my misery, right? How about if I take both of you? You make me look good in front of the guys? We all put each other out of our miseries?"

Julie and I stared into each other's eyes.

The bet had been who got an answer. We hadn't discussed anything about follow-up. I wondered if she had felt the same thrilling chill I had, listening to the guy's voice, if she felt the compulsion to pick up the phone Right. Now.

Her lips tightened.

We both reached for the phone.

My hand came down on top of Julie's.

It was my phone, of course, but I should play fair.

I sighed and sat back, let her lift the handset.

"Wait," said Marshall. "You're not seriously considering calling this kook."

Julie grabbed my phone log. I thought about changing one digit of the phone number. I could do it from here. But she could just listen to the messages again. Unless I zapped them, too. But—

She put the handset to her ear, hunched her shoulder to keep it there, and punched number buttons.

Marshall pressed the disconnect button. "Come on!

He could be some huge evil creepazoid! Do not do this!"

Julie bit his hand.

Marshall cried out and jumped back, and Julie dialed the phone again.

Whoa. Who was this rabid woman? Her eyes were sort of blank.

"This is Tricky Witch," Julie said. "When can we meet? Tonight? Great. Where?"

I could almost hear his deep voice. I wanted to rip the phone right out of Julie's hand and crawl in next to that voice.

"Your condo? Sounds great. What's the address?" She grabbed my pen out of my hand and started writing on the phone log.

"No," Marshall whispered. "No. Make him meet you in public, Julie."

"Seven," Julie said. "All right." She hung up.

She looked dazed.

"Tell me you're not following through," Marshall said.

Julie blinked, shook her head, frowned, looked around my room as though she'd never seen it before. She stared down at the phone log and the pen in her hand. "Huh?"

"You just called him, Julie! You just called the guy and made a date!" yelled Marshall.

I reached for the phone. I'd missed my opportunity earlier, and now—

Marshall hugged me from behind, trapping my arms against my sides. "Don't do it. Are you crazy? What's the matter with you?"

I shook my head and forced myself wider awake. I

so wanted to call the wizard! And Marshall was so right.

What was wrong with me?

Silver flashes. In his ad, and now in his voice. Compulsions.

A person had to be careful in the application of compulsions. I had made some dreadful mistakes right after I ditched my real home and parents at eight and found my new parents and home. At eight, you don't really know how people act, so you make compulsions way too strong to make sure you'll get what you want.

Eww.

It had taken lots and lots of counter compulsions to restore my new parents to anything near functioning level. And numberless minor tweaks later to make sure they were actually happy.

And some hard concentration to figure out what I really wanted, as opposed to what I thought I wanted. Which changed all the time.

But now the system ran itself, and I had lots of valuable practice behind me.

I took a deep breath, let it out. "Okay. You can let go now, Marshall. Stop squeezing!"

His hands had wandered a little high. Maybe he was taking advantage of the situation. Marshall, getting frisky again. Well, it was a long time coming.

He sighed and let go of me.

"I made a date with a stranger?" Julie asked. She stared at us, then looked at the phone log. "I wrote down an address and time. Eww, Brenda. Eww, Marshall. This is so not me."

"It was like you were possessed, and so was Brenda," Marshall said.

"Eww." Julie shivered. "Well. Let's move right along here." She dumped my phone log on my desk, grabbed her black leather-and-rivets purse, and marched out of my room.

Marshall and I looked at each other. "I was not hallucinating, okay?" he said.

"No. You weren't."

"Is she going on the date?"

"Oh, yeah."

"And we're following her."

"You bet."

He stared at the white rubber toes of his orange Converse high-tops. "This isn't something that happens every day, is it?"

"Depends on where you spend your days."

He glanced up at me through his fringe of hair. "I've been wondering about that, Brenda."

I had a reflexive urge to tweak him on the control bar. I had left control bars on him and Julie and Mom and Dad, even though I should have ditched the bars a long time ago. I almost never used them anymore, but I felt safer knowing they were there.

One tweak and he'd head out the door, having lost his memory of the last ten seconds. Two tweaks would make it thirty seconds. Too many tweaks and he would suspect something had happened, though he wouldn't know what.

"Sure you have," I said instead.

He bent his head and stared at his shoes some more. He glanced at the door. "Well," he said. Then his lips firmed and he grabbed my arm. "Don't let him get Julie."

"Okay."

We went down to the kitchen, where Julie was whipping up another one of her horrible smoothie mixes. We always shared one of these after school. It involved anything she could find in the kitchen and blend in the Osterizer. Today, Oreos, bananas, coffee ice cream, milk, a couple of eggs, and some orange juice. One of her better efforts.

Marshall and I met in front of Julie's apartment building around 6:30 that night. We were both wearing dark comfortable clothes, sneak outfits. I knew the address of the Wizard's condo from Julie's scribbles on my phone log, but we thought we should shadow her anyway. She gets lost easily.

She came out dressed to kill in a pink silk sheath and a black cocoon coat a couple minutes later. She had looped her long black hair up into a classy knot. She wore small tasteful earrings and makeup that made her look twenty-two, and black platform strappy sandals that made her look six feet tall.

"Wow," Marshall whispered.

I thought it. I didn't know Julie knew how to look like that. Obviously she had a secret life.

A cab pulled up in front of her building and she stepped in.

"God! She called a cab! What a grown-up!" muttered Marshall. "What are we going to do?"

Julie's cab was already pulling away. I grabbed Marshall's hand and dragged him toward the corner, running a Summon Taxi chant in my mind. There was a bus stop halfway up the block just in case, but I was pretty sure I had this covered.

Sure enough, a cab showed up about a minute later.

The driver looked confused. Marshall and I slid into the back seat, and I told the driver the Wizard's address.

Marshall and I sat back. "So," he said. "How'd you manage that?"

I looked out the window and wondered if I should tweak him.

"Brenda," he said. "I know you'll make me forget all this stuff later anyway, so you might as well tell me."

"Huh?"

"Sha, like I never notice my watch jumping around and slices of life disappearing. Or how half my sandwich is gone when I don't remember eating it, but the bite marks match my teeth."

"Maybe you have multiple personality disorder."

"Ding! Wrong answer. Hypothesized, tested, rejected. I narrowed it down to you and Julie, and now I'm pretty sure it's you. Did you *ever* tell me what you were doing?"

Once. When we were twelve, swimming in the ocean, and he had gone down and not come up. No grown-ups around to save him, and Julie had already gone home. It took me too long to realize he was missing, get scared, open up my tool kit, and find him. I got him out of the water. I got water out of him. I made him breathe, and I made him wake up, even though he didn't ever want to wake up again. He'd been so far gone I wasn't sure there was anything I could do to get him back, but I had gotten him. He had cried and asked me why I wouldn't let him go.

Well. He was my toy, and I wasn't through playing with him yet. I had told him that. I was so mad and scared and sad and shaken I didn't know what I was doing.

He tried to jump back in the ocean, then, and I wouldn't let him. I made him lie down. I tweaked and tweaked, almost an hour into the past, so he thought it was just after Julie left, and I told him we better not swim because I'd seen a bunch of jellyfish. We went home. He did ask me why we were both wet, but I said I didn't know.

Almost the most horrible memory I had.

"I'm not doing anything," I said.

Marshall shrugged. "Have it your way." He looked disappointed.

The Wizard lived in a building on the waterfront. It had a whole wall of windows facing the harbor. Julie went in the front door of the building just as our cab got there. I paid, and Marshall and I ran after her.

"Apartment number?" Marshall asked as we ran.

"Three-twelve."

Julie had already gotten into the elevator when we dashed into the foyer. Numbers flashed on the digital display above the elevator door. Third floor, stop.

Marshall found the staircase and we ran up. We made it to the hallway just as Julie went into a door, a flash of pink and black, then gone.

We ran after her and pounded on the door. It was a very thick door made of metal. No one answered. Marshall rattled the doorknob, but it didn't open. "Brenda," he said.

I reached for the doorknob. Lightning flared from it, crackling against the tips of my fingers. I screamed and jumped back, sucked on my burns.

"Brenda," Marshall said again. He gripped my shoulder. "Julie's in there."

I blew on my fingertips, shook my hand, reached out for another try at the doorknob.

The door opened. The smell of musky incense came from inside the condo. A tall, slim, unnaturally calm man with short silver hair stood there, casual in khaki pants and a navy long-sleeved turtleneck. He smiled at us, but he looked more mean than friendly. "Something I can do for you?" he asked. He had a slight British accent, and he spoke in the same voice as the one that had left messages for me and Julie on my machine. Thrilling and hypnotic. I blinked a couple times and took a step forward.

Marshall grabbed me from behind and locked his arms around my chest. "We want our friend back."

"Your friend?" He glanced over his shoulder. "Do come in." He opened the door wider and stepped aside.

The room beyond was floored with rush mats. I got a glimpse of exotic plants in ancient cement pots, and some kind of fireplace full of fire, with brass smoking things near it. I struggled. I really wanted to go in. Something big and wonderful waited in there, the best kind of surprise, I just knew it.

"Julie," Marshall yelled, holding me so tight he lifted me off the ground. I kicked back at his shins, but he was much bigger and taller than I was, and I wasn't wearing stomper shoes, only light Keds for sneaking. All I wanted was to walk past the Wizard and into his apartment. Longing to be in there burned in my gut. I couldn't think, so I just tried to wriggle and kick my way out of Marshall's embrace. "Julie, come out here!" yelled Marshall.

"No way," said Julie's voice.

The Wizard reached out and touched Marshall's forehead. Marshall's arms dropped. I spilled out of them, sprawled on the hall carpet. I looked up at Marshall. His face was dazed, his eyes blank. A tiny blue spot blazed on his forehead.

"Come," said the Wizard. Marshall sleepwalked into the apartment.

I scrambled to my feet and followed Marshall inside. Something in me was waking up. Was the Wizard tweaking *my* control bars? Who was this guy moving in on my toybox? What was his idea of play?

He closed the door with us inside.

Water trickled over black rocks in one corner, a waterfall down the wall that emptied into a small black pool with big orange fish and water lilies in it. Probably explained the somewhat swampy smell. Feather-duster-headed papyrus grew in a trough along one wall. Rush matting covered the floor. There was no furniture but two brass censers on hip-high stands in front of the fireplace. It was hot, smoky, and dank.

Julie stood in the middle of the room. She stared at the Wizard. Her face looked dreamy and stupid. Marshall, on the other hand, just stood there like a big dumb zombie whose will had been stolen, stupid without dreams. His arms hung from his shoulders, hands loose and dangling, and his mouth hung open. He kept blinking.

"Well, well," said the Wizard in that ultra-cool voice, fascinating and distant. "How nice to get three at once."

"Three what?" I said. "What do you want with us, anyway?"

He looked at me, his dark brows lifted, his eyes silver as ice. "Oh, ho," he said. "You can ask questions?"

I stomped as well as I could in Keds on rush mats over to Julie. I waved my hand in front of her face. Her eyes tracked. A little slow, but they did track. "Julie. Wake up."

She smiled and shook her head, then refocused on the Wizard.

"Which one are you?" the Wizard asked me. He snapped his fingers. "Secret Identity. Brenda. The woman of the message machine. Ah."

I stood beside Julie and glared at him.

"Secret Identity," he repeated. "Yours was quite an interesting letter, the most tempting of the batch. I was hoping you'd call."

"This is your idea of a fun date?" I shook Julie's shoulder. She didn't even glance at me.

"Oh, no. This is preparation for a fun date."

"What's fun about it if you turn them into zombies?"

"You mean you don't know?"

I glared at him some more. He smiled softly. "You do know," he said.

He reminded me of most of the people in my real family, the one I ran away from. The people I hid from, weaving my web of don't-notice, nothing-to-see-here, move-along-now around me and everybody I knew.

People like the one I was turning into.

I went to Marshall. I dipped my hand in my magic reservoir, huge, almost untouched, hidden inside my mind in a warm safe place that I rarely visited. When magic coated my hand like paraffin, I reached up and touched the blue glow spot on Marshall's forehead. It melted. Marshall blinked and woke up. He frowned.

I gripped his hand hard and turned to the Wizard.

"These are mine," I said. "Find someone else."

The Wizard smiled. "You can have the boy. I'm not interested in him. Do you really think you can get the girl back?"

I glanced up at Marshall. He stared down at me. I hadn't let him hear me talking about him like a toy since that day at the beach, when he spazzed out and I made him forget it. What was he thinking now?

I couldn't read his expression.

I dragged him over to Julie and shoved him into her field of vision. "Julie," I whispered.

She moved enough to see the Wizard over Marshall's shoulder, then stood there, smiling and staring.

I bit my lower lip. Dipped my hand into my reservoir again, and touched Julie's eyelids and ears with my fingertips, trying to strip off the glamour the Wizard must have dropped on her. She endured my touch, but when I released her, she spun like the arm of a compass toward the Wizard as magnetic north.

"She has my hunger in her now," the Wizard said. "What can you do?"

Like Bob. I hadn't even given him a hunger for me, but he still had one, and I didn't know how to make it go away.

I looked up at Marshall again. I closed my hand around a knot of magic, lifted it toward his lips. "If I touch you with this, and you kiss her," I whispered, holding my fingers in front of his mouth, "she might come back to us."

He licked his lips. He nodded. I pressed magic against his lips. He gasped. I guess it burned or tingled or something. I'd never tried anything like this before. I knew I wasn't thinking this through right, but I felt like we didn't have time.

"Julie," Marshall said. His voice sounded different. Deeper, more thrilling. She gazed up into his face. He kissed her.

She blinked rapidly, mumphed against his mouth, squirmed out of his grip and slapped him. "Marshall Lewis McLeod! What do you think you're doing?" she cried, and shoved him away from her.

He grinned. He grabbed me and kissed me. He tasted like caramel and the smell of burning leaves and the sadness of a stream locked under ice in deep winter. I hugged him, tasting my own magic flavored with the spices and syrups of Other. My heart beat faster. I wanted more. Marshall straightened, letting me go. I stared up at him. He looked like gold and chocolate, cool salt surf in midsummer, a credit card with no upper limit.

"Marshall!" Julie screeched. She punched his arm. "What the hell are you doing?"

Marshall smiled, and my heart turned over. I could stare at him for the rest of my life and be happy.

"Let's go," he said. He took my hand.

"Eww, yes. What is this low-rent place?" Julie glanced around. "Bad taste is timeless, and this place is eternity." She marched to the door and slammed it open, then stomped out into the hall. Marshall looked back at the Wizard, so I did, too.

"Interesting," said the Wizard.

"Good hunting," Marshall said, and led me out.

Julie stood by the elevator door, tapping one platform shoe on floor tile. The summon button was lit. "What just happened?" she asked as we joined her. "Brenda? Are you sane yet?"

"Huh?"

"Hey, Brenda," Marshall said. I looked up into his beautiful, beautiful face. "Will you go to the dance with me on Friday?"

"Oh, yes."

"Hey, Brenda," he said in a softer voice, "want another kiss?"

"Oh, yes."

"That is so disgusting!" Julie said. The elevator doors opened. Marshall drew me into the car in Julie's wake, then leaned down and kissed me.

Julie had to poke us hard to get us to leave the elevator on the ground floor.

"You're going to explain this to me," she said. "All of it. Over thick shakes. At the mall. Brenda's treat."

"We better book, then. This could wear off at any moment," Marshall said.

I dragged his head down and kissed him again.

"Stop that, you idiot children," Julie said. "It's incredibly irritating. I may hurl." She left the building and stepped off the curb, looking for taxis.

Marshall gently pushed me away and led me outside. "Hey, Brenda," he whispered, "can you get us another cab?"

"Oh, yes." I did my Summon Cab chant in my head. A couple of minutes later a cab arrived.

Julie sat up front, and Marshall and I sat in the

back seat. I snuggled up against him, and he put his arm around me. "This *is* going to wear off, right?" he whispered.

Julie told the cab driver we were tourists and asked him to tell us about local sights.

The driver made up stories about local monuments.

"Brenda?" whispered Marshall. "This is going to wear off, right?"

"Do you really want it to?"

"And that statue over there, that's the Unknown Soldier," said the cab driver, waving at General Burke, a war hero. "He's got an eternal flame burning at his feet."

"Fascinating," Julie murmured.

"It's already gone, isn't it?" Marshall tried to lift his arm from around my shoulders. I hung onto his hand.

"We got two ex-presidents buried in that cemetery."

"Really? I didn't know any presidents came from here."

"There's a rock star in there people come and put devil candles on his grave, too. And pennies and broken glass and sometimes small dead animals."

"Wow." Julie's voice dripped with just the right kind of awe.

"You're over it," Marshall whispered in my ear.

"I'm not," I murmured.

"You're just pretending."

"I'm not."

"What? So I could ask you anything and you'd obey?"

"Try me."

"They caught a serial murderer in that bus terminal. He was trying to get away from his last kill. FBI guys caught him right before he got on a bus," said the driver.

"Tell me what you've done to me." Marshall's lips brushed my ear, and I shivered with delight.

"When?" I asked.

"As long as I've known you. Have you always been manipulating me and Julie?"

I pressed my face against his shirt.

"Don't cry. Just tell me."

"Maybe," I whispered, rubbing tears off on his collar.

"Every single thing we do?"

"No." I sniffled. "I just wanted you to like me and not hurt me."

"Did you ever think we might like you anyway?"

"No."

"Last year there was a riot at City Hall. Protestors broke a bunch of windows. Police used tear gas."

"Amazing," said Julie.

"But now you're my love slave, aren't you?"

"Oh, yes."

He sighed. He stroked my head a minute, sighed again, and said, "Snap out of it, Brenda. That's an order."

I turned to stare out the window. All the fascination and super heartspeed and the butterflies in my stomach faded. I took a few deep breaths, then looked back at Marshall. The glow around him was gone, and he was just Marshall again.

He smiled.

"You're so dumb," I said.

"I didn't like my little stint as you."

"You liked it at first."

"Well, yeah. Some kiss, huh?"

"Some kiss." I sighed. "You forgot something."

"Oh, yeah?"

"You never told me not to do it again."

"Do what again?"

"Any of it."

"Well," he said after a minute, "I don't know what life would be like without it. Maybe not as fun."

"I haven't done anything in years."

"I wouldn't say that. Nothing else could explain that stupid suit I wore last Christmas Eve."

"Oh, that." He had actually walked around in public dressed up like a red velvet Santa, with a huge pillow stomach and a big white way real beard. Little kids had stopped him in the street, told him their Christmas wishes. He had even listened.

"You don't even know when you're doing it anymore, it's so automatic. What I really want is what we got today. Don't let somebody else take us over."

"Okay," I murmured, and snuggled against him.

"Will you give me kiss power again Friday when we go to the dance?"

"Maybe."

"How come it didn't work on Julie?"

Julie turned around and glared at us. The driver had stopped storytelling. He pulled up to the mall's front entrance.

"It did. It took one kiss to get her out of the Wizard's power. The second one would have brought her into yours."

"Huh," said Marshall.

"You're going to tell me *everything*," Julie said.

But first we got milk shakes.

DÉJÀ VU

by Michelle West

Michelle West is the author of a number of novels, including *The Sacred Hunt* duology, *The Broken Crown*, *The Uncrowned King*, and *The Shining Court*, all published by DAW Books. She reviews books for the online column *First Contacts*, and less frequently for *The Magazine of Fantasy & Science Fiction*. Other short fiction by her appears in *Black Cats and Broken Mirrors*, *Elf Magic*, *Olympus*, and *Alien Abductions*.

Old-fashioned girl, intimidated by singles scene, new to city. Likes: Libraries, men who understand that intimacy and sex are not the same, long, aimless afternoons wandering through a sleeping city. If you need to ask for a picture, I don't need to meet you.

When I was younger, the world was a harsher place. I realize that this sounds condescending; it's not. It's a lament for things past, and things that are passing even as I choose my words, as I rummage through memories made before you were born, before your parents were born. People knew me then. They prayed, and sometimes I was all the answer they received.

Hard, now, to remember that and not feel diminished by the age.

No, not age. Something as petty and ineffectual as that stains many things, but I shed it like a duck sheds water; when it's convenient, and as naturally as men breathe. Sometimes, though, I toy with it, holding it against the sheen of skin and the line of face and jaw until I can see myself as you—as many of you—have seen me.

Such influence.

The phone is ringing. If I wait long enough, it will be answered by a machine, and a voice will come into the stillness of the quiet room, distorted by speakers and electronics, distorted, as well, by things older than even I: fear, anticipation, curiosity. Hunger.

I know what I need.

This is something that it took years to learn. Something that no one is happy *until* they learn. But separating out necessity from luxury, separating out dream and desire from the reality of day-to-day life, is a task that has become harder and harder as the realities of life have become more abstract. There is no work beneath the rising sun; no hurried rush to catch the last rays of daylight, to save tallow or wax; there is no rhythm to life that is not set by artifice.

Life on the edge has taken on a different meaning. Were any one of mine still alive, they would walk into this land and think of it as paradise.

And they would learn that paradise is the thing that you carry within; that it is made in equal measure of the difficulty of your existence, day by day, and the dreams you have of overcoming that difficulty. Once, we hungered for food and shelter; now, we hunger for things less tangible. We huddled together in single rooms for warmth, and when we needed the society and comfort of our own, we gathered in groups, sharing work and labor. Now we speak through contrivances, watch through a window into a world of signal and noise.

You might ask me why I'm here instead of in a third world country that might better suit my memories of what life *was,* what it meant in the face of loss, and today, waiting for phone calls in the near perfect stillness of a single room in a vast, empty house, I might answer: in all ways, the spirit is diminished, except one.

In a land where death is expected to have so little dominion, its effect is strong.

I never answer the hone.

I let the machines play, I let people fence with tapes and digits, and when they have finished speaking into the absolute silence of something that remembers their words and pauses, their awkward sentences and their stutters, their smooth, memorized speeches or the way they fumble to remember what it was that drove them to phone at all, I let them go.

Some drift. I know that almost all of the men who call will not be for me. They are too young, or too hardened by age; they are too bold or too bored; they are too cold, too weak, too strong. But at least they give me this: the sound of their voices in the peace. Like a prayer.

The phone is one matter, but the door is different.

I live here between layers, in the stretching space between my birth and my death. Do I know what my death is? Yes and no; I know that mortality is not my bane, but no one of us is invulnerable, no one unchanging. I have seen others of my kind come and go, brought to life by one thing and taken from it by another. Accidents of fate. Carelessness.

No one comes to the door without my permission. And I give it so rarely these days it's easy to forget that it's given at all. Attrition takes us. Time. Almost all of my friends have forgotten how to leave their homes.

But one or two remember; they shake themselves out of slumber, stir, enter the world.

Carol smiles as she crosses the easy threshold that divides us. "You've been listening," she says, nodding at the phone, pausing in front of the television, running her hands along the keyboard near the vacant computer monitor.

"And you heard me?"

"No."

"Ah."

She pauses; it's this way with us; the words fall comfortably into the spaces between meaning. "You're looking . . . thin."

"You're looking well."

"Yes."

She is. Luminous, not youthful, but not crippled with age; the corners of her eyes are brushed with fine wrinkles that speak of laughter, and her lips are full and marked the same way. She is not slender; she is not weighty; she is impossible to hold in place, but not impossible to define: she is beautiful. Viscerally beautiful. "You found someone."

"Yes."

"Where?"

"I'm not going to tell you." Her smile is deeper, infectious; I feel my lips responding to it. I rise.

"It's quiet here."

"Yes."

Her lips lose that smile, but not that sense that the smile is only momentarily lost to gravity. "You have to eat."

I don't want to know what I look like. I rise. I realize as I do that I am not sitting on a chair. The floor is not cold. Bad sign. "I'm not so far gone."

"Who are you?"

"Don't ask."

"I have to ask. Who are you?"

"You always ask the questions I have no answers to."

"If I don't ask," she replies, her eyes wide and round and perfect, "you'll never find the answer."

"And that's important?"

She says nothing. But she touches the phone. Touches me. I look at her hand and we both stand in silence, staring at the place where we intersect: her hand is solid and sun-touched and real, and mine is made of glass, colored and tinted. "I'm very tired."

"You've been alone."

"Yes." Understanding, now; impossible not to understand when she stands there so *strong*. "You placed that ad."

She says nothing.

"You made a path for them."

"If I could, do you think I would have let you stay here for so long?"

"You made a way in."

"You made it, silly. The television. The computer. The phone. But . . . the windows are shuttered."

"There's light."

We've had this conversation before, each of us taking different parts, struggling against inertia and weariness, finding new inroads and new life for ourselves and each other. "You have to feed. Promise me."

"I—"

"I wouldn't have come, but I heard the phone ring. Listen. *Listen*. It's there. Everything you need is there."

She's right. Everything I need is there, on tape, magnetic fields of information that can be so easily retrieved if one can touch the right button. She leans over; our shoulders brush, hers vibrant with color and mine like melting ice.

I hear his voice. Numbers follow. At another time I would write them down, but it's only for show; I know those numbers almost before he finishes them the first time.

She knows it's hard. She leaves the room while I make the call—but she won't leave my home because she doesn't trust me *to* make it. She knows I love my silences. She should; she loves hers, although you wouldn't know it now. He picks up the phone as if he were sitting beside it, waiting for it to ring. I know that he is at work; that he has been working for six hours; that he is carrying a pen in one hand, and his desk is scattered with paper.

*　　*　　*

I don't know why we do this.

Understand that identity is not the same for us as it is for normal people. Identity is like a tide, a flavor, a taste; it comes upon us and we are overwhelmed, carried away, obsessed.

"No, you can't wear that. It makes Queen Victoria look promiscuous. Where on earth did it *come* from?" Rhetorical; she is on to the next item, fashioning it from the knowledge and roots of the life she has chosen. "This. It's black. Basic black is good for all important occasions."

It's a joke. I laugh politely, thinking it is darker than shadow, this clothing; heavy, tight, a cloth box. A coffin.

"Stop it."

"I don't want to go."

"Neither does he, I'll bet, and with better reason. You've been trapped in this place for so long—"

"It's *my* place. I—"

"Like it. I know. That's what we all say."

"And is that so wrong?"

"No. You know better than to ask me to assign a value judgment to death. This isn't about right and wrong. It's about you and me. I'm not in the mood to be deserted. This is a date, and you're going to make it."

When I step outside, truly step outside, there is no sunlight; the only light source is electricity, generated by falling water and vast man-made monuments, traveling up and down wire arteries and veins until it reaches clear glass through which to shine. Even so, it's almost enough to paralyze.

Carol is there. She lends me motion. She talks quickly, lightly, her voice falling into dangerous and familiar cadences as she loses—for a moment—the veneer of the life she's established for herself in this human world. She does this for me. She takes risks.

I know that I've done this for her before, when she wore a different face, carried the weight of a different name. Or when I did. But she can only drag me so far. She heard the phone calls, and she heard what I heard in them; she will lose too much of her own life if she circles too close; we will be hunting the same prey. And we learned, long ago, how disastrous that can be, but we survived. If god exists— and I believe that a god of some sort must exist, if only for the reason that life's bitter ironies can't be simple accident—he or she was kind; we survived. Others have not.

"You're here," she tells me quietly, letting go of my arm and putting her hand on the small of my back. "Go. Find what you're looking for. I'll be waiting."

And I enter the vast building, searching. I'm not afraid; I'm too numb to be afraid. The walk from Carol to the door is the longest walk I have taken in decades, perhaps centuries. Hard to hold form; hard to hold desire, to hold the memory of anything valuable; the lights are bright and the movement of city life is a tide against which I have no anchor. I turn back, and she is, as promised, waiting, her gaze forceful enough to bring me back.

If all goes well, she won't have to do it for very

long. Someone opens the doors for me, and I think I remember to thank them, if they see me at all.

I walk into the hushed light of a dining room in the modern era. The man in the suit doesn't seem to see me; the woman in the shirt and the smartly tailored slacks almost steps on my feet. Others walk by, conversing in a muted whisper, smiling, holding hands or averting their gazes in a public display of anger that they think draws no attention. No one notices me; no one at all. I don't look down at my hands. I don't look down at all; I'm afraid of what I will see. Or won't see. I had no idea . . . I had no idea that it had been so long. No wonder she came to see me.

But before I can be lost, I see him. A lone man, sitting in a booth, his hands in his lap, and in them— I can see this clearly, although there's a table, a cloth, unused plates and a layer of pressed paper above them—lilac. The scent is strong and sweet, laced with the bitter and the familiar. He cut those blossoms himself. For a second, as if shutters were opened onto a world so vivid the colors are bright enough to make me wince, I can see him standing in front of a tree on a neighbor's lawn, carefully choosing what to take and what to leave, all the while apologizing to the people who cannot hear him. The neighbors who aren't home. The previous person he once stole flowers for.

Everything you need is here.

There is a reason that we send no pictures. They are a limitation; no more, no less. We can be all things to all people, but until we are in the orbit of their gravity, we cannot know what things we *must* be, and we cannot be all things at once and still be real. He looks up when my shadow crosses the table.

"I'm sorry I'm late," I tell him, as I make a place for myself at his table. "I can't drive, and I turned east instead of west when I got out of the subway. I was afraid you'd think I stood you up, but I'm glad you waited."

His face freezes a moment in the neutrality of common expression that exists before something more extreme shapes the corners of eyes and mouth, the lines of forehead, the tilt of chin. Then he does smile. "You can't drive?"

"No. I know—it's stupid. But I've always lived in cities that were large enough to have decent public transit." I smile more brightly.

"You could have told me—I could have picked you up," he says. But what he is thinking is simpler: *Brenda didn't drive. Brenda never got her license. All those years she kept meaning to.*

All those years. The hands in his lap tremble into stillness. He lifts them, places them, empty, upon the table.

Intricate dance, this. Intricate negotiation. He wants to give me the flowers; it's what he brought them for. But memory has risen like a defensible wall around the action. They were her favorite flowers. She was a terrible gardener.

Truthfully, so am I; none of us are good at drawing life out of earth and air and sun. "I don't normally do this," I tell him. It's true; the methods change as the decades do. But at core, once you understand the language of the decade, people remain stubbornly similar.

"Neither do I."

"Then . . . let's pretend we met some other way."

"What other way?"

"I don't know. Let's say we bumped into each other at the library—that we had enough time to stop and talk there."

"Library is better than personals ad." He smiles.

"Or on the bus—no, that's too obvious. In a bookstore? We could try the museum, but I haven't managed to get there in over three years."

"I've never been to the museum here." A broader smile.

"We could be old friends from university?"

"I occasionally see my university friends; I'm not sure it would fly."

Friends are a problem. A serious problem, but I can deal with it once I have shape and form. "Okay. What about . . . we met yesterday at the supermarket when I was clumsy enough to drop a dozen eggs."

He freezes. Just like that. When he smiles, when he remembers that breath is necessary, his expression is both more guarded and less guarded; if a wall has gone up around his actions, it is harder, thicker, taller—but I now see the gates.

"A dozen eggs?"

"Two dozen."

His smile deepens.

"Two dozen?"

"One, when I was reaching for a better best-before date, and the other when I was trying to stop the first one from falling."

"And what would I have done?"

"Well, if you were anyone else, you would have laughed out loud or looked away and hoped that you didn't meet my eyes."

"Either of those sounds more like the real me."

I put a hand on the table. Light no longer passes through it. "Maybe we'll tell them," I say, leaning forward slightly, "that you told the very annoyed store clerk that you'd dropped the eggs because you knew I was embarrassed and you wanted to help me."

"That's a . . . a good way to meet," he says. But he is thinking, *the real me would have walked away on any other day, but I didn't—that one day, I didn't. Because she looked so tired and so ·awkward and so harried and·so real, and I thought she needed help. I'm not good at helping. I'm not good at reaching out. Just that one day, that done day . . .*

Over eggs, over a lousy two dozen eggs.

"It has the advantage of being original. Do you have a better suggestion?"

"No. No, I don't." *And I'd break every egg I could find if I could have the chance to do it over again.* The waiter comes with menus, and leaves empty-handed. They might be written in a foreign language, he pays so little attention to them. He is looking at me as if seeing me, truly, for the first time. As if he could comprehend what I am with work and effort.

"You're quiet. Am I boring you? Am I talking too much? I'm talking too much. I know it."

His smile is genuine. "No, you are not talking too much. Talking too much is when I do this—" and his face contorts as his eyes roll into the lids and he drops his head onto the table.

I laugh because it's funny and charming and familiar. I laugh, and the sound of my voice leaving my lips is foreign and familiar all at once. "Have you lived here long?"

"Here? In the city? No."

"Oh."

"You?"

"Not long. My mother lived here for all of her life; she died recently. I moved back to take care of her in the last few months."

He is absolutely still, face frozen again.

"I'm sorry—that wasn't a great move for a first date. But I told you—I'm not very good at this kind of thing. We can talk about anything else—I talk too much about the dead."

"No—no, it's all right." He reaches across the table, and I feel a shock of pleasure as his palm connects with the top of my hand. He is so very warm. "You're cold."

"Just a little. It'll get better soon."

"I—I don't want to sound like an idiot, but I know what it's like. You spend all this time caring for—for someone and then, they're just gone. But—if you talk about what you do day in and day out with most people, they get bored or uncomfortable. Because day in, day out . . ."

"I know. I know exactly what you mean." And I do. I really do. "Did you lose a parent, too?"

"No. Not a parent." He picks up the menu, and the small crack in the wall widens. I'm not a fool; I don't try to bludgeon my way in. He hasn't removed his hand from mine, and I take what I need from the contact. The waiter, like punctuation in a long sentence, closes the opening paragraph of the meal.

I don't want to bring up the dead too quickly, but that is what I do; I circle, I watch, I wait. I'm little better than an ambulance chaser, but I have managed, with time, to be less obvious and therefore less revolting. Manners and a certain grace are the masks that make the deepest of all flaws palatable. In human terms there are two types of people; those who grieve and move on, and those who are transfixed by death, who, standing too close to the dying, have thrown in a metaphoric anchor, and are moored in place by the history they have surrendered their present to.

And it is those people we seek.

The waiter brings a carrot and cheddar soup to the table; long slices of dark and light bread, hand cut, hang between us in a basket suspending from rope and hook. The napkins have been removed from their place of honor on our plates and set clumsily on laps. Eating is an excuse not to speak. He is afraid that he has made a foolish decision. He is afraid he's not ready, that he'll never be ready. He is thinking about broken eggs, about how broken eggs were always epidemic, and always a joke between them that took the sting out of that particular form of clumsiness. He is wondering who I am, that I could think of a story like that; he is hoping that if I can . . . if I can, I might be able to understand him enough to . . . the thought veers. Even in the silence of his mind, he cannot face what is not spoken.

"The soup is good," he says, after a silence that would be awkward under any circumstances.

"It is. I have a confession to make."

"Oh?"

"I'm a terrible cook."

He laughs. "That's serious. Anything else I should know?"

"I hate contact sports—or at least, I hate watching them. In fact, I hate watching most sports—I think golf is the worst, but that's only because there's been a lot of golfing on television recently. I'll watch equestrian and figure skating."

"Figure skating isn't a sport." The reply is graceful, natural.

"You always say that."

For a minute, his expression grows guarded. "I've never said that to you before."

I blush. Pleasing fan of warmth and a hint of guilt, more powerful because there's truth in it. "I'm sorry. It wasn't you. It's an old argument I used to have with a—with someone else." Subtext: I am comfortable enough in your presence I feel as if I've known you forever.

He relaxes. His hands, on the table, widen out like cloth being smoothed free of wrinkles. "All of my arguments seem to have lives of their own. And they always end the same way. See this?" He lifts his foot just above the line of the table and then drops it in a hurry once I've nodded. "It usually ends up serving the necessary function of stopper. I say too much."

"Which is different from talking too much."

He laughs, and the sound of his laughter *is* familiar; it's started. Finally, it's started. "All right. I say too much *and* I talk too much."

"So far, I've done all the talking. But if you haven't heard enough, I'm a small l liberal, I spend Wednesday nights doing volunteer work at the women's shelter, and I spend my days herding young computer programmers from place to place in the futile hope that herding them will make the deadline they're theoretically heading toward more solid."

He laughed again. "They've been giving you trouble?"

"The usual. The people on top can't figure out that programming is more work than marketing—if you want the program to do something other than crash—so it's not entirely their fault. But . . . it's nice to be out dealing with something other than the newest emergency."

He smiles, but the smile is strained.

"I'm sorry—I don't usually babble this much."

"No—it's fine, really. If you weren't talking, I'd probably start jamming words in sideways to kill the silence."

But he is silent. Too much that I've said tonight has been said before, and could have been said word for word, but the dead he doesn't speak of. I know this; I've taken the words from him and made them my own, modulating the voice I use, the cadence of the words themselves, into something that is not a duplicate, but a strikingly similar version, of one of the many things he cannot escape.

He is staring at his hands. If the table weren't there to support them, they'd be in his lap. At last, he rises. "I'm sorry," he says, and he looks it, "but I'm not ready for this. I'm just—I thought—"

"It's all right," I tell him, because it *is*. I know where he is going and I know why. All I have to do now is wait a few minutes—less—and follow him.

"No—it's not, I'm sorry. I'm sure you deserve better than this. Me, I mean. Do you—do you need a drive home?"

"No—I'm used to walking or taking public transit. I'll probably go for a walk before I head home anyway."

"Look—I'm sorry."

I touch his hand. "I'm not. You seem like a person I could trust, with time, and—well, you have my number. This time, I promise to pick up when I hear your voice."

He smiles, and I almost think he's going to stay, but whatever resolve he has comes out then and he pulls away.

The waiter is tactful and waits until he has truly fled the dining room before he brings me the bill. Except I know in advance it's not the bill, it's the receipt. I take it, smile politely, leave.

Carol is standing outside of the restaurant. She only points; she knows better than to speak to me or touch me when I am in this state. I want to thank her, but the words—I can't waste the words; they are gathered in the hollow of my throat, in another woman's voice.

It's funny. Once the process is complete, I am hampered in so many ways. For instance: he is driving now, his hands white on the steering wheel; I can see a glimpse of his profile through the window as he drives. I am keeping pace with the car without effort; he is driving slowly. When I am finished feeding, I will have no such freedom of movement.

And it is only at this time, caught between my own death and his, that I am truly free; I have power, but I have not yet paid the price for it; it sustains me as potential.

I circle him like a bird. And when he stops, when

his tires squeal and grind against the curb because he's always been able to set new lows when it comes to parking, I wait. I'm not patient, but I wait just to make sure that the car door is going to open.

When it does, I launch myself into the darkness, passing through trees and standing stones and mausoleum until I come, at last, to the solid place where I can—where I must—rest. Clothing settles around my shoulders like a shroud, and the smell of lilacs is strong and sweet. He is crushing blossoms against his palm. He has come here searching for answers, for forgiveness, for benediction, or for anger; he doesn't know which.

He cannot walk through bushes or trees; he cannot escape the sting of branches he can't see when he passes into the bands of darkness between the tall lamps in this well-tended, well-lit ground. This is a truth about humans: they take better care of their dead than they do of their living because the only thing that gives meaning and value to their lives is memory.

I stand in front of the tombstone, and as he approaches, I can see that he's carrying lilac as if it were incredibly fragile. As if he hadn't already crushed so many of the little blossoms, it might seem new or fresh, an unsoiled offering.

He stops when he sees me.

"Hello, Robert."

"What—what are you—didn't I leave you—"

"Yes, in the restaurant. You left me."

There is a hint of fear in his eyes, a hint of wildness that might turn to rage and might turn to something completely different. This is *his* space, in way that not even his home is; here, the tombstone is the center-piece for his rituals.

"How did you get here?"

"I flew." I smile.

He forgets to breathe.

"Why here? Why are you *here?*"

I say nothing now.

His face, in shadows both cast by light and insepara-ble from it, looks masked and streaked. "I brought you flowers."

"I know." I smile at him. In the old days, things were vastly simpler. Men and women lived in remote areas where, in winter, they might both die without any hope of discovery. We could hear their screams from half a world away, and we could feed in peace and silence.

We don't take life, per se. Once we did, and there are stories about us that span the continent in which our singular powers were used in order to kill. And perhaps they were true. Some of our kind have, in times past, become so bloated with power, so careless, that they can feed on fear, on the fear that precedes grief.

Not I.

I have always thought vampires singularly stupid in the careless way they propagate and spread; they are so very, very human. Feed indiscriminately, and with-out care for the environment in which you feed; create more who feed, while in the end doing nothing to protect and nourish the things upon which you feed, and you will wind up with a world of predators, a world without prey.

But perhaps vampires, in the end, are simply a disease that spread; or perhaps because in the end it is only the pumping heart that matters, they are confident that they can find what they seek in baser creatures.

Not so with us.

Humanity *is* precious.

Why are you here?

"To ask you a question."

He starts, curses silently for speaking out loud in this of all places. But having done so—which, of course, he hasn't—he gamely continues. I like this man.

"What question?"

"If you could have any one thing in the world, what would it be?"

He is quiet for a long time, and because the answer is important, because it is the key, I wait where the shadows are strongest.

"I don't know," he says at last, which surprises me. "If a man has already had his most important wish granted, what's left to ask for?"

"I don't know," I reply, mocking him gently although it's unwise. "I would have guessed that a man who had everything he wanted would not spend so much of his life seeking shelter in a graveyard."

"I buried the answer to your question nine years ago."

Men in the modern era have so little belief, so little faith, so little ability to conceive of the miraculous. It hampers us; binds our abilities.

I feel my shape slipping toward solidity, and it is *too soon*. I hear his shallow breath, and accompanying it, the thud-thud of heart, the movement of blood; we are sensitive to these things. I am almost at the nadir of my power, but that is the way with us: we teeter on the fine and narrow line between zenith and nadir, with little in between.

But in this place that he has hallowed through the years, he offers the gift of his grief, and that is enough. I take what I can.

I know how he met his wife. I know when they kissed—and as all first kisses are it was awkward. I know when they first argued, although that is a dim, dim memory, kept only because it was the first time she cried. . . .

He feels me touch these things; I had hoped that he would speak of them himself, but he is human and has attempted to hoard what I need.

"What are you doing?" he cries out, as these things slip away from him.

"I'm freeing you from the things that stop you from living."

"You're not—you're taking away—"

"Your grief, Robert."

"My life!"

"Is this living?"

"Yes!" But the word is wild, and if someone heard its cadence, the way it breaks, the emotion behind it, they would never guess its meaning.

There are some memories I must leave alone . . . the first time he woke beside her, for instance, although it is strong. But the second? The third? The fourth? I see the first time they went anywhere as a couple; the nervousness on her part, the confidence on his; it hurts him now because he understands her fear. But then? It made him feel stronger.

I am almost transfixed. Starting from the beginning,

as if his life were a tapestry, I traverse the colors and textures of the memories that compose it, grabbing at one or two threads and unraveling them, carefully and artfully, from the whole.

And then I follow them to their inevitable end. He is with me, of course; how could he not be? The memories I am bleeding from him are the memories that he has used to define himself. But as I approach the end, he struggles and twists; his anger gives way to fear, and his fear to hysteria. Although he has lived through these time and again, they have always been an echo of the reality, not the reality itself—he has never had to relive them as he does now: knowing where they are going, but unable to change their direction.

His pain is intense.

I feed from it, gathering strength.

They are arguing; she has always had the quicker temper; he is tired. Exhaustion is a wall they cannot climb, not tonight—although later, they will find a way around it. She does not drive.

Of course.

She leaves their home. She takes a walk. It is very late.

He is angry; he sits in the living room by himself, inculcating anger by revisiting every harsh word she said; his own slid past him the first time, but now, they share weight. He was cruel. He knew he was cruel. He was just *so* tired. He stares out the window, waiting. Thinking of all the things he should have said, and would have, had he been half as quick with words as she was.

And thinking of all the things he should not have

said, would not have said, if it could change the future that is coming, the past that he has lived with.

The clock marks the minutes. He listens.

He listens a long time to the monotone of the second hand as it traverses clock face.

Has a thought: *she is never coming home.*

Has another: *and I don't give a damn.*

And another: *she's not going to make me worry.*

Because, of course, he knows on some level that anger is not enough to destroy the history they've built together, memory by memory; that it is a storm that makes the sunlight seem stronger for its passing.

But she never comes home.

The police do, instead, hours later, when anger has given way to a numbness that can only barely hide his terror. Does he scream? No, and yes. At the time, in his memory, he could not break down in front of strangers; now, the strangers are just that: remote and aloof. Does he care what they think? No. He knows that judgment or no, they will vanish into the depths of memory only because they carry her name on their lips, speak it with rough voices that have been forced to softness.

I want this.

I want this, and he realizes, suddenly, what exactly it is that I want: this moment. The ones that follow it: the ride in the car, alone. The hospital. The morgue. The funeral arrangements, during which he was taken advantage of by a sonofabitch who used her death to make money—*you wouldn't want your loved ones to be buried like a dead cat in someone's backyard, would you*—the friends who come, before and after, the parents who never come again, the things that were buried with her.

All things at the end are given value only by their beginnings.

He looks up in the here and now, meets my eyes in the here and now; there are tears running the length of his beautiful face. He catches both of my hands, crushing them, unaware of how tight his grip is.

I ask him, wordless, and this time, when he answers, I accept it all.

He wakes in the cold.

"Robert?"

He sits up, in the dark. Looks around at the graveyard. Looks at me and smiles sheepishly. "I'm sorry," he says. He is always apologizing. Always.

"For what?"

"I—I don't normally pass out. I don't think I drank all that much."

"You didn't drink anything. You never do."

"Right. That's right." He touches the back of his head with the flat of his palm, searching absently for bumps or things that cause pain. "Why are we—oh—" His face falls again, and a hand is lifted to his lips to still yet another apology.

"I'm sorry, Brenda."

"For what?"

"I know you don't need to take care of me right now. I'm not the one who lost my mother." He looks at the tombstone. At the name. After a long moment of silence, he shakes his head, searches the ground for a moment, and comes up with crushed lilacs in his hands. "I brought these for you," he says to the headstone. "To thank you for raising such a wonderful daughter. To thank you for leaving her behind if you had to pass on."

"Robert—"

He hugs me.

"I'm sorry, love," he says quietly. "I've never lost anyone important to me. Not yet. I can't imagine what you must be feeling."

He can't. I take his arm. Mine is foreign to me; a middle-aged woman's arm, a solid arm. "Let's go home?"

"You haven't eaten."

"I'm not hungry."

He stops a moment, turns back to the graveyard, and then shudders. "Home, then."

As we leave the grounds, a woman passes us in the street; she looks very, very familiar; I can't quite place her face. But she's smiling as she walks to her destination.

And as I hold my husband, I smile; some part of me is being lost and even enjoys the sensation. We've been called so many things with the passage of time; is what we do really so wrong? I am better than the woman that died: I am entirely created by him; start to finish; all the memories he chose to treasure bind and hold me. I have no life outside of the life that has been created here. I will not leave him until his death, and if that death is sooner rather than later, if the life between then and now is content and happy, has a crime been committed?

I am content.

For now.

TRADING HEARTS AT THE HALF KAFFE CAFÉ

by *Charles de Lint*

Charles de Lint is a full-time writer and musician who presently makes his home in Ottawa, Ontario, Canada, with his wife MaryAnn Harris, an artist and musician. His most recent books are *Forests of the Heart, Somewhere to Be Flying,* and his single author collection entitled *Moonlight and Vines.* In 1999 he was the Guest of Honor at the World Fantasy Convention. For more information on his work, visit his Web site at <www.cyberus.ca/~cdl>.

CHERISH EACH DAY Single male, professional, 30ish, wants more out of life. Likes the outdoors, animals. Seeking single female with similar attributes and aspirations. Ad# 6592

The problem is expectations.

We all buy so heavily into how we hope things will turn out, how society and our friends say it should be, that by the time we actually have a date, we're locked into those particular hopes and expectations and miss everything that could be. We end up stumbling our way through the forest, never seeing all the unexpected and wonderful possibilities and potentials because we're looking for the idea of a tree, instead of appreciating the actual trees in front of us.

At least that's the way it seems to me.

Mona

"You already tried that dress on," Sue told me.

"With these shoes?"

Sue nodded. "As well as the red boots."

"And?"

"It's not a first date dress," Sue said. "Unless you wear it with the green boots and that black jacket with the braided cuffs. And you don't take the jacket off."

"Too much cleavage?"

"It's not a matter of cleavage, so much as the cleavage combined with those little spaghetti straps. You're just so *there*. And it's pretty short."

I checked my reflection. She was right, of course. I looked a bit like a tart, and not in a good way. At least Sue had managed to tame my usually unruly hair so that it looked as though it had an actual style instead of the head topped with blonde spikes I normally saw looking back at me from the mirror.

"But the boots would definitely punk it up a little," Sue said. "You know, so it's not quite so 'come hither.' "

"This is hopeless," I said. "How late is it?"

Sue smiled. "Twenty minutes to showtime."

"Oh, God. And I haven't even started on my makeup."

"With that dress and those heels, he won't be looking at your makeup."

"Wonderful."

I don't know how I'd gotten talked into this in the first place. Two years without a steady boyfriend, I guess, though by that criteria it should *still* have been Sue agonizing over what to wear and me lending the moral support. She's been much longer without a steady. Mind you, after Pete moved out, the longest relationship I'd been in was with this grotty little troll of a dwarf, and you had to lose points for that. Not that Nacky Wilde had been boyfriend material, but he *had* moved in on me for a few weeks.

"I think you should wear your lucky dress," Sue said.

"I met Pete in that dress."

"True. But only the ending was bad. You had a lot of good times together, too."

"I suppose . . ."

Sue grinned at me. "Eighteen minutes and counting."

"Will you stop with the Cape Canaveral bit already?"

Lyle

"Just don't do the teeth thing and you'll be all right," Tyrone said.

"Teeth thing? What teeth thing?"

"You know, how when you get nervous, your teeth start to protrude like your muzzle's pushing out and you're about to shift your skin. It's not so pretty."

"Thanks for adding to the tension," I told him. "Now I've got that to worry about as well."

I stepped closer to the mirror and ran a finger across my teeth. Were they already pushing out?

"I don't even know why you're going through all of this," Tyrone said.

"I want to meet someone normal."

"You mean not like us."

"I mean someone who isn't as jaded as we are. Someone with a conventional life span for whom each day is important. And I know I'm not going to meet her when the clans gather, or in some bar."

Tyrone shook his head. "I still think it's like dating barnyard animals. Or getting a pet."

"Whatever made you so bitter?"

But Tyrone only grinned. "Just remember what Mama said. Don't eat a girl on the first date."

Mona

"Now don't forget," Sue said. "Build yourself up a little."

"You mean lie."

"Of course not. Well, not a lot. And it might help if you don't seem quite so bohemian right off the bat."

"Pete liked it."

Sue nodded. "And see where that got you. The bohemian artist type has this mysterious allure, especially to straight guys, but it wears off. So you have to show you have the corporate chops as well."

I had to laugh.

"I'm being serious here," Sue said.

"So who am I supposed to be?" I asked.

Sue started to tick the items off on her fingers. "Okay. To start with, you can't go wrong just getting him to talk about himself. You know, act sort of shy and listen a lot."

"I *am* shy."

"When it does come to what you do, don't bring up the fact that you write and draw a comic book for a living. Make it more like art's a hobby. Focus on the fact that you're involved in the publishing field— editing, proofing, book design. Everybody says they like bold and mysterious women, but the truth is, most of them like them from a distance. They like to dream about them. Actually having them sitting at a table with them is way too scary."

Sue had been reading a book on dating called *The Rules* recently, and she was full of all sorts of advice on how to make a relationship work. Maybe that was how they did it in the fifties, but it all seemed so demeaning to me entering the twenty-first century. I thought we'd come farther than that.

"In other words, lie," I repeated and turned back to the mirror to finish applying my mascara.

I couldn't remember the last time I'd worn any. On some other date gone awry, I supposed, then I mentally corrected myself. I should be more positive.

"Think of it as bending the truth," Sue said. "It's not like you're going to be pretending forever. It's just a little bit of manipulation for that all-important first impression. Once he realizes he likes you, he won't mind when it turns out you're this little boho comic book gal."

"Your uptown roots are showing," I told her.

"You know what I mean."

Unfortunately, I did. Everybody wanted to seem normal and to meet somebody normal, so first dates became these rather strained, staged affairs with both of you hoping that none of your little hang-ups and oddities were hanging out like an errant shirttail or a drooping slip.

"Ready?" Sue asked.

"No."

"Well, it's time to go anyway."

Lyle

"So what are you going to tell her you do for a living?" Tyrone asked as we walked to the café. "The old hunter/gatherer line?"

"Which worked real well in Cro-Magnon times."

"Hey, some things never change."

"Like you."

Tyrone shrugged. "What can I say? If it works, don't fix it."

We stopped in front of The Half Kaffe. It was five minutes to.

"I'm of half a mind to sit in a corner," Tyrone said. "Just to see how things work out."

"You got the half a mind part right."

Tyrone shook his head with mock sadness. "Sometimes I find it hard to believe we came from the same litter," he said, then grinned.

When he reached over to straighten my tie, I gave him a little push to move him on his way.

"Give 'em hell," he told me. "Girl doesn't like you, she's not worth knowing."

"So now you've got a high opinion of me."

"Hey, you may be feebleminded, but you're still my brother. That makes you prime."

I had to return that smile of his. Tyrone was just so . . . Tyrone. Always the wolf.

He headed off down the block before I could give him another shove. I checked my teeth in the reflection of the window—still normal—then opened the door and went inside.

Mona

We were ten minutes late pulling up in front of The Half Kaffe.

"This is good," Sue said as I opened my door. "It doesn't make you look too eager."

"Another one of the 'Rules'?"

"Probably."

"Only probably?"

"Well, it's not like I've memorized them or done that well with them myself. You're the one with the date tonight."

I cut her some slack. If push came to shove, I knew she wouldn't take any grief from anyone, no matter what the rule book said.

I got out of the car. "Thanks for the ride, Sue."

"Remember," she said, holding up her phone. Folded up, it wasn't much bigger than a compact. "If things get uncomfortable or just plain weird, I'm only a cell phone call away."

"I'll remember."

I closed the door before she could give me more advice. I'd already decided I was just going to be myself—a dolled-up version of myself, mind you, but it actually felt kind of fun being all dressed up. I just wasn't going to pretend to be someone I wasn't.

Easy to promise to myself on the ride over, listening to Sue, but then my date had to be gorgeous, didn't he? I spotted him as soon as I opened the door, pausing in the threshold.

("I'll be holding a single rose," he'd told me.

("That is *so* romantic," Sue had said.)

Even with him sitting down, I knew he was tall. He had this shock of blue-black hair, brushed back from his forehead and skin the color of espresso. He was wearing a suit that reminded me of the sky just as the dusk is fading, and the single red rose lay on the table in front of him. He looked up when I came in—if it had been me, I'd have looked up every time the door opened, too—and I could have gone swimming in those dark, dark eyes of his.

I took a steadying breath. Walking over to his table, I held out my hand.

"You must be Lyle," I said. "I'm Mona."

Lyle

She was cute as a button.

("Here's my prediction," Tyrone had said. "She'll be three hundred pounds on a five-foot frame. Or ugly as sin. Hell, maybe both."

("I don't care how much she weighs or what she looks like," I told him. "Just so long as she's got a good heart."

(Tyrone smiled. "You're so pathetic," he said.)

And naturally I made a mess of trying to stand up, shake her hand, and give her the rose, all at the same time. My chair fell down behind me. The sound of it startled me and I almost pulled her off her feet, but we managed to get it all straightened without anybody getting hurt.

I wanted to check my teeth, and forced myself not to run my tongue over them.

We were here for the obligatory before-dinner drink, having mutually decided earlier on a café rather than a bar, with the unspoken assumption that if things didn't go well here, we could call the dinner off, no hard feelings. After asking what she wanted, I went and got us each a latte.

"Look," she said when I got back. "I know this isn't the way it's supposed to go, first date and everything, but I decided that I'm not going to pretend to be more or different than I am. So here goes.

"I write and draw a comic book for a living. I usually have ink stains on my fingers and you're more likely to see me in overalls, or jeans and a T-shirt. I know I told you I like the outdoors like you said you did in your ad, but I've never spent a night outside of a city. I've never had a regular job either, I don't like being anybody's pet boho girlfriend, and I'm way more shy than this is making me sound."

She was blushing as she spoke and looked a little breathless.

"Oh, boy," she said. "That was really endearing, wasn't it?"

It actually was, but I didn't think she wanted to hear that. Searching for something to match her candor, I surprised myself as much as her.

"I'm sort of a werewolf myself," I told her.

"A werewolf," she repeated.

I nodded. "But only sort of. Not like in the movies with the full moon and hair sprouting all over my body. I'm just . . . they used to call us skinwalkers."

"Who did?"

I shrugged. "The first people to live here. Like the Kickaha, up on the rez. We're descended from what they call the animal people—the ones that were here when the world was made."

"Immortal wolves," she said.

I was surprised that she was taking this all so calmly. Surprised to be even talking about it in the first place, because it's never a good idea. Maybe Tyrone was right. We weren't supposed to mingle. But it was too late now, and I felt I at least owed her a little more explanation.

"Not just wolves, but all kinds of animals," I said. "And we're not immortal. Only the first ones were and there aren't so many of them left anymore."

"And you can all take the shapes of animals."

I shook my head. "Usually it's only the ones who were born in their animal shape. The human genes are so strong that the change is easier. Those born human have some animal attributes, but most of them aren't skinwalkers."

"So if you bite me, I won't become a wolf."

"I don't know where those stories come from," I started, then sighed. "No, that's not true. I do know. These days most of us just like to fit in, live a bit in your world, a bit in the animal world. But it wasn't always like that. There have always been those among us who considered everyone else in the world their private prey. Humans and animals."

"Most of you?"

I sighed again. "There are still some that like to hunt."

Mona

You're probably wondering why I was listening to all of this without much surprise. But you see, that grotty little dwarf I told you about earlier—the one that moved in on me—did I mention he also had the habit of just disappearing, poof, like magic? One moment you're talking to him, the next you're standing in a seemingly empty room. The disembodied voice was the hardest to get used to. He'd sit around and tell me all kinds of stories like this. You experience something like that on a regular basis and you end up with more tolerance for weirdness.

Not that I actually believed Lyle here was a werewolf. But the fact that he was talking about it actually made him kind of interesting, though I could see it getting old after a while.

"So," I said. "What do you do when you're not dating human girls and running around as a wolf?"

"Do?"

"You know, to make a living. Or were you born wealthy as well as immortal."

"I'm not immortal."

"So what do you do?"

"I'm . . . an investment counselor."

"Hence the nice suit."

He started to nod, then sighed. When he looked down at his latte, I studied his jaw. It seemed to protrude a little more than I remembered, though I knew that was just my own imagination feeding on all his talk about clans of animals that walk around looking like people.

He lifted his head. "How come you're so calm about all of this?"

I shrugged. "I don't know. I like the way it all fits together, I suppose. You've obviously really thought it all through."

"Or I'm good at remembering the history of the clans."

"That, too. But the question that comes to my mind is, why tell me all of this?"

"I'm still asking myself that," he said. "I guess it came from your saying we should be honest with each other. It feels good to be able to talk about it to someone outside the clans."

He paused, those dark eyes studying me more closely. Oh why couldn't he have just been a normal guy? Why did he have to be either a loony, or some weird faerie creature?

"You don't believe me," he said.

"Well . . ."

"I didn't ask for proof when you were telling me about your comic books."

I couldn't believe this.

"It's hardly the same thing. Besides—"

I got up and fetched one of the freebie copies of *In the City* from their display bin by the door. Flipping almost to the back of the tabloid-sized newspaper, I laid open the page with my weekly strip "Spunky Grrl" on the table in front of him. This was the one where my heroine, the great and brave Spunky Grrl, was answering a personals ad. Write from your life, they always say. I guess that meant that next week's strip would have Spunky sitting in a café with a wolf dressed up as a man.

"It's not so hard to prove," I said, pointing at the byline.

"Just because you have the same name—"

"Oh, please." I called over to the bar where the owner was reading one of those glossy British music magazines he likes so much. "Who am I, Jonathan?"

He looked up and gave the pair of us a once-over with that perpetually cool and slightly amused look he'd perfected once the café had become a success and he was no longer run ragged trying to keep up with everything.

"Mona Morgan," he said. "Who still owes me that page of original art from 'My Life As A Bird' that featured The Half Kaffe."

"It's coming," I said and turned back to my date. "There. You see? Now it's your turn. Make your hand change into a paw or something."

Lyle

She was irrepressible and refreshing, but she was also driving me a little crazy and I could feel my teeth pressing up against my lips.

"Maybe some other time," I said.

She smiled. "Right. Never turn into a wolf on the first date."

"Something like that," I replied, remembering Tyrone's advice earlier in the evening. I wondered what she'd make of that, but decided not to find out. Instead I looked down at her comic strip.

It was one of those underground ones, not clean like a regular newspaper strip but with lots of scratchy lines and odd perspectives. There wasn't a joke either, just this wild-looking girl answering a personals ad. I looked up at my date.

"So I'm research?" I asked.

She shrugged. "Everything that happens to me ends up in one strip or another."

I pointed at the character in the strip. "And is this you?"

"Kind of an alter ego."

I could see myself appearing in an upcoming install-ment, turning into a wolf in the middle of the date. The idea bothered me. I mean, think about it. If you were a skinwalker, would you want the whole world to know it?

I lifted my gaze from the strip. This smart-looking woman bore no resemblance to her scruffy pen and ink alter ego.

"So who cleaned you up?" I asked.

I know the idea of showing up in her strip was troubling me, but that was still no excuse for what I'd just said. I regretted the words as soon as they spilled out of my mouth.

The hurt in her eyes was quickly replaced with anger. "A *human* being," she said and stood up.

I started to stand as well. "Look, I'm sorry—" I began, but I was already talking to her back.

"You owe me for the lattes!" the barman called as I went to follow her.

I paid him and hurried outside, but she was already gone. Slowly I went back inside and stood at our table. I looked at the rose and the open paper. After a mo-ment, I folded up the paper and went back outside. I left the rose there on the table.

I could've tracked her—the scent was still strong—but I went home instead to the apartment Tyrone and I were sharing. He wasn't back yet from wherever he'd gone tonight, which was just as well. I wasn't looking forward to telling him about how the evening had gone. Changing from my suit to jeans and a jersey, I sat down on the sofa and opened my copy of *In the City* to Mona's strip. I was still staring at the scruffy little blonde cartoon girl when the phone rang.

Mona

As soon as I got outside, I made a quick beeline down the alley that runs alongside the café, my boots clomping on the pavement. I didn't slow down until I got to the next street and had turned onto it. I didn't bother looking for a phone booth. I knew Sue would pick me up, but I needed some down time first and it wasn't that long a walk back home. Misery's supposed to love company, but the way I was feeling it was still too immediate to share. For now, I needed to be alone.

I suppose I kind of deserved what he'd said—I had been acting all punky and pushing at him. But after a while the animal people business had started to wear thin, feeling more like an excuse not to have a real conversation with me rather than fun. And then he'd been just plain mean.

Sue was going to love my report on tonight's fiasco. Not.

I'm normally pretty good about walking about on my own at night—not fearless like my friend Jilly, but I'm usually only going from my local subway

stop or walking down well-frequented streets. Tonight, though . . .

The streets in this neighborhood were quiet, and it
was still relatively early, barely nine, but I couldn't
shake the uneasy feeling that someone was following
me. You know that prickle you can get at the nape
of your neck—some leftover survival instinct from
when we'd just climbed down from the trees, I guess.
A monkey buzz.

I kept looking back the way I'd come—expecting to
see Mr. Wolf Man skulking about a block or so behind
me—but there was never anybody there. It wasn't
until I was on my own block and almost home that I
saw the dog. Some kind of big husky, it seemed, from
the glance I got before it slipped behind a parked car.
Except its tail didn't go up in that trademark curl.

I kept walking toward my door, backward, so that
I could look down the street. The dog stuck its head
out twice, ducking back when it saw me watching. The
second time I bolted for my apartment, charged up
the steps and onto the porch. I had my keys out, but
I was so rattled, it took me a few moments to get the
proper one in the lock. It didn't help that I spent more
time staring down the street than at what I was doing.
But I finally got the key in, unlocked the door, and
was inside, closing and locking the door quickly behind me.

I leaned against the wall to catch my breath, posi-
tioned so that my gaze could go down the street. I
didn't see the dog. But I did see a man, standing there
in the general area of where the dog had been. He
was looking down the street in my direction and I

ducked back from the window. It was too far away to make out his features, but I could guess who he was.

This was what I'd been afraid of when I'd first seen the dog: That it wasn't a dog. That it was a wolf. That Mr. Wolf Man really *could* become a wolf and now he'd turned into Stalker Freak Man.

I was thinking in capitals like my superhero character Rocket Grrl always did when she was confronting evildoers like Can't Commit Man. Except I wasn't likely to go out and fight the good fight like she always was. I was more the hide-under-the-bed sort of person.

But I was kind of mad now.

I watched until the man turned away, then hurried up the stairs to my apartment. Once I was inside, I made sure the dead bolt was engaged. Ditto the lock on the window that led out onto the fire escape. I peered down at the street from behind the safety of the curtains in my living room, but saw no one out there.

I changed and paced around the apartment for a while before I finally went into the kitchen and punched in Mr. Wolf Man's phone number. I lit into him the minute he answered.

"Maybe you think it's a big joke, following me home like that, but I didn't appreciate it."

"But I—" he started.

"And maybe you can turn into a wolf or a dog or whatever, or maybe you just have one trained to follow people, but I think it's horrible either way, and I just want you to know that we have an anti-stalking law in this city, and if I ever see you hanging around again, I'm going to phone the police."

Then I hung up.

I was hoping I'd feel better, but I just felt horrible instead. The thing is, I'd found myself sort of liking him before he got all rude and then did the stalking bit.

I guess I should have called Sue at this point, but it was still too freshly depressing to talk about. Instead I made myself some toast and tea, then went and sat in the living room, peeking through the curtains every couple of minutes to make sure there was no one out there. It was a miserable way to spend an evening that had held the potential of being so much more.

Lyle

I hung up the phone feeling totally confused. What had she been talking about? But by the time Tyrone got home, I thought I had a clue.

"Did you follow her home?" I asked.

He just looked confused. "Follow who home?"

"My date."

"Why would I do that?"

"Because we got into a fight and you're always stepping in to protect me or set people straight when you think they've treated me badly."

I could see that look come into his eyes—confirming my feelings, I thought, until he spoke.

"Your date went bad?" he asked.

"It went horribly—but you already know that."

Tyrone sighed. "I was nowhere near the café, or wherever you guys went after."

"We didn't have time to go anywhere after," I said, and then I told him about how the evening had gone.

"Let's see if I've got this straight," Tyrone said.

"She tells you she likes to dress casually and draws comics for a living, so you tell her you're a skin-walker."

"We were sharing intimacies."

"Sounds more like lunacies on your part. What were you thinking?"

I sighed. "I don't know. I liked her. I liked the fact that she didn't want to start off with any B.S."

Tyrone shook his head. "Well, it's done now, I guess. With any luck she'll just think you're a little weird and leave it at that." He paused and fixed me with a considering look. "Tell me you didn't shift in front of her."

"No. But from this phone call . . ."

"Right. The phone call. I forgot. You don't think you put that idea into her head?"

"She sounded a little scared as well as pissed off. But if it wasn't you and it wasn't me, I guess her imagination must have been working overtime."

Tyrone shrugged. "Maybe. Except . . . did you touch her at all?"

"Not really. We just shook hands and I grabbed her shoulders when I stumbled and lost my balance."

"So your scent was on her."

I nodded. "I suppose."

I saw where he was going. We don't actually go out marking territory anymore—at least most of us don't. But if another wolf had caught my scent on her, it might intrigue him enough to follow her. And if he was one of the old school, he might think it fun to do a little more than that.

"I've got to go to her place and check it out," I said.

"And you'll find it how?" Tyrone asked.

He was right. I didn't even know her phone number.

"That we can deal with," Tyrone said.

I'd forgotten what we can do with phones these days. Tyrone had gotten all the bells and whistles for ours and in moments he'd called up the digits of the last incoming call on the liquid display.

"It still doesn't tell us where she lives," I said. "And I doubt she'd appreciate a call from me right now. If ever."

"I can handle that as well," Tyrone told me and he went over to the computer.

I hadn't lied to Mona. I did deal with investments—on-line. I was on the computer for a few hours every day, but I wasn't the hacker Tyrone was. I watched as he hacked into the telephone company's billing database. Within minutes, he had an address match for the phone number. He wrote it down on a scrap of paper and stood up.

"This is my mess," I told him. "So I'll clean it up."

"You're sure?"

When I nodded, he handed me the address.

"Don't kill anybody unless you have to," he said. "But if you do, do it clean."

I wasn't sure if he meant Mona or her stalker and I didn't want to ask.

Mona

After I finished my toast and tea, I decided to go to bed. I wasn't really tired, but maybe I'd get lucky and fall asleep and when I woke up, it would be a whole new day. And it would sure beat sitting around feeling miserable tonight.

I washed up my dishes, then took one last look out

the window. And froze. There wasn't one dog out there, but half a dozen, lounging on the sidewalk across the street like they hadn't a care in the world. And they weren't dogs. I've seen enough nature specials on PBS to know a wolf when I see one.

As I started to let the curtain drop, all their heads lifted and turned in my direction. One got to its feet and began to trot across the street, pausing halfway to look down the block. Its companions turned their gazes in that direction as well and I followed suit.

He was dressed more casually now—jeans and a windbreaker—but I had no trouble recognizing him. My date. Mr. Stalker Man. Oh, where was Rocket Grrl when you needed her?

I knew what I should be doing. Finding something to use as a weapon in case they got in. Dialing 9-1-1 for sure. Instead, all I could do was slide down to my knees by the window and stare down at the street.

Lyle

It was worse than I'd thought. A pack of cousins had gathered outside the address I had for Mona. From the smell in the air, I knew they were out for fun. The trouble is, skinwalker fun invariably results in somebody getting hurt. We're the reason true wolves get such a bad rap. Whenever we're around, trouble follows.

The alpha-male rose up into a man shape at my approach. His pack formed a half circle at his back, a couple more of them taking human shape. I could tell from the dark humor in their eyes that I'd just raised the ante on their night of fun. I realized I shouldn't have turned down Tyrone's offer to help, but it was too late now. I had to brave it out on my own.

"Thanks for the show of force," I said with way more confidence than I was feeling, "but I don't really need any help to see my girlfriend."

"She's not your girlfriend," the alpha-male said.

"Sure, she is."

"Bullshit. That little chickadee's so scared you can smell her fear a block away."

"Well, you're not exactly helping matters," I told him.

He gave me a toothy grin, dark humor flicking in his eyes.

"I was walking by the café when she dumped you," he said.

I shrugged. "We had a little tiff, no big deal. That's why I'm here now—to make it up with her."

He shook his head. "She's as scared of you as she is of us. But tell you what, back off and you can have whatever's left over."

Some of us fit in as we can, some of us live a foot-loose life. Then there're the ones like these that went feral in the long ago and just stayed that way. Some are lone wolves, the others run in packs. Mostly they haunt the big cities now because in places this large, who's going to notice the odd missing person? People disappear every day.

"Time was," I said, "when we respected each other's territories. When we put someone under our protection, they stayed that way."

It was a long shot, but I had this going for me: we're a prideful people. And honor's a big thing between us. It has to be, or we'd have wiped each other out a long time ago.

He didn't like it. I don't know if I spoke to his honor, or whether it was because he couldn't place my clan affiliation and didn't know how big a pack he'd be calling down upon himself if he cut me down and went ahead and had his fun.

"You're saying she's your girlfriend?" he asked.

I nodded.

"Okay. Let's go up and ask her. If she lets you in, we'll back off. But if she doesn't . . ."

He let me fill in the blank for myself.

"No problem," I said.

Not like I had a choice in the matter. This was a win-win situation for him. If she let me in, he could back off without losing face. And if she didn't, no one in the clans would take my side because it would just look like I was horning in on their claim.

He stepped back, and I walked toward Mona's building. The pack fell in behind me, all of them in human shape now. I glanced up and caught a glimpse of Mona's terrified face in the window. I tried to look as harmless as possible.

Trust me, I told her, willing the thought up to her. *It's your life that's hanging in the balance here.*

But she only looked more scared.

Then we were on the stairs, and I couldn't see her anymore.

"Don't even think about trying to warn her," the alpha-male said from behind me. "She's got to accept you without a word from you or all bets are off."

The door to the front hall was locked when I tried it. The alpha-male reached past me and grabbed the knob, giving it a sharp twist. I heard the lock break, then the door swung open and we were moving inside.

Did I mention that we're stronger than we look?

Mona

I was still trying to adjust to the fact that the wolves really had turned into people, when my stalker led them into the apartment building. He looked up at me just before they reached the stairs, his face all pretend sweetness and light, but it didn't fool me. I knew they were going to tear me to pieces.

Get up, get up, I told myself. Call the police. Sneak out onto the fire escape and run for it.

But all I could do was sit on the floor with my back to the window and stare at my front door, listening to their footsteps as they came up the stairs. When they stopped outside my door, I held my breath. Somebody knocked and I just about jumped out of my skin. This uncontrollable urge to laugh rose up in me. Here they were, planning to kill me, yet they were just knocking politely on the door. I was hysterical.

"We can smell you in there."

That wasn't Lyle, but one of his friends.

I shivered and pressed up against the wall behind me.

"Come see us through the peephole," the voice went on. "Your boyfriend wants to know if you'll let him in. Or are you still too mad at him?"

I didn't want to move, but I slowly got to my feet.

"If you don't come soon, we'll huff and we'll puff, just see if we won't."

I stood swaying the middle of my living room, hugging myself. Wishing so desperately that I'd never left the apartment this evening.

"Or maybe," the mocking voice went on, "we'll go chew off the faces of the nice couple living below you. They do smell good."

I was moving again, shuffling forward, away from the phone, toward the door. It was too late to call for help anyway. Nobody was going to get here in time. If they didn't just smash through my door, maybe they really would go kill the Andersons who had the downstairs apartment. And this wasn't their fault. I was the one stupid enough to go out on a blind date with a werewolf.

"That's it," the voice told me. "I can hear you coming. Show us what a good hostess you are. What a forgiving girlfriend."

I was close enough now to hear the chorus of sniggers and giggles that echoed on after the voice had finished. When I reached the door, I rose slowly up on my tiptoes and looked through the peephole.

They were all out there in the hall, my stalker and his pack of werewolf friends.

God, I thought, looking at Lyle, trying to read his face, to understand why he was doing this. How could I ever have thought that I liked him?

Lyle

I knew it was over now. There was no way Mona was going to open the door—not if she had an ounce of sense in her—but at least I'd gotten the pack into a confined space. I couldn't take them all down, but maybe I could manage a few.

I could smell Mona the same as the pack did—smell

her fear. She was numbed by it. But maybe once I set on the pack, it'd snap her out of her paralysis long enough to flee out onto the fire escape I'd noticed running up the side of the building. Or perhaps the noise would be enough for the neighbors to call the police. If they could get here before the pack battered down the door, there was still a chance she could survive.

She was on the other side of the door now. Looking out of the peephole. I tried to compose myself, to give her a look that she might read as hope. To convey that I meant her no harm.

But then the alpha-male gave me a shove. Without thinking, I snarled at him, face partially shifting, jaws snapping. He darted back, laughter triumphant in his eyes, and I knew what he'd done. He'd shown Mona that I was no different from them. Just another skin-walker. Another inhuman creature, hungry for her blood.

"All you have to do is answer a couple of questions," the alpha-male said, facing the door. "Do you forgive your boyfriend? Will you invite him in?"

There was a long silence.

"Why . . . why are you doing this?" Mona finally said, her voice muffled by the door. But we all had a wolf's hearing.

"Tut, tut," the alpha-male said. "You're not playing by the rules. You're not supposed to ask a question, only answer ours."

I knew she was still looking from the peephole.

"I'm sorry, Mona," I said. "For everything."

The alpha-male turned on me with a snarl. I drew him aside before he could speak, my back to the door.

"Come on," I told him, my voice pitched low. "You know we had a quarrel. How's this supposed to be fair with you scaring the crap out of her and here I haven't even apologized to her? I mean, take a vote on it or something."

He turned to his companions. I could see they didn't like it, but my argument made sense.

"Fine," he said. "You've made your apology."

He turned to the door and let his face go animal.

"Well?" he snarled. "What's your answer, little chickadee? Your boyfriend says he's sorry, so can he come in and play now?"

Mona

I almost died when Lyle's face did its half-transformation. The wolfish features disappeared as fast as they had appeared. He turned to me with those beautiful dark eyes of his, and I couldn't see the same meanness and hunger in them that were in the eyes of the others. And I was looking for it, believe me. Then, while I was still caught in his gaze, he went and apologized to me. Like he was sorry for everything, the same as I was. Not just for what he'd said to me in the café, but because we'd liked each other and then we'd let it all fall apart before we ever gave it a chance to be more.

Call me naïve, or maybe even stupider still, but I believed that apology of his was genuine. It was something he needed to say, or that I needed to hear. Maybe both.

I was so caught up in the thought of that, that I didn't even start when the other guy did his half-wolf face thing and began snarling at me. Instead, I flashed on something Lyle had said to me earlier in the evening, back at the café.

These days most of us just like to fit in, he'd told me. Live a bit in your world, a bit in the animal world. But it wasn't always like that. There have always been those among us who considered everyone else in the world their private prey.

Most of you? I'd asked.

I remember him sighing, almost like he was ashamed, when he'd shaken his head and added, But there are still some that like to hunt.

Like this guy with his animal face and snarl, with his pack of wolfish friends.

But I was done being afraid. I was Rocket Grrl, or at least I was trying to be. I concentrated on this question the wolf-faced leader of the pack kept asking, focusing exactly on what it was he was asking, and why. It felt like a fairy-tale moment, and I flashed on Beauty and the Beast, the prince turned into a frog, the nasty little dwarf who'd moved in on me until an act of kindness set him free. All those stories pivoted around the right thing being said.

That doesn't happen in real life, the rational part of my mind told me.

I knew that. Not usually. But sometimes it did, didn't it?

Lyle

"Time's up, chickadee," the alpha-male said.

I got myself ready. First I'd try to knock as many of them down the stairs as I could, then I'd shift to wolf shape and give them a taste of what it felt like being hurt. I knew I didn't have a chance against all of them, but I'd still be able to kill a few before they took me down. I'd start with the alpha-male.

Except before I could leap, I heard the dead bolt disengage. The door swung open, and then she was standing there, small and blonde and human-frail, but with more backbone than all of this sorry pack of skinwalkers put together, me included. We all took a step back. Mona cleared her throat.

"So . . . so what you're asking," she said, "is do I forgive Lyle?"

The alpha-male straightened his shoulders. "That's it," he said. "Part one of a two-parter."

She didn't even look at him, her gaze going over his shoulder to me.

"I think we were both to blame," she said. "So of course I do. Do you forgive me?"

I couldn't believe what I was hearing. I wasn't even worrying about the pack at that moment. I was just so mesmerized with how brave she was. I think the pack was, too.

"Well?" she asked.

All I could do was nod my head.

"Then you can come in," she said. "But not your friends."

"They're not my friends," I told her.

The alpha-male growled with frustration until one of the pack touched his arm.

"That's it," the pack member said. "It's over."

The alpha-male shook off the hand, but he turned away and the pack trooped down the stairs. When I heard the front door close, I let out a breath I hadn't been aware I was holding.

"You were amazing," I told Mona.

She gave me a small smile. "I guess I have my moments."

"I'll say. I don't know how you knew to do it, but you gave them exactly the right answer."

"I wasn't doing it for them," she told me. "I was doing it for us."

I shook my head again. "It's been a weird night, but I'm glad I got to meet you all the same."

I started for the stairs.

"Where are you going?" she asked. "They could be waiting out there for you."

I turned back to look at her. "They won't. It's an honor thing. Maybe if I run into them some other time there'll be trouble, but there won't be any more tonight."

"We never finished our date," she said.

"You still want to go out somewhere with me?"

She shook her head. "But we could have a drink in here and talk a while."

I waited a heartbeat, but when she stepped aside and ushered me inside, I didn't hesitate any longer.

"I was so scared," she said as she closed the door behind us.

"Me, too."

"Really?"

"There were six of them," I said. "They could have torn me apart at any time."

"Why didn't they?"

"I told them you were my girlfriend—that we'd just had a fight in the café. That way, in their eyes, I had a claim on you. The honor thing again. If you were under my protection, they couldn't hurt you."

"So that's what you meant about my giving them the exact right answer."

I nodded.

"And if I hadn't?" she asked.

"Let's not go there," I said. But I knew she could see the answer in my eyes.

"You'd do that even after what I said to you on the phone?"

"You had every right to feel the way you did."

"Are you for real?"

"I hope so." I thought about all she'd experienced tonight. "So are you going to put this in one of your strips?"

She laughed. "Maybe. But who'd believe it?"

Mona

It's funny how things work. When I was leaving the café earlier, I could have happily given him a good bang on the ear. Later, when I thought he was stalking me, I was ready to have him put in jail. When the pack was outside my window and he joined them, I was so terrified I couldn't move or think straight.

And now I'm thinking of asking him to stay the night.

Science Fiction Anthologies

☐ **STAR COLONIES**
   Martin H. Greenberg and John Helfers, editors 0-88677-894-1—$6.99
Let Jack Williamson, Alan Dean Foster, Mike Resnick, Pamela Sargent, Dana
Stabenow and others take you to distant worlds where humans seek to make
new homes—or to exotic places where aliens races thrive.

☐ **ALIEN ABDUCTIONS**
   Martin H. Greenberg and Larry Segriff, editors 0-88677-856-5—$6.99
Prepare yourself for a close encounter with these eleven original tales of
alien experiences and their aftermath. By authors such as Alan Dean
Foster, Michelle West, Ed Gorman, Peter Crowther, and Lawrence Watt-
Evans.

☐ **MOON SHOTS**
   Peter Crowther, editor   0-88677-848-4—$6.99
July 20, 1969: a date that will live in history! In honor of the destiny-
altering mission to the Moon, these original tales were created by some
of today's finest SF writers, such as Ben Bova, Gene Wolfe, Brian Aldiss,
Alan Dean Foster, and Stephen Baxter.

☐ **MY FAVORITE SCIENCE FICTION STORY**
   Martin H. Greenberg, editor   0-88677-830-1—$6.99
Here is a truly unique volume, comprised of seminal science fiction stories
specifically chosen by some of today's top science fiction names. With stories
by Sturgeon, Kornbluth, Waldrop, and Zelazny, among others, chosen by such
modern-day masters as Clarke, McCaffrey, Turtledove, Bujold, and Willis.